I0725131

GHASTLY MISTAKE

MADAME CHALAMET GHOST MYSTERIES 6

BYRD NASH

ROOK AND CASTLE PRESS
SAINT CHARLES, ILLINOIS

Publisher's Cataloging-in-Publication Data
provided by Five Rainbows Cataloging Services

Names: Nash, Byrd, author.
Title: Ghastly mistake : a gaslamp ghost mystery / Byrd Nash.
Description: Saint Charles, IL : Rook and Castle Press, 2024. | Series: Madame Chalamet ghost mysteries, bk. 6.
Identifiers: ISBN 978-1-954811-57-7 (Amazon paperback) | ISBN 978-1-954811-58-4 (IngramSpark paperback) | ISBN 978-1-954811-10-2 (Kindle ebook) | ISBN 978-1-954811-16-4 (EPUB)
Subjects: LCSH: Women detectives--Fiction. | Ghosts--Fiction. | Murder--Fiction. | Fantasy fiction. | Detective and mystery stories. | Paranormal romance stories. | FICTION / Fantasy / Gaslamp. | FICTION / Fantasy / Romance. | FICTION / Romance / Paranormal / General. | FICTION / Mystery & Detective / General. | GSAFD: Mystery fiction. | Fantasy fiction. | Occult fiction. | Love stories.
Classification: LCC PS3614.A724 G53 2024 (print) | LCC PS3614.A724 (ebook) | DDC 813/.6--dc23.

Contents

BOOKS BY BYRD NASH

Madame Chalamet Ghost Mysteries

Ghost Talker #1

Delicious Death #2

Spirit Guide #3

Gray Lady #4

Haunted Grave #5

Ghastly Mistake #6

Contemporary, Magical Realism

A Spell of Rowans

College Fae Series

Never Date a Siren #1

A Study in Spirits #2

Bane of Hounds #3

Romantic Fairytales

Dance of Hearts (Cinderella retelling)

Price of a Rose (Beauty and the Beast retelling)

Fairytale Fantasy

The Wicked Wolves of Windsor and other Fairytales

It is a wonderful advantage to a man, in every pursuite or avocation, to secure an adviser in a sensible woman. In woman there is at once a subtle delicacy of tact, and a plain soundness of judgement, which are rarely combined to an equal degree in man. A woman, if she be really your friend, will have a sensitive regard for your character, honor, repute. She will seldom counsel you to do a shabby thing: for a woman friend always desires to be proud of you.

Edward Bulwer-Lytton, 1st Baron Lytton

Dedications
For all of those who have loved Elinor.

Chapter One

I awoke to the smell of death.

There was a hard surface under me and my head was splitting. Opening my eyes, I stared at a face. It took a moment for me to recognize Josephine Baudelaire, for her countenance was mutilated, her eyes gone, and her blood-coated mouth hanging agape without a tongue.

I tried scrambling to my feet, but the floor was slick and I slipped, my knee hitting the floor hard. The front of my dress was soaked with drying blood, and I panicked, wiping at it with my hands.

It took me a moment to realize that the blood wasn't mine.

It wasn't me. I wasn't hurt.

I felt a moment of relief before reeling up to my feet. Unsteady from shock, I gazed frantically around the room, trying to comprehend the situation. The small space had a low ceiling nestled among the roof rafters. I and the dead Josephine were the only occupants.

It smelled of rodent and was grimy and dusty, containing a lone chair with a precarious lean, a broken water pitcher on the floor, and a brass headboard from a bed leaning against the wall.

The door was locked, but there was one window, and I staggered to it. Using the sleeve of my dress, I tried wiping it clean, but the grime was stubborn and I only achieved an eye-hole view of a narrow street below me. Seeing people passing by, I tried lifting the window frame to yell for help, but it didn't budge. It was nailed shut.

All of this made no sense. How had I gotten here from Tristan's home to this? Who had brought me here? And why? The last thing I remembered was Dr. Devereaux and our experiment to break through my memories.

I was about to try and break the window glass when I heard heavy feet pounding up a staircase outside the door. In a moment, there was shouting.

"Get it open. Lean into it, man!" The door gave, bursting open to slam against the wall, revealing the Crown Inspector Sven De Windt and Marcellus Barbier, the gendarme detective and my friend.

"Marcellus!" I staggered forward with one hand reaching towards them. But my relief was short-lived.

"Arrest her!" De Windt barked.

The gendarmes behind him surged forward and they grabbed my arms pinning them. Confused, I stuttered, "W-w-what? W-what is happening?"

"Sit her down!"

They hauled me over and shoved me down into the only chair. It gave an ominous creak and pitched even more. I was prevented from spilling onto the floor by the iron grip of the two guardia who kept me there.

"What is going on?" I asked again, my voice gaining strength.

Without replying, de Windt made his way to the body of Josephine Baudelaire, and squatted to examine her. "See?" he retorted to Barbier, who had followed him to gaze down upon the dead noblewoman. "It is as the informant said. Murdered. By her."

Barbier cast me a worried, sideways look. "We should bring her to the station for questioning. Time is of the essence. With the murder of Lord Bridoux, a case like this must be handled swiftly."

De Windt stalked over to me. "Tell us how you did it."

"Did what?" I said faintly. A dark little corner of my mind recognized I was in dire straits. It screamed at me to mount some defense, but my limbs felt heavy and my mind was too fogged to take immediate action.

"The murder of Lady Baudelaire."

"No, that wasn't me." My protest sounded weak even to my ears.

He gave a heavy sigh, shaking his head. "Confess. It will go better for you."

I spoke louder, trying to make them understand. "I awoke and found her here. That is all."

"Eyes and tongue removed! How convenient for you, madame! Barbier, remind me again what Ghost Talkers need from the dead to communicate with them?" He said mockingly,

Barbier muttered something under his breath, refusing to meet my pleading gaze.

"Louder, please!" demanded de Windt.

"Eyes and tongue," Barbier repeated, still not meeting my eyes.

De Windt said triumphantly, "Both conveniently removed from our victim! To stop us from using another Ghost Talker to incriminate her."

"Why would I harm Lady Baudelaire? I barely knew the woman." I sounded shrill as I tried to tamp down my panic. My head was throbbing and their accusations made no sense.

"Really? Because I have several reports of heated discussions between you! At the Luminary, the night those creatures rioted, it was reported by several theater-goers that you were having a violent argument with her."

"Violent? It was not." I could barely remember our exchange. Where was Tristan? I needed him, fresh air, water, and a lawyer.

Ignoring my outburst, De Windt ticked off a the list on his

fingertips. "Those who know Lady Baudelaire say she feared you. Feared your influence over the Duke de Archambeau and His Majesty. The last report we have of her before she went missing was that she was seen leaving her residence with you, madame!"

"Ridiculous! I don't even know where she lives!"

"A short woman dressed in mourning black with a heavy veil was seen leaving Lady Baudelaire's residence with her in a closed carriage. You lured her away and murdered your rival in this dingy room of the Hells, hoping she wouldn't be found." My rival? What did he mean? Perhaps it was my blank face or just his love for oratory, but de Windt continued. "You couldn't deal with a lady of quality taking away the man you were bewitching."

"Are you referring to the Duke de Archambeau? He has no interest in Lady Baudelaire. Ask him."

"But you think he does in you? Remember, I saw what you were doing when at the Montaines'. Always trying to get him alone, separate him from his peers in hopes he would succumb to your wiles." De Windt sneered. "He might take you as a mistress, but it would be Lady Baudelaire he would marry. And your jealousy wouldn't allow that to happen."

"So I killed her? Are you a fool? Let me correct myself. You *are* a fool!" I squirmed against my captors but it was impossible to free myself.

Before he could respond, another guardia came into the room, breathing hard. "Sir, there's a crowd forming outside."

"Can't you see I'm questioning someone?" de Windt snapped peevishly.

Barbier made his way to the window. "He's right. There is a crowd forming. It would be best to leave before a riot starts. Rats living in the Hells have no regard for the law even in the best of times, and this is not the best of times."

De Windt rudely pushed the inspector aside. He tried rubbing more dirt off the window with his coat sleeve, but to no avail. "What are they shouting down there?"

The guardia who'd just arrived replied, "They think we are detaining one of their own, sir. Word on the street is that we nabbed a resident for crimes against the nobility, and they aren't happy."

"This hostility is because of the government crackdown yesterday after Lord Bridoux's murder," Barbier told de Windt. "Alenbonné citizens have not liked the door-to-door searches and arrests made."

Who was Lord Bridoux? The name meant nothing to me. If only I could think!

"Perhaps these rebel scum should stop murdering noblemen, if they don't like being made to toe the line!" retorted de Windt. "How did they find we were here? Someone in your department leaks, Barbier."

"Probably whoever gave us that anonymous tip set up a trap," the detective suggested.

"That makes no sense," scoffed de Windt. "If some citizen wants to see justice done, why would they also attack those dispensing it?"

I interjected, "You are accusing me of murder because of some anonymous information?!" I was so angry that if I hadn't been raised to be polite, I would have vulgarly spat at him.

"Be quiet, prisoner," snapped de Windt. Turning to Barbier, he added, "Your police wagon should be here shortly and my mounted unit. We shall take her in without incident. Meanwhile, cover that body."

They had nothing in the room to use, so in the end one guardia shed his coat to conceal Josephine's ravaged face. I closed my eyes, trying to think. Obviously, this was a trap set for me, but this accusation surely would not stand. I had friends, such as Tristan and Charlotte, who would come to my defense. Yes, I had argued with Josephine and been found with her blood-covered corpse. But other than that, there was no evidence at all.

The only saving grace was that at least Josephine's ghost wasn't standing here mocking me. She must have transitioned after being murdered, or she was haunting some other location.

De Windt and Barbier kept arguing. The police inspector was urging de Windt to leave now, while de Windt wanted to wait for backup.

During it all my head kept aching, occasionally giving me double vision. Far off there was music, but I couldn't concentrate on listening to it. I felt the cotton mouth and fogginess that made me think I had been drugged. I barely suppressed the urge to vomit. Why couldn't they be quiet and let me think?

"Besides, I don't think Madame Chalamet did this. She isn't that type of woman," Barbier said. *Thank you!* "No. Elinor would be more subtle. She might scare someone to death with a ghost."

De Windt gave an exasperated snort. "I brought you along because I needed men immediately to hand. What I don't need is your opinion."

Barbier's back stiffened. "So I'm only useful when you can use my men?"

The guardia had been quiet, but these words seemed to cause a subtle shift of power in the room. The one who had warned us gave Barbier a nod before returning downstairs. My two guards stopped restraining me.

A rock shattered the glass window, and we all gave a nervous start.

"What?!" yelped de Windt, jumping back from the flying glass.

"I tried to warn you! Get five or more people together, and a mob forms in a heartbeat. Alenbonné is a powder keg, and anything can be a match. Arresting a woman in the heart of the Hells? One they think is one of their own? Let's leave while we still can." Going to the top of the stairs, Barbier shouted down. "What's happening out there?"

"The crowd's getting bigger," answered one of his men.

"Well, don't let them!" Barbier limped tiredly back into the room. He gave me a passing glance, frowning with concern. "We need to get out of here."

Outside, someone yelled, "Let her go! You have no right to keep her!" Suddenly, there was the sound of horses and wagon wheels on cobblestones, and a voice I recognized was shouting. "Move back! Make way." It was Jacques Moreau. I sagged in the chair.

"I told you my men would be here soon," said de Windt triumphantly.

"So can we leave?"

"Of course. But it will be I who will conduct the interrogation and gain her confession to murder."

Chapter Two

Barbier gestured to his men to move away and, with a hand under my arm, gently assisted me to standing. "Be quiet until we get back to the station. We'll figure something out there," he murmured for my ears only.

We left the room, the guardia in front, me and Barbier next, and de Windt last. De Windt talked the entire time, but I ignored his gloating, which was easy since my head was aching.

The stairs trembled under the heavy boots of the guardia. It was a narrow staircase and, between my lightheadedness and nausea, I found it difficult to stay upright. At the bottom of the staircase, I mis-stepped and fell against the guardia in front of me, causing the other to grab and rudely shake me as if I had caused the trip on purpose.

"Gentle, lads," Barbier bade them. "No need to handle her like she's a parcel."

As we exited to the street, the cool air hit my face and I gasped with relief. There was indeed a crowd. For a moment I feared they were Ghastlies, but they were only ordinary folk, the rabble of the Hells looking for something upon which to vent their anger about their poor existence. Faces with fiery eyes and hands with mean fists.

Barbier and de Windt had moved away to handle their men while the crowd shouted. "Let her go!" "Death to all aristos!"

Perhaps their message of support should have buoyed me, but it only frightened me more. I was abruptly thankful for the guardia on either side of me. If I died from violence, the crowd would not care. I was only a reason to vent their spleen upon those in authority. Another rock flew by, narrowly missing a guardia's head.

A gendarme wagon to transport criminals with its two horses was shoving through the crowd with the help of the king's men, who were mounted on horses and waving their sabers. One of them was a uniformed Jacques Moreau. He was maneuvering his mount backward, the horse's hindquarters pushing people back. There were five other cavalry men, but their horses were so closely crowded that they had little room to maneuver so the black wagon wasn't making much progress towards us. Trying to reach it would leave us exposed in the crowd, with no space for retreat.

De Windt took his frustration out upon Barbier. "Why haven't your men cuffed her yet? She's a dangerous murderer!"

"She isn't going anywhere. Let her keep her hands. She may need them if things go belly-up."

Ignoring the inspector, de Windt stared hard at the guardia standing next to me. "Shackle her."

The man looked at his commander, and Barbier nodded reluctantly.

One of the guards, a man I recognized from a previous investigation, whispered, "Sorry, madame." He snapped open a manacle, and I felt the cold steel go around one wrist.

This couldn't be happening!

A voice as powerful as Death summoning one to the Afterlife rang forth. "You shall relinquish what is mine."

Tristan Fontaine, in his tailored suit of charcoal gray, stood at the front of the crowd. His face was a storm, and his eyes promised murder. Seeing him, I felt a wave of lightheadedness. The guardia's hand on my wrist dropped away, leaving the other cuff to dangle loose from my wrist.

"Elinor, come here."

When I reached his side, one of Tristan's arms came around me, moving me behind him. "Farrow, I shall need a horse."

"Here now!" cried de Windt in protest. He was ignored.

From behind Tristan, Farrow pushed backward through the crowd, his head above many as he went to the horse and rider closest to him. Thankfully, it wasn't Jacques who was struggling to keep his horse from rearing. The chestnut with its long bow nose was panicking as its rider sawed hard on the reins, pulling back at the same time as he tried to spur the horse onward. Confused, the animal spun in a tight circle and caused his rider to slip sideways from the saddle, his boots losing their stirrups.

My bodyguard took advantage of it. He put his hand under the man's boot sole and gave it a shove upward, unseating the rider completely. The soldier landed hard on the cobblestones. The crowd cheered, and he was quickly pulled away by them.

"Now, now, my beauty," Farrow told the horse, gripping the reins tightly under its chin and bringing it to Tristan. "Your mount, Your Grace."

Grabbing the reins, Tristan mounted in one smooth motion. The horse made its displeasure known with a small rear; Tristan didn't seem to notice. Like a dance, his hips swayed to the animal's rhythm as it pranced sideways, pushing away protesters who feared its kicking hooves.

"Put your foot in the stirrup, Elinor." I couldn't. I didn't have the strength or the knowledge. "Farrow, assist the lady."

Bear-sized hands seized me, hoisting me onto the horse's back. Before I could fall, I wrapped my arms quickly around Tristan's waist to hold me fast. There was no room in the saddle, so I was behind it, and I could feel the horse's powerful hindquarters moving below me, the heat of its body, and the smell of its sweat.

Tristan made the horse spin, producing open ground as the mob jumped back, fearing to be trampled. From behind him, I saw them all: de Windt's face contorted with rage, Barbier hiding a smirk, and Jacques' white face. The Crown prosecutor was frothing at the mouth. "You can't take her, Fontaine! Give her back. She murdered Lady Josephine Baudelaire!"

Tristan politely touched his hat in goodbye. "Good day, gentlemen. De Windt, give His Majesty my regards."

Jacques was no longer looking our way, but behind me. I followed his gaze and saw one of the king's men raising his gun to shoot. Down on its barrel came the flat blade of Jacques' sword, and the rifle went flying, just as our horse sprang forward.

Of course I'd been around horses in terms of them pulling quick-cabs, but had never ridden one. The sensation of its powerful hindquarters driving us forward was mystifying and terrifying all at once. How could he control it? Why would it not throw us off?

Hands tried to grab my dress, to stop us, but Tristan gave some command, and suddenly the horse became a lethal dancer. It was spinning, turning, rearing, and leaping into the air, all at Tristan's command.

Suddenly, we broke free. Past the black wagon, past the crowd. We turned and took a narrow path through a market filled with barrels, baskets, and carts. As we flew past, I heard shouts: "Hey!" "Who are you?!" "What's happening?"

But we were flying, the horse entering a smooth canter, its shoes ringing against the cobblestones.

It was only then that I tried to ask a question. "How did you find me?"

"Long story. I shall tell you later."

"Josephine Baudelaire's been murdered." It was horrible how they had desecrated her corpse. With my arms wrapped around him I felt more than heard his grunt in reply. "Where are we going?"

"We need a place to regroup."

I nodded against his back.

Gone were the winding old streets of the Hells. Houses replaced tenements, and people going about their business watched us with some curiosity. Tristan brought the horse down to a jolting trot and started taking alleys.

We were in a part of Alenbonné that I knew nothing about, but he seemed familiar with it, as he brought the horse to a halt in front of a horse-high wooden gate. Bringing his mount sideways to it, Tristan pounded a fist on the wood. The gate opened revealing an enclosed courtyard of a working stable. It was quickly closed behind us by a heavy-set man wearing a leather apron.

Tristan threw his leg over the neck of the sweaty horse and jumped to the ground.

"Here, Elinor, let me help you down. Just slide."

With his arm steadying me, I brought one leg over and slid down the side of the horse, mixing its wet horse hair with the dried blood on my dress. My legs were jelly.

Tristan greeted the man who opened the gate. "Dixon. I need the horse and gear to vanish."

"Aye. Could be a bit difficult with the king's brand on his rump. You want him cut up for the soup pot?" Dixon was clearly a blacksmith, from his leather apron and the hammer he held.

Tristan gave a chuckle, probably more from relief than genuine humor. "He's a bit of a bad boy, but no, I don't think he deserves that. Deliver him back to barracks if you can do it without causing comment. Say you found him wandering in a park."

Dixon took the reins, leading our four-hooved savior away. Tristan put his hand around my waist, bringing me into the shadows of the barn. "Dixon is one of mine. He can be trusted. Now, tell me what happened."

The words rushed out of me. "Dr. Devereaux visited me at your house. I agreed to be hypnotized."

"What?! Elinor!"

"I'm sorry. It was a stupid idea, but I thought I would be safe at your house."

"As you should have been," he muttered.

"During our session, the secret passage behind the painting opened, and a woman stepped through." I rubbed my forehead, trying to recall. "She hit Dr. Devereaux, and that's all I remember until I woke up in that house." I gripped Tristan's arm and shook it. "Josephine. She is dead."

"That explains why you are covered in blood."

I nodded, trying not to cry. "De Windt accused me of murdering her! He said I was seen leaving with Josephine from her house. Someone described seeing a small woman in black with a veil."

"Easy enough to find a body double. But it makes me believe that our master criminal is about to make his final move. He sacrificed Josephine in an attempt to take my queen."

Looking up, I asked faintly, hopefully, "Am I your queen?"

"Of course, my dear. And I will sacrifice a king to have you."

His kiss was intense, and I gladly welcomed it. Being drugged, waking up next to a corpse, and being accused of murder made one feel fortunate to be alive. Tristan's fingers tangled in my knotted hair as he tugged my head back for another kiss. I did not care. We were both feeling frantic and wild.

I had always felt I was strong enough for any task, but having Tristan with me, his maleness, his strength, made me realize how much sometimes even I wasn't enough. His grip around me was so firm, a physical strength that I knew would somehow support and protect me. Perhaps it was primal, but I found my intellect agreeing to it.

"You really need to stop getting into these scrapes," he said affectionately.

Scrapes? He just committed an act against the man who was the king's chief law enforcement officer!

I cried out again, this time with worry. "Tristan?"

He read my mind. "Don't worry."

The soft words made me start to cry. "What will happen to you?"

"Don't worry," he repeated, stroking my hair.

It just made me cry harder.

Behind me I heard someone clear their throat. It was the blacksmith, Dixon.

"My wife set up a bath inside. Fresh clothes for the lady."

"Good, Dixon. Good."

Chapter Three

The bath was a hip-tub set in front of the kitchen fire. Sheets were hung on a rope for my privacy. Behind the screen, I pulled off clothes that were stiff with blood. When I finished, my hands were trembling.

On the opposite side, perhaps because of my silence, Tristan wondered how I was doing.

"I'm fine." I climbed into the old washtub. My knees came to my chin, but I didn't care. The hot water felt so good that I groaned.

"Are you sure you're all right?"

"Yes, Tristan. It just feels good." I slipped down, letting the water come across my shoulders and neck, embracing the heat. "How did you know where I was?"

On the other side of the hanging sheet, Tristan explained. "I was standing in the gallery listening to them arguing about the death of Lord Bridoux—"

"De Windt mentioned him! Who is he?"

"Lord Bridoux? I wouldn't think twice about him except that someone walked up to him and his wife in the park this morning and shot them. He died on the spot. She is not expected to live."

After a moment, Tristan continued. "Bridoux had a minor government position, something he gained because of his title. His death exposes the vulnerability of the aristocracy. Imagine someone bold enough to commit such an act in broad daylight! No wonder his murder has caused outrage."

All sound was muted as I ducked under the water to rinse my hair. When I resurfaced, some of the water splashed over to the stone floor. The blacksmith's washtub was a paradise I could have stayed in forever, or at least until the water cooled.

"So you didn't know of my abduction?"

"No," he said shortly. There was a pause. "What I will tell you will sound crazy. Though in my time with you, I've seen the dead speak, so perhaps this is no stranger."

"What happened?" Now he had my full attention.

"I had no idea anything was wrong. I thought you were secure at my house, perfectly safe." He started to describe the hall where the lords and commoners argued the law. "The building has windows in a row set high above the gallery. It lets in light, but not a view. It's not unusual to see light streaking down when the early morning or late evening sun hits it right. There was shouting and arguing, but my attention was captured instead by a shaft of golden light that was illuminating a statue behind the dais of the head speaker."

"What statue?"

"Ah. Right, you haven't been inside and seen. There are white marble statues in niches along every wall. They each symbolize some noble virtue or person."

"What was this one?"

"Elysia. She's a virtue, a protector of mothers and children. Then I heard music."

"Music," I whispered.

"It sounded like chimes. Bells? Or a clock striking. I suddenly wondered what you were doing, and I felt an overwhelming urgency to talk with you. I left parliament and went to my office to tell Stephan I was leaving for the day when he handed me a note from Jacques Moreau."

"Jacques!" I gasped in surprise. The soap slipped from my hands, disappearing into the murky depths of the tub.

"It warned me that you were about to be arrested and gave an address in the Hells."

"Jacques," I repeated. "He stopped us from getting shot during our retreat." I explained about his sword hitting the gun of his fellow officer.

"Hm, I might need to rethink my estimation of that man. I thought he hated me."

"Probably he still does, but I doubt he'd want to harm me."

I picked up the pitcher near the tub's side and poured it over my head to rinse my hair. "Oh!"

"What's wrong?!"

"The water is getting cold."

I used a faded towel to dry myself, making sure I stood by the fire. To rid it of water, I twisted my hair into a rope and squeezed it before rubbing it briskly with a towel.

Tristan said, "Dixon brought you some boy's clothes, as it is a better disguise than a dress. I hope that doesn't bother you?"

"No. That's fine."

He handed them through the slit where the two sheets met. The clothes were made from a rough, coarse fabric, a laborer's outfit, with trousers too long, and a wide waist that slipped down past my hips. I rolled up the cuffs and used suspenders to keep them from falling down. The fullness of my bust made it difficult to hide the fact that I was a woman. Perhaps the coat was bulky enough that if I met someone in the dark, in the fog, who was blind in one eye, I could pass as a short, fat boy.

On the other side of the curtain, I heard heavy boots and the blacksmith's gruff voice. "Your Grace. The horse will be found running loose near the royal stables, with no one the wiser."

"Good. Now I need a few other things. Perhaps a quick supper before we leave? If that would not inconvenience you and your wife?"

"Certainly, Your Grace. I'll let her know."

After I heard the door close again, I pulled back the sheet. Tristan was alone. He was no longer wearing his immaculate trousers and coat. Instead, he was garbed in a laborer's outfit of baggy trousers, a worn work shirt stained by long use, and a wool coat of poor manufacturing. A cord worked as a belt around his waist.

He appraised me critically. "Not very convincing in the light, so be sure to remain silent and slouch. We shall head out after midnight and darkness will help."

"What about the curfew? Won't we be noticed by the patrols?"

"Don't worry, Elinor. I know what I'm doing."

I pursed my lips to stop from saying more. It wasn't like I had experience running from the law.

In the courtyard, someone had set up a table with food and drink. In my half-starved state, the dumplings and chicken soup tasted better than anything Chef Perdersen could make. Across the yard, Dixon was working the bellows on a fire, and we talked to the hammering of iron on his anvil.

"Apple cider to drink." Tristan put a pewter cup beside my plate.

When my spoon was scraping the bottom for the second time, he said, "Once you finish, we need to do something about your hair."

My hand went up to touch it. "What do you mean?"

"We need to conceal it."

"Is that a *horse* brush?" I exclaimed when he picked up something from the box resting on the bench.

"I work with the tools I'm familiar with." Taking up my long hair in one hand, he started parting it into sections. It took time to work out the knots, and I grimaced when he hit a snag. "I was once in the cavalry. Long, long ago. Before my father died. It's what first brought me to King Guénard's attention."

"You were that good?"

"I'm afraid to disappoint you, Elinor, but it wasn't my brilliance that caught his attention. It was my disregard for status. When the king's horse took off with him during the dress parade, I was the only one who didn't consider his dignity. I ran his nag down while the rest of the company stood frozen at attention, like lumps on logs. I was quietly discharged because of dereliction of duty for that bit of heroism."

"You probably saved his life, and that was your reward?!" I said, outraged.

"Afterward, I learned that he had requested the discharge so he could call me back to court, for he had plans for me. Thus, my life changed because of a runaway horse."

"How unfair!"

"Elinor, working for King Guénard has never been about fairness. It's about what you can get away with that suits his wishes. Anyone in his orbit must dance to his tune, like planets around the sun."

His words made me suddenly feel fearful. What would happen to us now? "What will His Majesty think of you saving me? Stealing me from his own men?"

Tristan had finished the brushing and started to braid my hair. "He may see it as a joke— or an attack on his authority. You never know. Guénard has the mind and temperament of a spoiled brat."

"Tristan!"

He gave me a lopsided smile. "Those who are raised with power and wealth don't always grow up, Elinor. They sometimes become stunted, and such is the case with His Majesty."

"It sounds like you don't like him."

"I've seen too much and understand how things really work. Nepotism and corruption sticks to everyone."

"So you agree with the rebels? The system is corrupt?"

"Yes, and no. Things do need to change. Improvements. But the government cannot be reformed in this warlike manner. Killing members of le beau idéal is not the way to make change."

"What will happen to me? Where shall I go?" My bottom lip started to quiver as I thought of my rooms at the Crown and my friends. Anne-Marie was at Hartwood, probably still waiting for me. Twyla was certainly in some sort of danger. And those that knew me would soon hear I was accused of murder.

Tristan sat down beside me on my bench and gave my shoulders a gentle shake. "No self-pity. That isn't the Elinor I know."

I sniffed, wiping the back of my hand indelicately across my nose. He handed me a fine linen handkerchief initialed in the corner with his family crest. Seeing it made me blubber more. "You can't wear those clothes and carry a handkerchief that looks like this!" I shook it in his face. "You'll be caught and hanged as an accessory to a murderer!"

Tristan appeared very calm for a man who might soon be standing next to me on the gallows. "Good point. I shall need to burn this in a fire before we leave."

He didn't seem to be paying attention. I needed to make him understand. "De Windt is sure to tell the king you saved me. He thinks me a murderer and is bound to paint you very black, as he dislikes you so."

"I imagine he's telling His Majesty right now that I am a villain of the worst type." Tristan actually smiled.

"You cannot be taking this so lightly! What will become of you? You are the Duke de Archamebeau, master of the Chambaux estate. You can't be rescuing would-be murderers."

His smile remained, but his eyes were serious. "You forget I know all about being accused of murder. Somehow, I weathered the storm. And you, Elinor Chalamet, are the least likely murderer I know. You shall also sail this storm to calmer waters."

I opened my mouth, and he put his finger over my lips, stopping me from speaking. His gaze mellowed and took on an aspect that made my breath catch.

"Dear one, let me protect you the way I want. Will you marry me?"

Of course I said no again.

"Is it because of my title?"

I tried the same argument although it sounded tired even to my ears. "I'm an independent woman. I'd lose my identity if we married. Remember?"

"Yes, so you've told me before. But I've thought about your words and I think they are utter nonsense. You know our union would never subjugate you. You'd walk out on me if I ever did so."

I said weakly, "I'm a wanted criminal. What would your mother think?"

"She chose the first woman; I shall choose the next and last. Dearest, please listen to me. If you married me, the Chambaux name would protect you. De Windt would think twice before arresting a duchesse."

That made it all the worse.

"I don't want to be a duchesse." My protest came out as a wail.

His thumb brushed over my cheek as he held my gaze. "Really? Well, if you don't want the title, don't use it. Just use the simple address of lady. That has a nice catch. Lady Fontaine."

"Sounds like your sister." My lip trembled.

"What's the real reason, Elinor?"

My hand came up to capture his, and I held it tightly. "Marrying me would bring you many problems. Your family wouldn't like it. Your peers would never accept me. It wouldn't advance your career. It would be a bad idea. For you."

"I love you. Do you love me? Or are you only toying with my affections?" The last he said with a smirk.

"You know I love you! How could I not?"

He wrapped his arms around me, drawing me tight. "Then it's time you made me an honest man."

Chapter Four

I was married over an anvil.

As a blacksmith, Dixon could officiate. However, I insisted that he understand I was determined to make our union be morganatic, much to Tristan's initial irritation.

"I dislike your insistence on this left-handed marriage," he protested. "You are my wife and should be treated equally."

His pride was pricked, but I was considering my own in the matter.

"You can't deny that we are not the same in social standing. As soon as you register our marriage officially, I shall be accused of using you to elevate myself, not marrying you because I love you dearly. This way I make it clear that I will not inherit anything from your ancestral home, Chambaux."

"I don't care what society thinks." He crossed his arms and looked sour.

"As you've told me many times! But I am not so lofty as to think I can ignore tittle-tattle. Anyway, this should appease your sister and mother. You have a cousin in charge of Chambaux who you've led to expect that he will inherit it. It would be harsh to deny him something you have given the impression is his."

He protested again. "But what of our children? You've robbed them of their inheritance by insisting on this."

"Surely you have other lands or property you can give them?" I put my hand on his arm, attempted to cajole him. "Besides our children might want to make their own way in the world, without the burden of vast wealth or titles."

Tristan was not convinced. "Have you ever tried living with a title or vast wealth? It makes the world very comfortable."

"Why are we fighting over this? If you wish to be married to me, you could bend a little. I know I am."

"We are not fighting, Elinor. At this point, I'm just glad to get you committed to matrimony."

"And this legality will make me feel easier about it."

He bowed his head. "Fine. If this is your condition."

"It is."

~

The ceremony was a simple one.

First, Dixon had to cut off the come-along on my wrist. As the metal broke with one strike of his chisel, he joked, "Off with one shackle and on with another."

Despite what others might think I reminded myself this wasn't a marriage of gratitude or desperation. As the ceremony started, my heart calmed. This was right.

We stood facing each other, and crossed our hands over the anvil, my right hand holding Tristan's right, our lefts similarly joined. From somewhere, Dixon's wife had found a red ribbon— faded to pink and evidently much loved— that she tied around each of our wrists.

After cleansing a blade in the flames, Dixon started the ceremony:

Right is bound to right,
Left tied to left,
Red is the ribbon,
That ties the heartstrings together.
Join the bodies,
Unite the minds.
And bind the spirits,
Thus two, become one.

The cut of his knife on the inside of my wrist barely registered, for his blade was sharp and he did not hesitate. After he cut Tristan's wrist, we held the flat of our left wrists together to mingle the blood. Our eyes held so much emotion that it filled my heart until I had no words.

Dixon's wife pulled the end of the ribbon and it fell from our wrists. It had been a symbol of our heart's blood, but as ours mingled together, it was no longer needed.

Passing the blade over the smithy fire once more, Dixon directed us to hold our wrists up so he could cauterize our slight wounds. My nostrils flared at the smell of burned skin. We both would have our two scars; marks that proclaimed our ceremony to the world.

"Iron seals the union," said Dixon, solemnly. A sigh seemed to fill the room, and the fire flickered as if being blown by a wind. Somewhere down the alley, a dog howled.

Tristan swept me up into a crushing hold, and gave me a deep kiss that made Dixon's wife exclaim, "Ain't these two lovely!"

The next few hours were spent drinking. We were brought cups of mulled wine and hunks of salted bread.

"No cake," mourned the blacksmith's wife, whom I'd learned was called Lucy.

"Bread is more traditional, I believe," I told her as I dipped the end into the wine and held it out for Tristan to take a bite. He bent forward and, flashing his teeth, nipped off the end while he arched his eyebrows at me in a devilish way.

"Wife," he said, holding out his own piece of wine-dipped bread.

"Husband," I replied, taking my bite.

And so we began married life.

It seems when you marry a man with property, he always has coin to tip. He gave Dixon and his wife a set of coins in the traditional manner, with each representing a distinct part of the ceremony: the copper penny for blood, the silver knight for body, and the gold royal for spirit.

Talking and drinking went on for hours, and I was half-asleep leaning against Tristan when he shook me fully awake. "Time to go. Our ride is here. Dixon reports that the entire city is in an uproar. Lord Bridoux's death is the reason given, but my contacts state they are looking for a short, blond woman and a tall, dark-haired man."

We shook hands with Dixon and his wife, thanking them for their hospitality, before exiting the gate doors to find a wagon filled with horse dung waiting in the alley for us.

"You must be joking," I exclaimed.

"I'm not," said Tristan. "Manure must leave the city regardless of what politics are happening, for the horses make too much of it. No one will expect the Duke de Archambeau to be driving a wagon filled with horseshit."

Before I could protest any further, he grabbed me around the waist and lifted me up to the driver's box. He mounted after me, settling next to me and picking up the reins. The wagon shook as we rattled down the lane pulled by the biggest horse I had ever seen. Tristan told me his plan.

"My name is Tom and you are John. You're my nephew, who is helping."

"Where are we going with it?"

"Outside the city."

"We can't leave!"

"Elinor." He shook his head. "You've obviously never been hunted. We are the fox being chased by the hounds, and we need to obscure our trail, backtrack, and double track in a direction they won't expect."

"Why leave and come back?"

"Those helping us need time to do their work. Meanwhile, we can make it easier for them by not getting arrested or shot."

We were only stopped five times before we got out of Alenbonné. By the third time, it was routine. I stayed quiet and let Tristan do all the talking. He said everything in such a broad country accent that I could hardly follow his words. Whenever a guard looked my way, I slumped and tried to imitate my street friend Marcus. Sulky, but confident.

The guardia were almost at the end of their shift and were thinking of home. They didn't care about a manhunt and while they poked the mounds of manure with a fork, no one was hiding under it, so they sent us on our way. We went out while wagons bearing country produce entered the city.

I kept waiting for someone to ride after us, shouting for us to stop, but they didn't.

"That was too easy," I commented.

"Our hunters don't expect us to leave, and surely not in this manner. My guess is that your rooms at the Crown, your servant's home, and Hartwood are already being searched. Once they discover we are not there, they will set a watch upon those locations they think we shall return to. They will expect you to reach out to someone you know, and will look for you among the class to which you belong."

"But they know I'm with you! What about your family? *Your* connections?"

"I wish them well with that. If the situation wasn't so serious, I would enjoy having de Windt going through my private papers and watch his frustration grow as he comes up with exactly nothing! Stephan and my staff only know about my official duties, nothing of my other life."

"What do you mean?" I cuddled up close to him and sunk my hands deep in my trouser pockets. With an hour until sunrise, the night air felt chilly.

"De Windt and Barbier are bureaucrats. They manage people who are known— the guardia and the king's men. Their actions must be public, for they serve the public."

"Aren't you a public servant?"

"Not like de Windt and Barbier are. I serve the king so I'm a free agent, given tasks that the king doesn't want others to know about. Hence, my network is all in my head. People like Dixon. There is no indication that he is connected to the Duke de Archambeau. No money trail, correspondence, or recorded visits."

"Oh. But what of Stephan? Wouldn't he know about Dixon?"

"No. I only use my staff to take care of the work that is public. Meetings with other officials, letters. I never want someone to face the accusations I did because of Minette's actions. Ignorance is their protection."

After leaving the city boundary, we were quickly in the flat farmlands that surrounded the city, with their drainage canals and stalks of corn and wheat. The tedious view made my head nod, and I eventually fell asleep, leaning against Tristan.

It was probably an hour later that the jolting halt of the wagon woke me. We had reached a farm. A man was crossing the farmyard, a few chickens dramatically running out of his way, squawking and beating their wings. He listened to Tristan's request, nodded his head, and ambled back to the barn.

In the end, he took our wagon and horse and gave us a pony with a cart loaded with metal canisters filled with milk. Back on the main road, Tristan told me to check under the seat.

"There's a basket! Biscuits. Cold ham, cheese, apples, and some milk."

"Good man. I'll have to send a thank you to his wife. Now, eat up, for we shall be awhile on the road."

It took about an hour before we reached a hamlet of roughly five buildings situated around a town square. It seemed we were delivering milk, and Tristan knew every house where we dropped off a canister. If we met anyone, they called him Louis, and while a couple gave me a curious glance, no one asked about me outright. Tristan did not volunteer any explanation for my presence.

At the last house on the edge of the village we got down from the wagon. Two men exited the back door, and the elder shook hands with Tristan while the boy took the pony and cart. After a brief conversation I could not hear, they left. I was about to ask why we were standing there when up drove a large wagon filled with cabbages and squash, driven by a broad-shouldered farmwife.

"Come along, you two. I'm already late to market."

We climbed aboard the tailgate. I found a nice pumpkin to sit on, though when the woman clucked to her horse the wagon's jolting movement almost made me fall off.

"Hang on to the sideboard," said Tristan, demonstrating how he moved sideways to lay his arm along the side of the wagon.

It was probably mid-morning when she stopped at a cross-roads, and Tristan jumped down. He held out his hand, and I gripped it before scrambling off. The driver didn't say goodbye, only slapped her reins on the horse's broad back, and started down the road.

Instead of waiting for someone else, Tristan took my hand and started walking.

Before I had kept silent, fearing my girlish voice would give us away; now we were alone. "Where are we going?"

"A place where we can rest."

"Good. I hope there's a nice bed." My headache had faded, but now I was feeling incredibly tired.

"Now that's the spirit I like to see in my new bride," quipped

Tristan, and I gave a bit of a breathless laugh. I kept forgetting our marriage was less than six hours old!

Our path eventually became narrower until we had to walk single file. We had been traveling downward, and the trees were thickening. I was stumbling by the time Tristan stopped, and he pulled me alongside him, his hand around my waist.

"What do you think of our getaway?"

We had arrived at a canal, and floating on its serene surface was a narrowboat.

Chapter Five

The bed was soft, and the rocking boat quickly lulled me to sleep after such an exhausting day. Hours later, I awoke, disoriented.

"It's all right. Bad dream?" Tristan's voice was husky against my neck. He was lying behind me, his arm draped over my hip.

"It took me a moment to recall everything that's happened." I blinked, trying to dispel the image of Josephine from my mind. Her face would haunt me for some time.

"I hope one thing you remembered is we are married." His warm fingers pulled back the braid of my hair, exposing the small hairs on my neck. He leaned in and kissed my skin.

"Yes, of course I do." I could feel the ache on my wrists, the burn that showed to the world we were united by oath and law.

Tristan's hand came across my chest and he started unbuttoning my blouse.

We hadn't lain together since that fateful day in the grass at Hightower when he had told me the truth about Minette. Again, I smelled the fresh grass and the wildflowers, felt the breeze that blew over skin as we'd made love that day.

The cabin was dim, with a faint sunset light coming through

the porthole, suggesting we had slept the day away. I rolled over to see his face and found his eyes very serious. "I didn't force you into marriage, did I?"

"You did rather, but I think I wanted to be forced. Otherwise, I would be too afraid to ever agree."

His fingers went back to toying with the buttons. It being a boy's shirt, it took only a moment before they were all undone. He pulled the tail out from under my trousers and rubbed his warm, flat palm along the skin of my stomach. I closed my eyes, feeling the pleasant tingle that the path of his hand caused.

"Are you happy, Elinor? Truly?"

"Yes."

"I doubt it was the ceremony you had dreamed of as a girl," he remarked dryly, as his hand caressed my hip and the curve of my waist.

Opening my eyes, I pulled myself up to kiss his cheek. "I was far too busy to moon over how I would marry. If I put much thought into it, I doubted it would ever happen."

Tristan moved, shifting a leg over my thigh to hold me. I discovered boy's trousers didn't have the padding that layers of women's clothing did, and I felt the warmth of his body and the muscle in his thighs. It was very distracting.

"I don't want you to feel I forced you. That I took advantage of your situation."

"Do you think you forced me at Hightower?" I felt rather insulted by the implication.

"I thought perhaps that was done from pity."

How strange men are!

"I didn't give you the greatest gift a woman has out of pity. And you aren't forcing me now." I returned the favor and started unbuttoning his shirt, exposing the dark curly hairs on his chest. "I love you, Tristan Fontaine, and want to be with you for the rest of my life."

He pulled me against him, interrupting my action with a

forceful kiss. He murmured against my cheek, "My dear girl. You were so beautiful at the restaurant. I wanted to forget going to the theater and take you home to my bed instead."

"Well, a good thing you didn't! If we hadn't gone, the Luminary would have gone up in flames!" I reminded him.

He chuckled in a gruff, masculine way. "Elinor, how can you be so pragmatic when I'm trying to be romantic?"

"It's only the truth!"

His teeth made little nibbles across my collarbone. "I've wanted you ever since I first saw you in Dr. LaRue's morgue — so sure of yourself, making me look a fool with that little whistle thing. Taunting me."

"Who would have thought a visit to the morgue would be the start of a romance?"

"Ah. But I couldn't help it. You were so tiny, with that spark in your eye. And that impertinent mouth of yours, challenging me. Laughing at me." Tristan kissed me, tugging on my lip. "But sadly, I quickly discovered you were only interested in investigating cases, so I brought you one, like a cat brings a mouse to someone they love." He grimaced, remembering. "I should never have brought you the Losendahl case, risking you."

"Without me, you would never have found her," I pointed out.

"Better to have lost her than you. I could have killed Parnell for what he did to you!"

My hand slid up his forearm to his bicep, feeling the firm muscle underneath. "Well, you did give him a good thrashing, according to Twyla, so I'll accept that in the spirit that it was meant."

He grinned and gave me another fierce kiss followed by others that were undecided if they wanted to eat or caress me. I knew what I wanted.

He paused between nibbles. "Tell me when you first realized you loved me?"

I wrapped my hands around the back of his neck and considered his question. "Well, I admit I was a bit disappointed when you were possessed and only kissed me because the ghost of Bastiaan Hagen mistook me for his lost love."

"What a waste of a first kiss!" He made up for it now. "But when did you love me, Elinor? When did you know?"

"Oh, I think it was when you shot Lord Buckard for his attempt to molest Lady Tulip. It was done so quickly and efficiently." As soon as I spoke, I wished to take the words back. Honestly, I had forgotten about Minette. My hand cupped his face. "I didn't mean—"

He turned his head and kissed my palm. "I know, I know."

Wanting to think of something else, I changed the subject. "But what of you? When did you know you loved me? You have only mentioned an attraction. When did you love me?"

His hand toyed with my braid, pulling it apart so my hair scattered over my bare breast.

"I kept telling myself that I was only physically attracted to you. You were so small, and full of fire. Your eyes were always laughing at me, daring me to counter your outrageous statements. How many times did I imagine doing this to tame you?" At my gasp, he laughed. "Oh, Elinor, if only I had been brave enough!"

"You still haven't answered my question."

"It is hard to define the when. My need to see you, hear your laugh, your voice and smile, made me come back despite my family's insistence on leaving you alone. They knew before I did that I wasn't going to forget you. When you left with Parnell and we couldn't find you — you cannot imagine the horror I felt thinking I would not find you alive."

Our fingers tightly intertwined.

"But you did find me! And all was well."

"But for weeks I did fear I was too late. That your fate would be like Ebbe's, living a half-life. When your doctor friend came to me with her concerns that you were not recovering, I panicked.

You needed rest and encouragement. I thought Hightower would give you a ghost hunting treat without any danger. How wrong I was!"

"Hightower was perfect!" I insisted. Especially as we had first made love, first confessed to our feelings, there. "Didn't you enjoy our time there?"

He chuckled again. "Elinor, we had to deal with a murder, cemetery ghosts, and accusations of treason from de Windt. It wasn't the holiday I had envisioned."

"Anne-Marie said you invited me only to seduce me."

"I think it was you that seduced me!" Grinning, he tapped the tip of my nose with his forefinger.

"Well, maybe. A little," I confessed, blushing.

"Talking about seduction, I'd like to stop talking and concentrate on other matters." The placement of his hands emphasized his meaning.

"Well. Hm. I feel a bit nervous about this."

"Nervous?" He was surprised. "After Hightower, why would you be nervous?"

I couldn't meet his eyes, so looked at the porthole. "That was an impulse. Unplanned. This is. Well, we're married!" I blurted out.

He reared back, astonished. "Wouldn't being married make it easier? More natural for you?"

Confused and uncomfortable, I started to babble. "It's just now you are in charge. The man rules a marriage. Before I was free, my own woman. What if I do the wrong thing? Make you despise me for my ignorance? Marriage is forever and I could mess this up."

"My dear girl, even when you argue or chastise me, I know how lucky I am to be with you." He locked his hand into mine again, clasping it, the matching burn marks evident on both of our wrists. "It is more likely that I will disappoint you than you me! I made a muddle of my first marriage. I work for a childish tyrant, and my mother is such a gorgon she makes the king blanch whenever he sees she is a guest at the table."

He searched my face, seeing my doubt. He nodded, making a decision. "I see I shall have to woo you."

"Woo me? We're married."

"The courtship should always continue. Will you let me show you how to come together in joy?"

I nodded, feeling embarrassed and excited at the same time.

Of course, Tristan was far more experienced in making love than I, who had only one dalliance amongst the grass and wildflowers to my name. On the little rocking boat he was kind and patient, helping me to relax, but it wasn't until hours later, after a brief nap, that we came together without the burden of talk, and with only our feelings showing the way.

This time it was he who fell asleep first, his head resting on my hair and his hand on my bare belly. Looking down at his profile, I kissed the top of his head. Dear boy, how much I loved him.

Stroking where his hand lay, in an instant my mind put the jumbled pieces together, and I realized that I was now carrying his child six weeks later. Counting back, I realized I hadn't had a womanly cycle since my time at the lighthouse.

It was a good thing I was married. And that I had sworn away Tristan's title and wealth.

Chapter Six

"What are you dreaming about, sleepyhead?"

I was half awake and opened my eyes at Tristan's comment, stretching my arms overhead. Sun was streaming through the porthole, showing it to be morning, a day after our escape from Alenbonné.

"Breakfast, I think."

"Should I serve you in bed?" He dipped down and gave me a kiss.

Married life had its advantages. Waking up in the early morning to a naked man lying next to you. Taking advantage of him and snuggling up to return to sleep. Having him make breakfast? Well, that was just another bonus.

"I'd much rather get dressed and see where we are. I was too tired yesterday to notice much."

"Tired? It didn't seem like that to me." He waggled his eyebrows at me, and I blushed. Grabbing the sheets, I pulled them up to my chin to give myself coverage. "Could you give a woman a bit of privacy, mysir!"

He laughed, but turned his back. "I've set a table up top on the deck. Though there isn't much space, you can get some fresh air."

"How did you find anything to eat?"

"Oh, this is one of my bolt holes. It's kept stocked with things someone on the run and needing to lie low might want."

His words reminded me that my old friend at the guardia would now be hunting me down to arrest me for the murder of Josephine Baudelaire.

Tristan started up the ladder, telling me, "I'll meet you up top. There's a hand mirror hanging on the wall, with some kit. If you want to freshen up, I've put water in the pitcher."

Next to where the mirror hung was a mug, brush, and razor for Tristan to shave. Curious, I leaned over and smelled the soap. How strange it was having a man's things in my space!

The mirror revealed wild hair. Luckily, there was a real brush and comb, not just a horse brush. After bringing some order to my hair, I opted for one long braid, as it was easiest to manage when I did not have pins.

My neck was tender from where Tristan's appreciation last night had left its mark. Moving down, I touched lightly where my father's watch had marked me so long ago. Taking the mirror off its hook, I used the glass to examine my breasts. Yes, they seemed a bit heavier, somewhat swollen, and definitely tender. My cycle had been due two weeks ago.

My hands went down, and my fingers flared over my stomach. Was it bigger, or was that my imagination? Was a baby really growing inside me? I wasn't nauseous or feeling sick at all. I wasn't sure what to think of the possibility as I hadn't considered being a mother, let alone married. In two weeks, if I missed another cycle, I would ask Charlotte for advice.

I left off my stockings and climbed up the ladder barefoot.

It was a beautiful day. Mist was coming off the river with birdsong filling the air. Except for a few trees near the shoreline, the horizon was flat farmland, empty of people. No buildings, no shouts from vendors in the street to buy their wares, no carriages wheeling past. It wasn't the type of morning this city girl was used to experiencing.

"It seems so desolate, and unnaturally quiet," I said to Tristan as I took the seat he held out for me.

"It's called nature, Elinor."

Breakfast was not anything fresh. It all came from tins, but I wasn't going to complain about the lack of eggs or bread, although eating canned shrimp with peas was a strange combination. At least there was tea and coffee.

"Now, we need to discuss our plans."

"Agreed."

Tristan used his knife to point at a can of tuna. "Alenbonné." Next, he pointed at a group of peas that ringed the can. "First, a geography lesson on where we are. We left the city from the north side, but have since been traveling south, circling the city limits. We aren't as far from Alenbonné as you might think. Only a half-day away by the canal; at most a day, if we take it slow."

"So close? Why did we leave at all? Couldn't we have stayed at the blacksmith's?"

"The best way to throw off pursuit is to keep moving. Staying with Dixon would have caused too many questions from his neighbors. Our presence would have been hard to conceal, especially as he runs a thriving business. In the city, there are always gossips peering out their windows."

"Wouldn't our presence be talked about more in the countryside?"

"Country folk are a clannish lot, Elinor, and will discuss our presence only with their neighbors. The men here know me. I work beside them in the fields, drink with them, at least twice a year. If de Windt or Barbier sent someone, he would be viewed with hostility."

He reached over and tucked a stray lock of hair behind my ear. "I hope you won't be angry with me, but I've done more to keep you safe."

I narrowed my eyes. "What do you mean? And why do I have the feeling I won't like it?"

His reply was in what I always thought of as his duke's voice: arrogant, confident, and a bit possessive. "My rank protects you in ways that being Madame Chalamet would not. In a legal sense, you are now my property."

I opened my mouth to protest, but he laid his finger across my lips. I promptly nipped it, and he quickly removed it, shaking the digit in mock pain. "You little beast!"

"That's why I didn't want to get married!"

"You see it as a negative, but this is an advantage. I sent out letters while we were at Dixon's. By the time we return, our marriage will be filed as public record. I've ordered my lawyers to set a time and date for an official interview by de Windt so you can state the facts of the matter. Because I am your guardian now, this interview cannot take place unless I am present. Naturally, I will bring our lawyers. Note the plural. That is the advantage of money, dearest."

His high-handedness exasperated me. "You seem to have it all figured out! If I'm so safe, why are we on this houseboat?"

"It's a narrowboat," he corrected me. "I needed time for messages to be sent and for them to be received. To set things into motion. However, my plans provide only a superficial safety that the king could override at any time. I've sent a letter to Lady Talleyrand, asking her to notify King Guénard of the situation and get his forbearance in the matter."

"To accept that I'm a murderer?"

"Not at all. You have been falsely accused of a crime and as your husband, I have taken steps to see that you are protected. If we want to win His Majesty to our side, she can do it."

I had met Lady Talleyrand only recently. While she seemed a pleasant woman, my fate seemed to rely entirely upon her reputation as a diplomat and what Tristan believed her capable of doing with her silver tongue.

"I know you are impatient, my dear, but the noble class, le beau idéal has never been my friend and could turn on you in the same manner. We must step carefully to win the day. There is a reason I have elaborate bolt-holes set up. After Minette, I learned never to trust my peers."

His hand came over and cupped my cheek, his thumb stroking my jaw. "I would feel much better if you would let me send you to Chambaux. You could be on the Zulskaya border in an hour from there."

Sent away from him, to hide at his country estate where his mother lived? No! I would definitely not be telling Tristan my suspicion that I was pregnant, or I'd end up being locked in my room by the Duchesse de Chambaux, surrounded by vineyards.

"No." I shook my head. "There are people I care about in Alenbonné. Anne-Marie, who certainly is being questioned. Twyla. They could have been ensnared in this plot to smear me."

Tristan reluctantly nodded. "I understand. You have responsibilities, as I do, to people you love. But we shall move slowly and carefully. What if Dr. Devereaux is involved? Who used the passageway to kidnap you? This outlandish accusation could be just a distraction to stop Valentina's dinner party."

I had completely forgotten that Lady Talleyrand had been to meet Theodoor Vischeer and discuss a compromise to quell the voices moving against the king. "Surely, with the murder of Lord Bridoux, that dinner won't happen now. No noble would want to risk their neck meeting the rebels!"

"Now it's needed more than ever!" Tristan said vehemently. "If the unrest is not calmed, we risk total chaos, perhaps even the overthrow of a dynasty."

My eyes widened. "But surely all of this will blow over when the king restores order."

"I would not take that bet, Elinor." Gazing over the flat fields, Tristan saw other things. "We know that someone at the Morpheus Society made a drug to create these Ghastly beings. Who knows how many of those creatures are waiting to be called forth to destroy our city, our government? Unfortunately, the nobles are filled with fear by the recent assassination of Lord Bridoux, and they will react, predictably, by tightening their grip on a population already on fire to rebel. It's a powder keg."

"We must get back!"

He turned his head back to gaze at me, his eyes sad and serious. "We must."

It seemed he was taking this property idea way too far, for when I got up from the table, he grabbed my wrist and pulled me down into his lap. "I don't think I've gotten a kiss from you this morning, lady wife."

I gave him a peck on his nose. "How about that?"

"Not nearly enough. After all, I married a criminal. I think she should reward me far better."

"Why should I pay? We are married, as you keep reminding me."

"And I'll keep reminding you, as I have the feeling if I don't, you might slip away." His hand slipped up the back of my shirt, his palm warm on my back. It made me vastly aware of how little boys wore compared to young ladies.

"Tristan! What if we're seen?"

"Are you worried the birds and fish will carry tales? There is no one here. You weren't shy at Hightower."

"I was distracted by your sad story."

Both hands slid up under my shirt, across my ribs. "I can tell you another sad tale. How about when I fell off my pony, *Friponne*?"

"You are the rascal! I thought you said we should get back as soon as possible?" I said breathlessly.

"I'm newly married. A condition that has not brought me much pleasure in the past so I fully expect to enjoy myself this go around."

Chapter Seven

It was two hours before we left. Like many lovers, we ignored the world when it suited us.

The boat was powered by coal, and while we waited for it to gain the heat it needed, Tristan showed me the cheap art of disguise. Getting some mud from the shore and mixing it with old ashes, he smeared his hair, face, hands and arms. It aged him as the dirt settled into the wrinkles around his eyes and mouth.

"Should I do the same?"

"It would be best. And we should darken your hair." The ashes did that, dulling my blond to a dingy gray. "Now, a kerchief around your neck will help disguise your face." The cloth was greasy and smelled. Tristan pulled down a fisherman's knitted cap with a fishy perfume down on my head. Finished, he took a step back and examined his work.

"It won't deceive those who truly know you, but it may fool the casual glance."

"I thought getting a disguise would be romantic. Not dirty and smelly."

"Sacrifices have to be made, Elinor. Though I would prefer you just stay hidden when we meet people. Let me show you."

A panel in the floorboards lifted at a certain point to reveal a long rectangular cavity that would fit one person, two if they were children. It had airholes discreetly hidden by how the furniture was fixed into place.

"Hm. So I hide while you are in danger?"

"They'll be looking for a man and a woman."

Tristan did the steering, which made him a visible target, while I stayed concealed in the cabin. As the narrowboat glided across the water, bringing us closer to the city, we talked, sharing memories that had nothing to do with murder or ghosts. How my father had trained me to identify jewels with a memory game; a bedtime book with illustrations of bears that wore clothes and walked on their hind legs; and the time I tried to make my father a cake. Too busy reading, I had caused a kitchen fire when the cake burned.

Tristan talked of fishing. At one point in our journey he stopped and showed me how to use a sardine on the end of a hook, but we caught nothing. He spoke of long summers spent on his family estate, the dirt between his toes, running between the rows of vines, and the very fat pony who taught him how to take a fall.

Our childhoods seemed very far away. Perhaps that was why we chose to talk about them, for it took us both back to simpler times and avoided discussing a complicated present.

"Do you miss Chambaux?"

From where I sat, I could see his upper body and profile as he steered the rudder. He shrugged. "It was the place of my childhood, long gone, and can't be repeated. Sometimes I do miss the fields, smelling the air after a rain, seeing the mountains in the distance. What I really miss is the privacy, for in the country there are no prying eyes judging your every move as there are in court. No machinations. Life is simpler."

"But would you enjoy a simple life?" I asked skeptically.

"Now that I'm married to you, I do not think I'll have one." Tristan waggled his eyebrows at me to emphasize his words.

"I'm serious. It's hard to imagine you not getting bored living in the country."

He thought about what I said, finally agreeing. "I do enjoy a challenge. Perhaps that's why I haven't returned to Chambaux. The place runs smoothly without any guidance from me. It is set in its ways, and those ways will continue long after I'm dead."

We must have passed someone, for he suddenly gave a wave, calling out "Fine weather!" There was a returning shout from a farmer in the field, lost on the wind as we glided by.

"At Chambaux, I always felt like a caretaker. It is more of my mother's place than mine. Valentina was not joking when she said our mother would be out in the vineyard giving non-stop advice. When I think of her officiousness, I pity my cousin."

"You don't want to go back?"

"Not at all. Why this sudden interest?" He seemed wary.

"I was just trying to imagine you as a farmer."

"Do you not believe my stories of working out here during the harvest? I make a pretty mean haystack, let me tell you."

I cocked my head, for even though he was covered with dirt and ashes, Tristan's fastidiousness was still evident to my eye. "It's just — hard to imagine."

"And what of you, Elinor? Would you leave the Crown? Alenbonné?"

Where would we live as a married couple!? I realized we had not discussed that.

"I've been at the Crown for three years, almost four. Before that I was at a boarding house for unmarried ladies. And prior to that, I was with Madame Granger after my father died."

"A nomadic existence," he mused.

"A little. I've been thinking it would be nice to have my own home where I could do as I please, and not hear a guest on the other side of the wall, or have people notice my guests and when they arrive." Tall pencil trees in a column, a hilly vineyard, and an old crumbling mansion near a candy-box town — a crazy thought entered my mind, but I did not voice it.

"Complete with a world-class chef, I expect?" teased Tristan.

I laughed. "I can't cook, so someone had better know how! Ours was a masculine household, as my mother died when I was nine, so I had no one around to teach me how to bake bread or braise a chicken. Though I am proud to say I can boil an egg and make toast."

"You'll find that the women of my class do not cook. They prepare menus, choose wines, and request the best dinnerware to be laid if she wants to impress, but if dining at home with her husband, she tells the butler to lay the second best."

My heart flinched. I wasn't suited for this life. Even without seeing my grimace, Tristan knew by my silence that I was upset by his statement.

"I've been thinking about how we should arrange things. Valentina can always stand in for you if you do not wish to entertain. She does for our mother and has for me since Minette's death. I think she would prefer to do so if I remain at Hartwood."

Wouldn't his peers mock him for not having a wife capable of hosting a dinner party? Tristan really hadn't thought through the ramifications of being married and I didn't want to spoil the day with being negative.

"Why is it called Hartwood? I've always wondered."

"Oh, it has nothing to do with deer or a forest. It's named after the man who built the house."

Hours later, he docked the narrowboat at a small wharf next to two other boats and told me, "Stay here. I'm going up to pay the toll and get more fuel."

"Should I hide?"

"Just wait here. If I return with a guardia, dive into that hole."

From the porthole, I watched Tristan cross the dock. It took me a minute to realize what was wrong: he was disguising his height. Slightly crouched and leaning to the left, he carried a sack over his back which all created an illusion that he was shorter than he was. He had put on two sweaters, stuffing the inside of them with sacking, and topped with a coat, it thickened his build. From afar, no one would have thought him to be the tall and impeccably dressed Tristan Fontaine, Duke de Archambeau.

Luckily, the only person who returned with him was someone local, who gave Tristan instructions on how to line up the narrowboat to receive its load of coal. Tristan clambered back on board and steered us into position. Facing away from me, he reassured me that there was no threat, but cautioned me to stay hidden for safety.

While the coal was being loaded, he and the man on the wharf talked about water levels and any canal obstructions we might face along our route. Before we pulled away, Tristan waved goodbye.

Once we rounded the bend, he called me up top. "I got us a lunch basket. They fix them up for those traveling by canal. Bread, bacon, hard-boiled duck eggs, cheese, and apples."

I had boiled some water on the stove for tea and put some aside to cool so we could use it for hand washing. "When will we be home?"

"I'm trying to decide when we should go in. During daylight hours, we can merge in with the other boats, but we won't have the cover of darkness to disguise ourselves. But if I was de Windt or Barbier, at this point I'd be expecting us to use darkness to aid our movements."

"Whichever is fastest!" Whenever I thought of Anne-Marie or Twyla, I became fretful and nervous.

"I understand," he said sympathetically. "But I don't want a noose around *your* neck."

I almost said 'They don't hang pregnant women,' but swallowed down my secret. Once things calmed down, I'd let him know, if it was even proved to be true. For now, it would just add to his worries; besides, I wasn't sure. "Once we get inside the city, what's the plan?"

"Meet up with Farrow and Marcus. Learn the news."

"Marcus!" I exclaimed, surprised.

"You think I didn't see the potential in that boy? He's far too smart to become just a gutter thief."

"Don't let him hear that! He says being a gutter thief requires only the best of brains." Worried, I added, "Marcus is keeping an eye on Twyla for me. So much seems to point to the Morpheus Society that I cannot feel that she is safe with Madame Granger."

He looked down at where I sat. "What troubles me most is that you were removed from my house, and Valentina is still there."

"And what of poor Dr. Devereaux?"

"At this time, I am undecided if he is victim or partner in whoever removed you from my house."

After our luncheon, the traffic on the canal picked up, and we started passing other boats. Greetings were shouted, salutes given, and information exchanged about avoiding a fallen tree. In the distance, was the Alenbonné skyline and coiling above their rooftops was a snaky column of smoke.

"I don't like that," I told Tristan, who was watching the black plumes and frowning.

"Neither do I."

A half-hour later and you could smell it.

"Bodies. Someone is burning bodies."

CHAPTER EIGHT

We entered the city at dusk. I had to hide five times, only hearing the tromp of heavy boots and Tristan speaking in a country accent so thick with round vowels I could barely understand him.

Reaching down to me, he pulled me out one last time. "Almost there, Elinor."

"Have they told you anything?"

He didn't have to ask me to explain. We both knew what I meant.

"It's the Ghastlies. They've been dropping like flies. In the middle of the street, the store, businesses. The city is afraid of infection."

Inside the city, the smoke smell was intense, and I pulled up my kerchief to cover my nose. Peering out the porthole, we passed buildings I didn't recognize. When I asked where we were heading, Tristan explained. "There's a dock where the farmers bring their goods for the market. We'll be tying up there."

After our arrival, I waited as Tristan left to gather news from his contacts. I was strung tight as a wire, but eventually, as the hours passed, tired from worry and suspense, I fell asleep on the bunk bed.

In the twilight between waking and sleeping, I heard my name, *Elinor.*

Twyla?

Help me.

But the thread of communication was cut, and I startled awake to the sound of someone boarding.

"Elinor," Tristan called in a low voice. "It's me. Marcus is with me."

I sat up, swinging my legs over the bunk as the two climbed down the ladder. Tristan lit a lantern and turned the wick down low. Behind him was the skinny, shorter form of Marcus. My heart leapt to see them both safe.

"He's got some news for us," Tristan said.

"Twyla is in trouble, isn't she?"

"Unfortunately, she is. Marcus tells me she left a message on the window to be removed."

Marcus was clearly as upset as I. "I don't think she's there anymore. No one is answering the door."

Feeling defeated, I rubbed my eyes, trying to rid them of sleepy grit.

"What of Madame Granger? Her manservant, Cédric Durant?"

Marcus shook his head. "I don't know. The house is dark. It looks abandoned."

I grabbed Tristan's arm. "We need to go there first."

He put his arm around my shoulders. "I agree. But first I want you to get something to eat, while I tell you everything I've learned."

The city was in an uproar. Rumors were flying that the Ghastlies carried a horrible affliction that could be passed to others. After the City Cough wiped out a third of the population taking my mother and brother, Alenbonné feared the spread of disease.

City officials were meticulous in dealing with any looming health threat.

"That is not true! The Ghastlies are not contagious! Their death is only postponed because of Lafayette's drug."

Tristan shrugged. "Marcus says they drop to the ground in a mound of bones, sinew, and blood. That doesn't indicate a pleasant death."

"No death is pleasant. Peaceful would be a better choice." Death being my profession, it was important to me it was portrayed accurately.

"You know what I mean. A quick, explainable one that doesn't cause the flesh to fall off your bones."

Marcus had been looking between us, waiting for a chance to join in. "It's horrible, madame. They claim that a dozen things fell dead in the marketplace square. Stank right bad."

"So the city is burning their remains?"

"Yes," said Tristan, shortly. He evidently did not want to dwell on it. "Now, for some better news. Dr. Devereaux was found in a closet under the stairs, with quite a large lump on the back of his head. He seems innocent of the matter of your abduction. My lawyers have a signed statement from him which places you with him when you were supposedly murdering Josephine. They have sent a notarized copy of it to de Windt."

I let out a sigh of relief, my shoulder's sagging. "Then I'm cleared."

Tristan corrected me. "Until we find her actual killer, you are not cleared. It's your word and Devereaux's against whoever they have paid to give false witness. And we don't know how much the doctor remembers. You could still be arrested. We need more to bolster our case to protect you."

"A ray of sunshine, aren't you?" I couldn't help the sarcasm, as my mood had been dashed by his summary of my situation.

Tristan ignored my peevishness. "Marcus, tell her about Hartwood."

The young man excitedly explained, "They have it all under guard. No one was allowed out without an escort, not even Lady Fontaine. Mysir de Windt has taken over and is ordering His Grace's staff around."

"But what of you?" I asked him.

"I cleared out as soon as I saw how the wind was blowing. No one holds me." He boasted.

"Anne-Marie?"

Tristan told me, "She's still at Hartwood."

Surely nothing could happen to her or Valentina with de Windt hovering. It was my stray apprentice I was concerned about most.

"We must get to Madame Granger's house and find out what happened to Twyla."

Tristan agreed. "The silence at the house Marcus reports is disturbing. We shall go there first."

From the narrowboat cupboards, he pulled together supplies.

"Do you know how to shoot a gun?" He asked Marcus, but the boy shook his head reluctantly. "I'm more comfortable with knives."

Tristan gave him several options and Marcus opted for a folding knife, the smooth handle made from a black wood I did not recognize. The slender blade brought back the unpleasant memory of the killer Vonn chasing me in the Beyond. I looked away, my hand instinctively going to the place where he had cut me on my arm although it wasn't aching at this time.

"Elinor?" Tristan asked. "What about you? What do you have to protect yourself?"

"I don't have my manstopper, as it was left at Hartwood."

Tristan didn't actually roll his eyes, but he said in a superior tone, "When things calm down, I'm going to train you on using a proper weapon. Your manstopper is only effective at close range, and it's better never to be that close to your enemy."

While speaking, he had removed a leather strap from another

box. He positioned it over his right shoulder, buckling it into place. It crossed over the front of his chest, and under his arm, so that a leather holder rested against his ribs. Tristan retrieved a pistol from the same box, loaded it with ammunition, and then placed it in the holster. When he pulled on his bulky jacket, it concealed the weapon from view.

The entire process was carried out with a well-practiced ease that was disconcerting.

"Is all of this necessary?"

"We do not know who killed Lady Baudelaire or why they did it. We need to be prepared."

Money at the wharf changed hands as Tristan paid for the docking. The three of us quickly blended into the crowd of those loading or unloading the boats. In a port city, commerce could not be stopped, it seemed, though I imagined the crowds were greater when the city wasn't under threat.

It was below sea-level, fog and smoke settled in Alenbonné and I coughed to rid myself of the coarse air that tickled my throat. A good hard rain was needed to make everything fresh again.

Marcus helped us maneuver through the streets, showing me a part of my beloved city that I'd never known existed. To him Alenbonné was one big labyrinth, and he held all the clues about on how it worked. He had a sixth sense for guardia patrol routes, and so avoided being stopped. We climbed through a basement window, crossed an underground room, and exited through a vacant building's back door. This accessed an alley that took us within a block of where Madame Granger's house was.

The house appeared dark, despite the fast-approaching evening. Most disturbing was the vacant look to the building. Where was Madame? And Twyla?

We did not have our lock-picking tools; my set was still at the Crown, Tristan's at Hartwood. Tristan gained access by wrapping his hand with his coat and breaking a pane of glass in the back door. The glass falling inside to the floor sounded horribly loud, but it was not greeted with any alarm from inside. He reached through and unlocked the doorknob.

"Marcus, stand watch." The young man nodded. Tristan handed him his coat, and, drawing his weapon, entered first.

The kitchen, as with most houses, was in the rear. The stove was cold, and dishes filled the sink. On the counter was a cut loaf of bread with an open butter dish beside it. I nodded towards it. Tristan's mouth tightened.

We walked down the hall, past the parlor entrance, and reached the front door foyer. I suppressed another cough, strangling it. Tristan stopped, and I hit his back.

The prone body on the floor was why he had halted. Kneeling, he turned the man over, revealing his face in the dim light. "Dead. Do you recognize him?"

I whispered back, "Yes, he's Cédric Durant. Madame's man."

"What's upstairs?" Tristan asked, stepping over Durant and putting one foot on the first step.

"Three bedrooms. One faces the street, and two look to the back. The larger room at the front belongs to Madame, while Twyla has the back one."

He reached out a hand to steady me as I stepped over Durant. In working with Charlotte and Barbier I had seen many dead bodies in all conditions. Judging by the blood and the smell of the body, Durant had been dead for a day, maybe two. Considering the state of his face and hands, he had put up a good fight. Confirming what had actually killed him would take an autopsy by Charlotte, but I guessed it had been a knife.

A small girl stood at the top of the stairs startled me until I realized she was the little repeater ghost; the first spirit I had ever contacted. She passed through a wall, where a doorway used to be, and vanished. Tristan showed no indication he had seen her.

Twyla's room was empty, but showed signs of a struggle: a chair on its side, and a crushed hat on the floor. In the window was the handkerchief, the symbol she needed our help. Seeing it made me almost cry out, and I bit my lip, feeling my eyes grow wet.

It took a moment to settle my emotions and to follow Tristan to the other room. We found it empty.

We exchanged a grim look before entering Madame Granger's bedroom.

The door was ajar. Pushing it wider, revealed her corpse primly tucked under blankets. Perhaps part of me expected to see her gone, whatever the reason I felt a wall around my emotions. I wasn't going to let anything in or out.

Reaching out, I touched the back of her hand to find it dead cold. At least her body showed no signs of violence.

"Thoughts?" Tristan asked me, coming to stand on the opposite side of the bed.

"Twyla did not go willingly. Durant tried to stop them but failed."

"And Madame Granger? She looks peaceful, no signs of a traumatic death."

"I don't think violence was used against her." I took a deep breath and let it out slowly.

The ghost of Madame Granger, who was now standing beside Tristan, spoke. "You were always late for your lessons, and now you are late for my death!"

Chapter Nine

"Elinor, you look like you've seen a ghost," said my husband.

"I have. Madame Granger is standing beside you."

Of course, he did not see her. I gestured for him to come around the bed to me.

It was my mentor, but much changed. Leona Granger was no longer an elderly woman, half crippled with rheumatism, but now in her early thirties, tall and slim, her features showing an unearthly beauty. Cast off was the role of aged invalid, and her soul revealed itself at an age when she'd been at the height of her power, about two decades before I had met her.

Her personality, though, was the same.

"Stop standing there gawking, Elinor. Let's discuss important matters, as I won't be able to tarry. The Afterlife is calling me strongly, and I find this Beyond an uncomfortable waystation."

Now that Tristan was beside me, I reached out to hold his hand.

"Do you see her now?"

"Yes," he murmured.

Leona wore an expensive gown of ivory silk, with a sheer overlay beaded with silver beads and pearls. The style was out of date by decades, but it showed her long neck, shapely shoulders, and bust to every advantage.

Others who'd known her during her heyday had told me that Leona Granger had once been a fascinating beauty. Seeing this face with its apple cheeks, wide mouth, smooth pink complexion, and large dark eyes, I saw that she would be a striking woman in any company.

The room behind her faded away to be replaced with another bedroom. Rich furniture, heavy full drapes that puddled on the floor, a fur tossed across the top of a dressing screen, and the most extravagant ballgowns draped over a couple of chairs.

I sharply turned to glance behind, only to see the original room we had entered. Somehow, Madame Granger had blended reality with the Beyond. "Where are you?"

She gave a relaxed, throaty laugh of a woman who knew everything. "Halfway between. I'm stepping through my life, Elinor, leaving that dried husk behind." Her head, coiffed with an enormous pile of hair and feathers, nodded towards the bed where her corporeal body lay. "It was you that stated ghosts shape the Beyond to their favorite haunts. Pulled from their memories."

"What does this remind you of?"

"My love nest, Elinor. Does that shock you? Is it hard for you to believe I once had a lover?"

"I do not remember you mentioning any man in your life before," I replied calmly.

A dangerous energy surrounded her, as volatile as gunpowder. Where I had expected her to be sad, perhaps melancholy, her mood was triumphant. I was glad that Tristan said nothing and only watched.

She touched a five-strand choker of pearls and emeralds around her throat, as her eyes viewed me from lids at half-mast. She exuded danger, and I held my breath.

"Once I thought I was in love. Like you do with your duke." Her glance at Tristan was disdainful; I squeezed his hand, trying to communicate with him not to be baited. He squeezed back. "We met at one of my demonstration séances and he immediately offered himself as a patron. At first I paid him little attention, but once he gained his title and access to his family's wealth, well, it was hard to ignore such a persistent suitor. My gowns were from the best milliners, with jewels that would have fascinated your father. A carriage with four horses at my command."

Her eyes glistened as she remembered her former glory days.

"I think he was fascinated with having a mistress who conversed with ghosts. His mother had died when he was a baby, fostering a morbid interest in death." The edges of her mouth grimaced, and she looked away from me. "I am sure the mind-doctors you admire so much would love to examine our relationship!"

"Perhaps it was merely because you were so beautiful?" I said quietly.

She gave me a smile, her eyebrows arching, as she wiped away a tear that never fell. "I'm sure that played a part in it. But love between the high and low never works out. You'll find that out yourself, Elinor. You and your baby."

I swallowed. "Your precognitive sight is as strong as ever, even in death, Madame."

Tristan said nothing, but his hand squeezed mine hard, and he did not release his hold. Well, I hadn't thought he'd hear about my pregnancy from my dead mentor, but life cannot always be managed.

Leona shrugged. "I've always lived in two worlds. In my infancy, unseen playmates entertained me, and as a debutante, I danced to unheard music. As a woman I was the premiere psychic of the Morpheus Society. Now, in the Beyond, my powers are even more glorious in their scope. Seeing the soul-spirit that rests between your hips in this in-between place is easy for one such as I."

Still, I could not decipher the root cause of her jubilant

manner. I had never seen a happier ghost, and her joy made me suspicious.

"I am sorry I wasn't there when you crossed over."

She flicked her hand at me, dismissing me and her death.

"Brain aneurysm. Silly me. I believed my double-vision and light sensitivity were because of my involvement with the supernatural. The pressing of the Beyond on my soul made me realize I was dying. It's why I sent for my son."

I blinked, my world tilting.

"Surprised, Elinor? Do you believe you're the only woman to have an untimely pregnancy? My only mistake was thinking a child would be a well-played ace that would convince my lover to marry me. Not he! The larger my belly grew, the less interest he showed in us. A woman was acceptable, but a crying infant demanded too much generosity."

"I'm sorry."

My sympathy did not go down well. Her chin came up, and she sneered. "When your lord abandons you and your child, you'll truly be sorry."

Tristan spoke for the first time since she had appeared. "I won't do that."

Her eyebrows rose mockingly. "Believe what you wish, Your Grace, but when your peers snub you, you will dump my poor apprentice and her child quickly enough. The aristocracy cares only for their lineage to an outdated monarch that should have died off ages ago."

Despite her fervor, Leona was already fading around the edges. Sometimes the room behind her blurred like a watercolor in the rain. The Afterlife was hungry for her presence; she would not be a ghost.

I asked quickly, trying to get the information we needed. "Did your son come?"

"Oh, certainly. But he was too late. I was already dead when he entered the house."

"Who is he?" I had the sinking feeling I already knew.

"Marcellus Barbier." She gave a gleeful laugh. "Oh, how I've longed to tell you! It's why he brought you to me. You needed to be watched, taken care of, and I agreed."

"Watched?"

"Because he murdered your father, my dear."

All the breath left my body, and suddenly I couldn't catch any air. Tristan's arm came around me, holding me tight so I could continue standing.

"Tell me. Tell me all of it."

Chapter Ten

What Leona Granger told us:

My high born lover gave me a house, jewels, a carriage, and money for gowns and anything else I might wish. My powers made me very popular among le beau idéal and he escorted me to exclusive parties as his special find.

Overall, the relationship was comfortable for me. I accompanied him to elite society events, mingling with high-ranking nobles. He only requested me in the evening, so during the day, I could pursue my studies.

You do not know, Elinor, what it was like for a woman back then. I was a curiosity, a freak to gawk at, but it increased my clientèle of people who paid me well to be scared by my spook stories. So what if what I showed them gave them nightmares? They deserved it for treating me so lightly. Anyway, soon, they would come running back, desperate to lay their fears of death to rest, and always they did it with a heavy purse.

My powers were at their zenith, and as I demonstrated my expertise with summoning the dead, my lover was both excited and frightened. At the time I did not credit that his fear would eventually grow. But I believe that, coupled with my pregnancy, made him decide to set me aside.

There I was, my hands and feet swollen, unable to hold down a morsel of food. He made arrangements for me to go to the country where I could conceal my condition. After my labor in some horrible farmhouse, I handed it off to people Lucas had found who would adopt it.

When I returned to Alenbonné, it all seemed like a dream. Lucas, though, had no plans of risking me getting pregnant with another child, so I was given farewell gifts. What a sniveling coward he was!

I took a year off to travel to Perino, letting society forget me. When I reappeared, I drove through the park in an open carriage wearing black and a heavy veil that obscured my features. I spent the season talking to no one, which only made their jaded faces perk up with interest. When the time was ripe, I let a few friends back into my circle and told them in hushed whispers about hair-raising séances which produced terrifying spirits. But no, I could speak of it no more!

Oh, how their snobby faces made me laugh! They would swallow any mystic tale I told them. When you measure intelligence, I learned that the highest noble in the land may not have a thimble's worth! They lack the common sense that our class has in buckets.

It helped that the Morpheus Society was looking for a leader. The organization was in a lull. Our founder, Lady Alouette Sarte, had passed away, and contrary to what she had promised no one could ever summon her, no matter how many talented mediums tried. They floundered, and I was practically forced to take charge. It was I who started the sponsorships, the apprenticeships, and the home for mediums who had lost their way.

I was exceptionally busy organizing and growing our reach. A decade passed, and another. It was easy to forget I had a child.

The next time I saw my son was when he visited me dressed as a sergeant for the guardia. He made some pretext to see me, such as burglaries in the neighborhood, I think. At the end of our interview he introduced himself as my well-forgotten child. His foster parents had never told him who I was, but he had snooped through their things, old letters written by Lucas, and by hook and by crook traced me.

At first I was angry, but he wanted nothing from me. He did not want to reveal my secret. As the months passed, I realized we had much in common: brilliance, impatience for advancement, and greed for the good things life could offer. A camaraderie grew between us, and while we did not announce our blood connection, he was often a guest here for private dinners.

He shared his disgust that some criminals lived a better life than he and his fellows. He passed it off as a joke, but I knew he envied them their freedom to do what they wanted. The human face cannot fool me! As our friendliness grew, I pressed him about his unhappiness, and he finally admitted to me that he sometimes played a harmless little game. He skimmed the money out of the safe of a man they had just arrested. Or he'd lift jewels from the room of a lady who had reported a missing dog. It made him laugh that he was never caught.

They trust the uniform, he told me. *They never suspect that it is I who robbed them.*

I see from your face you think it was petty thievery, no more. But it was more, I tell you! His mind, like my own, was too lively, and needed some preoccupation, a testing of his mettle to keep himself amused. Without some challenge, he would have turned inward, and committed far worse crimes.

For months, that was the situation until he chased a suspected murderer and fell while running across rooftops. He landed wrong on a coal shed, breaking his leg. The guardia used a drunk physician, and it was set badly, so it took a long time to heal. The gendarme refused to pay Marcellus when he could not work. He asked the nobleman who had been threatened by the killer if he would help, but my son had the door slammed in his face!

The harshness of the situation only deepened a natural resentment. He had done his job and was being punished for it! His eyes opened, as had mine when my lover abandoned me!

He saw the fat king who pays his mistresses off with the people's hard-earned money, but says he doesn't have enough to feed the citizens. The rich merchant who gambles away his fortune, while accusing his manservant of stealing some ornament in the house. The silly ornamental woman who wheedles money out of her husband with professions of love, but uses that same money to fund her base-born lover.

Confined to bed, he had time to think about the unfairness of his situation. It was only natural that he thought to blackmail the nobility. They deserved it!

For a blackmail scheme to succeed, there first must be an example set. Someone whose fate can be shown as theirs if a victim does not comply.

From his sickbed, Marcellus went after the noble who had denied him assistance. Lord Doriac was easy to destroy, for he had fudged his taxes for years to the Crown. All he had to do was inform the proper authorities, and they descended like locusts to seize the man's estates and bank accounts.

His next target was Lucas. That is when I discovered what Marcellus was doing — for after decades of neglect, Lucas visited me and begged me to stop our son. When I confronted Marcellus, he said that if Lucas would beg my forgiveness on his knees, he would cease bleeding the man dry. Of course, Lucas complied. As I've said, the man was a coward, without dignity.

Sometimes if I came across a family secret found through my work, I'd pass it along to him. But only when the client treated me poorly or deserved to be punished.

Marcellus, though, was meant for bigger things. He expanded into other areas which could use a man of intelligence. Extortion.

Bribery. Embezzlement. He was open to anything that presented a challenge and made him think.

Women rarely have money to pay their bills, let alone for their secrets. Compromises sometimes had to be made, so Marcellus started taking jewelry if they had no allowance. She could tell her husband she had lost the ring at card play or that the bracelet must have slipped off her wrist, as the clasp was weak. If the piece was too valuable and the loss would have been noticed, the lady commissioned a facsimile to prevent the loss from being discovered.

That is how your father lost his life.

If he had not been so foolish, he could have pocketed his share, maybe even worked with Marcellus, but he was a man of principles.

Mysir Chalamet was asked to make a replica of a necklace but the woman became frightened and gave the game away. Or perhaps your father sensed something was odd about her request and guessed. I do know she told him the real reason she needed the work done.

Within days, Marcellus heard that your father had requested an appointment with King Guénard. He feared your father was going to talk and expose him.

That could not happen.

He made sure it did not.

I felt like I was being strangled. "Why did he bring me to you?"

"You kept asking questions. He didn't want to kill you, so he thought I could give you some peace, calm you down. You were so young, we thought it best to have you looked after."

Her sanctimonious statement infuriated me, but I needed information and showing temper would not get me it. The room behind her was fading, revealing reality. Madame's strength was fading and she could cross-over at any moment.

"Was it true what you told me? That you couldn't reach my father beyond the grave?" I asked. My voice didn't sound like my own. It was high-pitched, almost like a child's.

"Yes. Your father transitioned immediately. There was nothing I could do."

No. I didn't believe that. She said it too quickly, and her eyes were those of an accomplished liar. I didn't know who she was any more, but contradicting her would gain me nothing.

"Dr. Devereaux hypnotized me, and I found where you closed off my mind."

Leona's hand came back to her throat, stroking the pearls. "For your safety, Elinor. When you came here, you had horrible nightmares. Sleepwalked. I had to take away those memories and tuck it all away. For your safety."

For my safety! Hypocrite. Liar.

She continued speaking as I stood there, dumbstruck by the tale she had told me. "I do care about you. That's why I'm telling you now about Marcellus. Look after him, just like I did. He enjoys working with you, and I think he'll listen to you."

"Listen to me!?" I repeated, astonished. I couldn't imagine something less likely.

"He respects you. He's often told me how smart you are. So clever. I hoped you two would marry someday."

Was she insane? Marry the man the man who'd betrayed me and murdered my father?! I was living a nightmare. The world had become upside down. Tristan, who had listened quietly, squeezed my hand. But I had no time for his reassurance. My voice was cold and hard. "Where is Twyla?"

Leona's mouth made an exasperated pout. "That girl!"

I repeated myself, this time loudly. "Where is she?! We got here, and she was gone. Mysir Durant is dead in the hall."

"Marcellus took her. He needed someone to manage his dead army. A conduit, as Parnell used those girls."

"Twyla will never do that for him. She'll escape into the Beyond before she'd let him control her."

Leona looked away from me. Her hair was now translucent. Time was running out. "He has his ways of making one do what he wants."

"Where did he take her?!" I screamed at her.

My mentor sighed. "I'm sorry about Cédric. It was his loyalty that got him killed, for he protected the girl, thinking I would have wanted that. But Marcellus was not going to stand for his desires to be countermanded by a mere man servant. If only I had been here to intervene - that's why he needs you! A woman who understands him, and can be his helpmate."

Leona's form flickered, and fury shook me. "Where is she?!"

"Parnell's palace." It was the last thing she said before her vapor faded away.

Dropping Tristan's hand, I lunged forward, but my hands gripped nothing but air.

CHAPTER ELEVEN

I gave an inhuman howl of anger, frustration, and grief.

"How dare they?! How could they?! What a fool I've been! How could I have not seen it?" My words spilled forth in a vomit of emotion, my hands shook with rage. "He was the constable for our street. He actually found me when I ran from the house after finding my father dead! After he murdered him!"

My hands balled into fists; I wanted to punch Marcellus, slap Leona. Hit something. Tristan watched me in concerned silence, his face grimly intent.

"He took me to Madame Granger's so I could be *managed*."

"Madame Granger said her lover's name was Lucas," said Tristan. "Lord Bridoux's first name was Lucas."

I stopped, pivoting to face him, my hand flying to my open mouth. "The man shot at the park? Murdered with his wife? How did I not see that Barbier was a monster?!"

Tristan came to me and placed his hands on my shoulders. "I'm sorry, dearest. Unfortunately, monsters don't wear signs."

I started sobbing, gulping air between my words. "I thought of him like a brother! A protective guardian during those horrible years." I drummed my clenched fists against Tristan's chest, wailing. "I helped him solve crimes! How he must have laughed at that!"

"He's a scoundrel. You gave him more than he ever deserved." Tristan's words barely made an impact, for I was in a tailspin. My mind whirled with memories that now looked different.

"He's a rotten-to-the-core bastard! He used me. Watched me search for my father's killer, knowing himself guilty of the deed. Did he enjoy my suffering? Did he and Leona laugh at my futile attempts?"

Tristan's arms slipped down from my shoulders to my back, and he brought me tight against him. I made rasping, choking cries against his chest.

"My dear girl," he repeated, his hand stroking my hair.

I was so lost in my suffering, I had no idea how long we stood there before Tristan stiffened. "Did you hear that?"

"A whistle?"

"Marcus."

He took me by the hand and when to the stair's landing where we could see Madame's dead manservant in the foyer. A shadow passed across the glass of the front door. Someone was on the front stoop.

Tristan drew back so he could not be seen and gripped my arm. "I think we had best be leaving."

"The stairs?"

"We shall exit via a window."

As Tristan worked to get a back window open, I returned to Madame Granger's room for one last goodbye. Leona's face was white-gray, her eyes peacefully closed, and her mouth held a slight smile as her head rested on a lacy pillow.

"How could you?" I hissed at the corpse. "I knew we had our differences, but this? How can you justify what you did? I will hate you until I die."

"Elinor," Tristan called quietly. I went back to the spare room. He was already half out, steadying himself on the roofed shingle projecting out over the first floor. His hand took mine. Thankfully, I was still in my boyish disguise and not skirts, which made climbing over the rooftop easier. The houses on this street all shared walls and roofs, so we traveled over three units before sliding down a downspout to the ground.

Our roof traveling made me think with nostalgia of dear Lindengaard and when Tristan and I had pursued Count Westergaard — though, that memory was also tainted with sadness, for he had died a few months after being placed in the sanatorium, still believing he was the rightful ruler of Sarnesse.

From the shadow of the building opposite, Marcus said, "This way. Be quick." He hustled us down the alley, around a corner and through a gate into a secluded walled garden. Behind the cover of trash cans, we shimmied down into a broken cellar window. Marcus first, then me, and last, Tristan. When we were all in, Marcus said, "They almost had you that time."

"Who?" Tristan asked. Their conversation seemed to happen far away; my mind was still too full of what I had learned to concentrate on everyday concerns.

"The gendarmes. They came prowling about. I think someone finally got wise that the house was too quiet and that the old lady hadn't been seen for a few days."

Tristan laid out his next plan. "Elinor and I should return to the narrowboat. Do you think you can get us there?"

The fact that Marcus paused before responding showed me more than anything how dangerous it was that we were back in Alenbonné. "That's pretty far to go. Stay here and let me bring some of my crew, Your Grace. I need time to set things up."

From his interior coat pocket, Tristan handed him a leather pouch that clinked with coins. "Go. But find Farrow. He knows my wishes and can coordinate with you. You know where he is?"

Marcus nodded. The pouch disappeared into his own jacket. He gave me a nod-bow. "If you return and we are not here, we have either been caught or were forced to find another place."

Marcus used a crate to boost himself up to the window, where he wiggled out and was gone. It was just us two. There was some light from the window, but the cellar smelled of dank and rats. It mirrored the darkness of my mind.

"Elinor?" Tristan put his arm around my shoulders and brought me close to kiss the top of my head. "I'm sorry, love. Very sorry that this evil has touched you."

"Now we know who it is. The Master Criminal we've been chasing. How he must have laughed." My voice sounded like a tapping on tin - metallic and high.

I was surprised by his next statement. "I would like you to go to Chambaux."

I pulled back, breaking out of his arms. "No!"

Since he was the Duke de Archambeau, he did not beg me nicely, but said it sternly, with that arrogant command that alternately amused or infuriated me. "The city is on the edge of a knife. What if it falls? Chambaux is close to the border. You could get over to Zulskaya, where I have friends who will look after you. I cannot have you — and our child— at risk."

Later I would realize that it was my anger and grief which made me snap at the one man who truly supported me. "I knew this is how it would be! Not a marriage of equals, but you lording it over me, deciding about my body as if I was some horse you just bought!"

His hand tugged through his hair, disarranging it. His face was pale under his dirty disguise, and there were shadows under his eyes. "Be reasonable, Elinor! You know that is not why I make this suggestion! Barbier has shown that he will kill when someone gets in his way. Do not think your long acquaintance with him will protect you. Or believe Madame Granger's insistence that he will be guided by you."

My voice was deadly; it was an arrow hitting a target. "Oh, trust me, I don't think Barbier will spare me at all! Or that he will listen to anything I have to say. He has fooled me for over a decade with his lies, but no more. I want to see him pay for his crimes, my father's murder. Which is exactly why I need to be here. Have you forgotten Twyla? He has her. And that is my fault! I should have insisted she come and stay with me instead of Leona." My voice cracked on her name. A harsh wind swept over the desert of my heart.

Tristan's voice was softer but still stern. "Elinor, you are losing your perspective. Now is the time to be coldly logical. If we go into this emotional, he can trip us up and we will lose everything, including your apprentice. Where is my pragmatic Ghost Talker?"

I laughed scornfully. "Do you think that I cannot act with enough logic to put a noose around his neck? Being a woman, I'll be too hysterical to act? Be a burden on your investigation? Is that what you think, Tristan?"

He must have known he was treading dangerous ground. "Not at all. Do not put words in my mouth. If you were a man under my command who had been so deeply betrayed, I would ask you to step aside. We make mistakes when we operate from a place of heated emotions. I know that to my cost."

"I don't want to talk about Minette!" I screamed at him, uncaring if any passing guardia heard me. In the mood I was in, I could throttle a guardia barehanded if they came to arrest me. *Let them come! I'll relish it!*

Once, when he had been unreasonable, flushed with anger over a misapprehension, I had pursued him. Calmed him down. Now it was he who remained calm, trying to get me to see his side.

"I'd rather talk about our baby. How long have you known? When were you going to tell me?" His hurt stopped me like nothing else would have. I put my hand to my forehead, sliding it over my hair. "I only suspected it a day ago. It was not a secret I was holding from you. I wanted to be sure before I said anything."

He stared at me, unblinking, and I returned it level-gazed. After a moment, he nodded, deciding to trust my words. "All right. I believe you. I will not force you to go, but I beg you to reconsider

Chambaux. It is your decision and I will abide by what you want. All I ask is that you truly weigh it as an option."

"Let's say I go there. What happens if the city does fall? The king does not keep the country? Goes into exile, is imprisoned, — or worse, killed. What will happen to you!? Barbier hates nobles. Your danger equals, if not surpasses, mine. Shall I slink off to safety and let my husband die alone?"

"No one is going to die, unless it's Barbier," was Tristan's cold evaluation.

Chapter Twelve

By the time Marcus and Farrow returned, I was cold and tired. Shock and adrenaline had drained me, so I was happy to see that Farrow had secured a carriage and we wouldn't be crawling through basements.

Tristan lifted me up and followed me into the coach. Seated, I gave Farrow a nod before sinking into the corner opposite him and Marcus.

He handed Tristan a stack of newssheets. "No word of the woman's murder." Why would Madame Granger be in the newspaper? *Oh.* Josephine Baudelaire. "I'm guessing they're covering it up. The only mention of you and our lady is your wedding announcement."

I almost laughed. I must have given some sort of exclamation, for Tristan reached over and squeezed my gloved hand.

"Any news of my sister?" he asked Farrow.

"Originally, Hartwood was guarded by the gendarmes, but those men have been replaced by de Windt's men."

"Then I shall need to see the king."

"Looks like it. Or go straight to de Windt. Confront him."

"Hm. An option. I have a few others I am considering."

They discussed the state of the government, players I knew nothing about and did not care to know. I was mute, my mind busy slamming itself against the same brick wall, flooded with memories of Marcellus Barbier, the comfort he had given me after I had found my father, his occasional visit at Madame Granger's house to check on me (*oh yes, to check on me!*), and later my medium work with him to solve crimes. The encouragement he'd given me. What about that? Did Charlotte know what he was? Was she part of this? *Surely not!*

Farrow's eyes kept shifting my way. He clearly saw I was upset, but wasn't comfortable about asking why.

Tristan asked, "Have you arranged the house like I asked?"

"Yes, Your Grace. I even got Madame Chalamet a little surprise she'll be quite happy about, I think."

I was not up for surprises. Only if it was an unending flow of wine, a supply of chocolate, and a warm bed where I could hide for the next decade or so.

"Where are we going?" My voice sounded flat.

"Not to the houseboat, unfortunately. It's too public. Best to go to ground elsewhere."

The neighborhood was unfamiliar, but the houses were well kept. We halted in front of a nondescript building like the others on the street. As I exited the carriage, my nose and eyes stung from the smoke that had penetrated the very bricks and cobblestones of the city. It was a horrible smell.

Tristan scooped me up into his arms. "Farrow, you get the door."

"I can walk," I protested.

"Let me do this for you."

I didn't have it in me to fight him and just rested my head on his shoulder. Being carried wasn't a bad thing.

Farrow opened the door, and we were immediately greeted by his surprise.

"Madame!" It was Anne-Marie! Her smiling face almost made me cry again.

Tristan told her, "Your mistress needs a hot bath and some food."

"Bath first, please," I said, ready to be done with clothes that smelled of fish and greasy hair.

Anne-Marie trotted up the stairs and Tristan followed, carrying me as if I was an infant. Upstairs, we followed her into a bedroom, where he set me down on the bed while she disappeared into the bathroom. I heard the squeak of bath taps turning and the rush of water.

"I'll be downstairs."

I nodded. When he left, I was alone with Anne-Marie, and I stood up to embrace her in a fierce hug. Here was someone real, someone I could trust and believe in!

"How did you get here? I thought you were locked up at Hartwood?"

"Lady Fontaine and Marcus got me out. Through a secret door, behind a painting. She told me you and her brother needed me and that she would take care of de Windt herself. Oh, madame, I was so worried about you when you disappeared!" Anne-Marie's youthful face crinkled, her eyes full of fear and doubt.

I patted her shoulder. "It is all right, Anne-Marie. The duke has everything in hand." Not exactly, but it wouldn't do to worry her any more than necessary. "I have some news I think you will be pleased with." Holding up my wrist, I showed the burn mark on it made by Dixon. "I'm married to His Grace. I've given you a very troublesome master."

"Oh, madame!" She hugged me again, practically dancing from foot to foot. "I knew the first time I saw you two that you were meant to be together!"

I couldn't help but smile despite the weight on my shoulders. "I'm glad you are pleased. You'll have to put up with his outrageous demands."

"Oh, I'll let his valet, Luca, deal with him."

Unbuttoning my coat, I asked, "Do you have some clothes for me? I can't stand these a moment longer."

"It's all been arranged. His Grace has managed it all."

As I sank into the hot bath, feeling the water soak into my muscles, I felt I could excuse some management.

After my bath, I crawled into bed. The bedroom door opened and Tristan came in carrying a tray, causing Anne-Marie to rush forward to take it from him. The tray was set down on a lap table that she'd found resting against the nightstand, and afterward, she gave us a little bob before exiting.

"Curtsying? You have made an impression," I told him.

Sitting on the bed, he uncovered the plate. "I'm afraid food supplies are running a bit short. Because of panic buying, we bought this for double its market value."

"What would a duke know about market value?" There were thick slices of ham, a roasted potato with butter, and an apple. "Besides, it looks far better than tinned shrimp and peas. Did you eat already?"

"Yes." As I ate, he explained that the house was one of the rental properties he owned under a pseudonym. "Marcus, Farrow, and Anne-Marie will be staying with us. When the trouble started here, the renter left for an extended trip to Perino. They may not fit, but there are clothes in the wardrobe. I will reimburse the renter for anything we end up using, so choose what you want without worry."

The potato smothered in butter was delicious. "What about the neighbors and their curiosity?"

"They are used to seeing newcomers come and go because the house is often rented to short-term residents. We won't be here long. Valentina has sent me a message via Marcus about what has been happening since they tried to arrest you.”

“Am I strong enough to hear it?” I felt a sudden rush of dread and braced myself.

Tristan, though, smiled and his eyes sparkled with mischief. “I think you’ll find this amusing. De Windt has overstepped himself. He acted on an anonymous tip to find you with Josephine. When we disappeared, he invaded Hartwood with his men when Lady Talleyrand and Lady Langenberg were there discussing the diplomatic party. I think you can anticipate what happened next.”

I covered my mouth, containing a giggle. “Tell me!”

“He gave orders to his men to show no quarter and to search whoever they found. It seems the king’s cousin was displeased with being searched by one of his female officers who followed his orders to the letter.”

“How horrible for Lady Talleyrand!” The lady had struck me as one who took pleasure in being refined and dignified.

“And how stupid of him!” Tristan was not above crowing over his old enemy. His eyes had a devilish glee. “Of course, he was all apologies, but the damage was done. She gave quite a colorful report to King Guénard about the matter. It does not bode well for de Windt since a political cartoon in the latest edition of The Gazette mocks the color of her intimates and implies she’s a bloodsucker.”

“What color were they?”

“Peach, which rhymes with—”

“Leech. Oh, how devastating for her! Is she all right?”

“I daresay she will survive, though her pride might have taken a bit of a beating. If she makes light of it, or turns it as a joke back upon them, she will have won some points. But de Windt will pay the cost of placing her in a position to become such a joke.”

He looked down at my plate, satisfied that I had eaten it all. “Do you feel up to coming downstairs? I thought we could do a planning session together about our next step?”

It was an olive branch for making the suggestion I should hide at Chambaux. "Yes." He picked up the tray and lap table and set them aside.

I slid out of bed, belting my robe. "I refuse to wear those boy's clothes again!"

"Anne-Marie is probably burning those. Look in the wardrobe and pick out something."

I went through the wardrobe, picking out dresses and holding them next to my body. They were made for someone a little taller, but eventually I found a dark blue dress that offered the best fit. The drawers offered some intimate apparel, though none of them peach. I wondered about the woman who had picked them out and why she didn't take them with her? Fishing down to the bottom of the drawer, I picked out the plainest cotton chemise, short and long petticoat, and corset I could find.

As I dressed, Tristan lay on the bed watching me.

"Are you just going to sit there and stare?"

"I can think of no better place to be. Why would I want to miss that beautiful view of you bending over to pull on your stockings?" He grinned as I blushed.

Still, I could not stop my thoughts returning again to what Madame Granger had told us. "I cannot believe that he tricked me."

I was standing close to the bed and Tristan reached out for my hand, pulling me closer. "You thought he was the man he presented himself to be. Do not feel guilty for thinking him as honorable as you are."

"Right now, I'm just feeling stupid and angry."

"I understand."

Of course he did. His first wife had betrayed him.

"If I hadn't heard it from madame myself, I would never have believed it. I thought him a man who worked on the side of justice, and now I'm told he's a criminal mastermind? It makes me question all the cases we worked on together. Did he play a part in those crimes that I missed?"

I sat on the edge of the bed, and Tristan wrapped his arms around me. He chucked me under the chin. "You can drive yourself crazy thinking about those things, Elinor. I imagine one part of him was the man you imagined. There are parts of a person's soul you will never know. Hungers they conceal. I understand how such a betrayal rattles you to the core. Who can you trust? Are your friends who they seem? If you can be tricked once, why not again?"

"You are thinking of Minette?" I was reluctant to mention her, but there was an undeniable parallel.

He shrugged. "We were mismatched. She enjoyed taking risks, the excitement of living dangerously. Upon reflection, she wasn't satisfied with her life. I always knew she thought others were fools to be manipulated, but I never realized she considered me one of them." He gave a laugh that was actually more lighthearted than I would have expected when discussing her.

I reached up and touched his cheek lightly. "How can you view that so lightly?"

"It's taken time. For years, I was suspicious and distrustful of others. Her betrayal made me bitter, but finding you, loving you, enabled me to let it go. See it in a better perspective for what it was: two mismatched people on a collision course. After all, when we married I was only twenty-five, she twenty-one."

"So young."

"Indeed! Too young and foolish on both of our parts. I'm thirty-five now. Ten years gives you perspective." His hand came up to caress my jaw, and I leaned my head into his palm. "You are a shining light in the darkness, Elinor. You illuminate all my dark corners, and bring warmth to where it has ever been cold."

"I'm nothing special or unusual."

His hand stroked the top of my head. "You are pretty special to me. And I think others too. For every Barbier, there is an Anne-

Marie. For a Madame Granger, there is a Charlotte La Rue. You are loved and respected. Very few are outright villains, my dear."

I gave a little sniffle. "I'm so worried about Twyla. We need to find her."

"We shall. That is why I want you downstairs with us. I was wondering if you could sketch the place Parnell created in the Beyond?"

"Yes, I could do that. As long as you don't expect something artistic."

"I hope that one of us might recognize the place."

CHAPTER THIRTEEN

We came downstairs hand in hand to find our friends sitting at the dining table. We were greeted by them all in their varying ways and congratulated on our marriage.

Tristan waved them to silence. "Settle down. You can all send the wedding gifts around to Hartwood once we rescue Twyla Andricksson and clear Lady Fontaine's name."

For a moment I wondered why he was talking about his sister, until I realized dazedly that was me. Married. Tristan sent Marcus to gather paper and pencils while he received an update from Farrow.

Farrow was a large man, who made the round table where we all sat look doll-sized. He was taller than Tristan and twice as wide, and despite short white-blond his round face made him look young. He cleared his throat and began his report.

The Ghastlies' rapid collapse throughout the city showed that Barbier had planted the creatures everywhere. In banks, shipyards, taverns, boarding houses, they fell over as if they were puppets suddenly without their animator. Even those who died at home alone were quickly found by those terrified of an epidemic.

While the Ghastlies weren't collapsing because of disease, there was no guarantee that what was left behind would not foster it. Perhaps it was best they were being quickly disposed of by cremation. The gendarmes were conducting a door-to-door search to discover them.

"What about here? Will we be found?" My heart beat faster thinking of a guardia knocking on the door. Once, I had seen them as my friends — but no more.

"The house was searched before we arrived," Tristan reassured me. "We shouldn't be bothered."

Farrow continued imparting the intelligence he had gathered. "One thing I've heard is that the numbers are dwindling. Only a couple were found yesterday."

"Which could mean that the cause for their collapse is no more." Tristan speculated. "What I wonder is how many Ghastlies remain, if any? Why did only some die? Was that Barbier's plan?"

When Marcus returned with paper and pencils, Anne-Marie jumped up from the table. "The cake! I've got to take care of it before it burns, Your Grace!" She rushed down the hallway to the kitchen door. When she swung it open, a delicious smell wafted our way, and I sincerely hoped the cake had not burned.

Picking up the paper and a pencil, I started sketching. Tristan asked Farrow, "Any line on the Lady Baudelaire investigation?"

"No. That subject is locked down tight with not even an obituary in the news sheets. Her husband is away, as are any nobles able to travel. If you discount the ones without funds or a country property, the only nobility remaining are the ones closest to King Guénard."

"Rats leaving a sinking ship," commented Marcus. He wore clean clothes and looked more like an errand runner for a merchant's import business than a gutter rat who would pick your pocket as you asked for directions. His hair was brushed and his nails were clean. From the looks of admiration he kept giving

Tristan I deduced what had generated this new attention to his personal appearance.

"That leaves the king vulnerable." I imagined him deserted, roaming empty halls, demanding cake and wine with no one answering.

"He has the military, Elinor," Tristan reminded me. "Your friend Jacques and the army will protect him. Which rather begs the question of what Barbier will do next. It also presents another problem that could become bothersome. Without the number required in attendance, Parliament won't be able to meet, forcing our government to a standstill, which could play into Barbier's hands."

"So the dinner party that Lady Valentina and Lady Talleyrand planned won't be happening," I said, relieved. That entire scheme had seemed too dangerous to me.

"No. It's still happening," said Tristan. He was pouring coffee from a pot sitting on the table and handed me a cup. "Before Anne-Marie was smuggled out, Valentina gave her a note. Plans are moving forward, despite delicate peach-colored intimates."

Farrow stifled a laugh behind his hand. Marcus, who could not read, was puzzled, and Farrow leaned over to whisper in his ear about the recent Gazette's political cartoon.

"If Barbier isn't watching the house, where is he?" I asked.

"Gone. Did a flit," said Marcus.

Farrow grunted in agreement. "It seems the inspector is nowhere to be found. A few other guardia are also missing, but with the force commanded to search house to house for Ghastlies, his desertion has gone unnoticed. I believe there are men on the force who are covering for him."

Tristan put in, "I doubt the gendarmes realize what is happening within its own ranks. They are in chaos, with too much to do, and too few men to do it. I am not surprised we could leave the city."

"But what is his next move?" Everything was so upside down, I couldn't make any sense of it. "Alenbonné keeps going; the king still has his throne. How did he think he would seize power? No one would let a guardia of base birth rule. The nobility would never stand for it."

"If the king falls, it opens up possibilities for looting, seizing property, killing those you hate without compunction," suggested Farrow.

"Whatever Barbier wants, he has spent a great deal of time, effort, and reputation in an attempt to gain it," surmised Tristan. "I wonder if he will try to claim his rights? File as Lord Lucas Bridoux's son?"

"He'd still be illegitimate."

"Do you think so, Elinor? What if Barbier produces a forged marriage certificate between Bridoux and Madame Granger? I could see him being brash enough. How do we know that a secret marriage did not take place? If Lord Bridoux's wife dies, there would be no one to dispute it. He could take his father's seat in parliament without one word of complaint, especially as most are out of the city."

"Stop, Tristan! That would be horrible!" His betrayal showed that Barbier was cunning. He wore a mask for years and I had believed he was loyal to upholding law and order, satisfied in serving the king only as a guardia. How many had he murdered to further his ambition?

Marcus asked excitedly, "But he can't take a seat in government. Ain't he a commoner?"

"Isn't he. Not ain't," Tristan corrected him absentmindedly. "We need to get you some elocution lessons, Marcus, so you can expand your spy skills. Words make impressions." He continued, thinking out loud. "What we know at this stage is that Inspector Marcellus Barbier has most likely murdered his father, Lord Lucas Bridoux. I assume it was an act of personal revenge since Bridoux did not acknowledge Barbier as his bastard, but the boldness of the act indicates that we are nearing Barbier's endgame. We need to know more about Bridoux. Farrow, can you research this for us? I know little of the man."

Farrow nodded and scribbled the request in a tiny notebook, an act that reminded me of my lost apprentice. Meanwhile, Anne-Marie had returned and placed a ginger cake dusted with sugar in the center of the table, along with a knife, a stack of plates, and forks. I stared at its sweet goodness, thinking how incongruous it was with our serious conversation of murder and betrayal.

"Barbier has Twyla. We must find her." I couldn't help but tremble, thinking of the danger she must be in. "Barbier must be behind whatever circumstances forced Sergeant Dupont's soul from his body. It only follows that it was he who murdered Lady Baudelaire and set me up to take the blame."

Tristan placed his hand on my shoulder and gave me a reassuring squeeze. "Madame Granger said he had lost control of his Ghastlies. Why do you think that is?"

To help the others understand, I explained the situation more fully. "The Ghastlies we encountered at the theater had their souls suspended in the Beyond. They were not ghosts, since they had a physical body on the earthly plane, but they were so close to dying their souls were suspended in the Beyond, struggling to cross to the Afterlife. Maybe the person Barbier was using to control their souls died or lost his mind? Mediums often suffer mental confusion from prolonged time in the Beyond. Could this be what happened to who was controlling the Ghastlies?"

I tapped the pencil against my lips, managing my thoughts. "If they were using Parnell's drug, it is not a healthy elixir. The collapse of the Ghastlies indicates that Barbier can no longer rely upon the person he was using to control them. He needs another puppet-master for his creatures. Twyla?"

"Which puts the girl in grave peril. What about Granger's comment about Parnell's dream palace? What did it look like?"

"I described it to Barbier at the time." I gave a harsh laugh. "But nothing came of that! Not hard to know why. How he must have laughed up his sleeve the entire time we trusted him!" I took a deep breath to calm myself. "A cavernous hall, with stick-like supports of an arched roof. A maze of connected large spaces. Does that sound familiar to any of you?"

"No." Tristan, Farrow, and Marcus shook their heads.

"Perhaps this will help. This is my drawing of the place." I turned my sketch around and slid it across the table. Farrow shook his head again. Marcus picked it up to examine it closer. "These thin supports and the arched ceiling make me think of the Hollow Works. What do you think, Anne-Marie?"

The girl took the drawing he handed her and bit her lip in concentration. "Yes, I can see that. The rows of pillars and the arching roof."

Tristan and I asked at the same time. "What are the Hollow Works?"

Anne-Marie explained. "It's an old shipyard where they had a dry dock and offices, but it's abandoned now and hasn't been used for years."

"Why?" asked Farrow.

Anne-Marie reflected. "I must have been about ten, when the piers holding up the building collapsed. Something was wrong about the foundation, and the sea destroyed some supports."

"So the structure is no more?" I asked.

"There's some left. The building shifted over the dry dock and is half falling into the sea. It's very unstable. Dangerous even. No one goes there except the homeless or gangs."

Tristan and I exchanged glances. I asked her, "Is your father in town?"

"Yes, he's been trying to convince us to leave to Perino. He thinks it's too dangerous to stay here, but Ma isn't going to be pushed out of the only home she's known."

"Can you send a message for him to come here?"

"Certainly."

I explained to Tristan. "Anne-Marie's father is a sailor. He will know the area and have resources we could use."

Tristan nodded. "Farrow, I need you and Marcus to investigate this place. Send some of the street imps or dock rats to watch, but no risk-taking, Marcus. I'm serious. We think that Barbier may be holding Twyla Andricksson there."

At Twyla's name Marcus stiffened, and Anne-Marie's hands came together to clasp each other tightly in alarm.

"We want to get her out, but safely, so absolutely no heroics." Tristan stared at Marcus. "This man is extremely dangerous and unpredictable. Do not approach him. Report to me."

To Farrow, he started outlining the type of information he wanted. "Who goes in and out. Entrances, exits. Are there any Ghastlies about? Any evidence that the girl is there? They will need food and supplies. Whatever you can find, but do it quietly. We cannot alarm them."

Chapter Fourteen

Before falling asleep, I tried again to summon Twyla through the Beyond. Nothing happened. Not even a whisper. Every few hours when I woke from sleep, I immediately tried again. A final time in the morning, before going downstairs for breakfast. But I only found silence.

I refused to think she was dead. No, they needed her to control the Ghastlies. Since she had not escaped to the safety of the Beyond, I guessed she was unconscious, probably drugged. Probably Madame Granger had told Barbier about Twyla's trick of evading her lessons and vanishing into the ghostly plane. And I had told him of how, when Vonn had threatened us, Twyla had removed us physically to the Beyond.

Barbier had gone to a lot of trouble to capture her. He would not risk her running away to where he could not go.

It was obvious from the shadows under my eyes, and my depressed demeanor that I was upset. As he poured out tea for me, Tristan reassured me, trying to cheer me up. "We will find her. Mys Andricksson has spirit. She won't be suppressed for long."

That was another thing to fear. Barbier needed the girl compliant, and that was antithetical to Twyla's nature. She would fight him, and like Madame's manservant, might lose that battle, for Barbier had showed he was ruthless when countermanded.

After breakfast we scanned the newspaper. News of the Ghastlies was dropping to the back page. Coverage of the road-blocks was still hostile, and the newspaper editors demanded that they be removed. The discussion of the assassination of Lord Bridoux had shifted to articles about his wife's health, which painted her survival as unlikely.

The lawyers had sent paperwork for us to sign, stacks of documents for me to waive any claims on the Chambaux title or the vast estates attached to it. I signed them with a flourish, leaving Tristan bemused.

"Are you sure? Now that you know—" He meant since I was bearing his child, but to mind it made it all the more reason to get it done. We would forge our own way.

"Yes. I have absolutely no regrets." I handed the stack back to him and gave him a kiss. "Besides, I hear you have plenty of other properties."

"A cowshed on a dairy farm that makes delicious cheese. The other property is mostly swampland. Maybe we could harvest mushrooms for a living?"

"So we won't stay at Hartwood?"

He eyed me speculatively. "I'd rather keep my second and best marriage far away from my first and failed one. Would you want to live with Valentina?"

Despite being finally on good terms, I did not. Also, I didn't know what she thought of our recent marriage. "What about using one of your Alenbonné houses, like this one?"

He shrugged. "None of them speak to me as a home."

It was mid-morning when we received word from Farrow and Marcus about the Hollow Works. The locals had been evicted by a new group of roughs who now guarded entrances, and the area residents found them unfriendly so avoided them.

"We found four by the entrance street-side, and three more on the roof. During meal times they change their shifts. Someone is picking up food from local taverns, and from the amount they have about ten people at any given time. No one has seen a girl. Only men," said Farrow.

Marcus nodded. "I talked to the wharf rats, and they said this lot showed up about six months back and chased them off. They aren't happy. I'm sure they would be up for a ruckus with these gents."

My last gold soul-sister, Renee Bassett, with her delicate flute voice, stirred. Usually she lay quiet, nestled in my heart, but this talk was drawing her attention. How I wish I could speak one-on-one with her! She might have been able to help us. Instead, my arms tingled all the way to my fingers, and an icy tremor went down the knife scar where Vonn had sliced my soul-form in the Beyond.

Perhaps that was answer enough.

"That's the place. Twyla is there." Tristan, Farrow, and Marcus were seated around the dining table, and all heads turned my way. "I feel it."

Anne-Marie came in with three men. Her father, Claude Draper, greeted me with a cheeky, "Still have that little pistol, madame, I gifted you?"

"Certainly I do, Claude. It has come in very handy." We smiled at the same time, shaking hands. "It's good to see you. We appreciate your help in this matter."

"Anne-Marie says they've taken that friend of hers — the one who talks too much. It's a dark world when a young girl from a decent family can't be safe in Alenbonné. If it was Anne-Marie that was taken, I know you'd do anything to rescue my gal."

"Of course she would!" said Anne-Marie.

Claude had brought two other men with him, sailors like

himself, to assist in our plans. "Fabien, Luis. Both worked on the Hollow Works back in the day, before it all came tumbling down."

Claude was on the small side for a man, with a round bald head, big ears, and eyes that loved jokes. His wiry physique could scale a ship's mast in under a minute. The other two were broader of shoulder, a little taller, but also in their early fifties. Fabien was dark-skinned and black-haired, like many from Perino, but he spoke with an Alenbonné accent. Luis was burned brown from the sun, and seemed quieter. Both had only nodded during introductions, though they gave Tristan, who was clearly a lord, a bit of a twice-over glance.

Through a connection, Tristan had gained the early architectural drawings of the shipyard from the National Archives. He spread them over the dining table and the men leaned forward as if they were at a starting gate.

Tristan addressed the room at large. "We have a belief that a young girl, Mys Twyla Andricksson, may be held here against her will at the Hollow Works. It is the same group that is causing alarm and violence throughout the city."

The three sailors exchanged looks but said nothing.

Tristan asked Marcus and Farrow to share what they knew. Marcus repeated what he had told us earlier. "They've chased the thieves and beggars away, often with violence. Locals dislike them, but rumors say gendarmes protect them."

"Organized," said Farrow. "They have shifts, men who change guard. A few seem to be guardia, as they still wear parts of the blue uniform. So that fits with what we know of our man, Barbier. If he isn't concealing Mys Twyla there, he's hiding something he wants protected."

Feeling a rush of anger, I clasped my hands in my lap under the table so they wouldn't show my agitation.

"Why we asked Anne-Marie for your assistance, Mysir Draper, is that we hoped you could advise us on how to get in without being noticed. What can we expect inside?" Tristan asked.

Claude leaned over and started pointing out features of the architecture on the paper with a calloused finger. "This here area is gone. It all sank when the piers gave way. It's dangerous to come in that direction. Not only because it's underwater, but the debris would make it tricky in the depths."

The other two gave their professional thoughts on the matter.

"Suicide going that way," was Fabien's comment.

"Even if you could dive it, you'd get lost underwater," Luis agreed.

Claude's finger swept along and ended up tapping at another point which faced out to the harbor. "This was the original entrance for the ships to be pulled in using cables and winches. The warehouse has slid sideways over it, making an overhang. It's still accessible by water, but not from the land, so a small boat could get in."

"Use rope and climb up through the hatches." Fabien's suggestion was countered by Claude.

"Hatches are bound to be rusted shut after all this time."

"What hatches?" asked Tristan.

Claude tapped the map again. "Wagons came through the ground floor to bring in equipment, machinery and the like. It could be hoisted up using block and tackle to the next floor through the trapdoors they cut into the flooring planks." His hand showed where this had been done.

Before Tristan could say otherwise, I interjected, "I shall go with you. I must be there for Twyla."

It was obvious Tristan wished he could deny me. "You can come in later, after we've cleared the place."

"No," I said firmly. "When Parnell held me captive, Twyla went with you and she was the only reason I could return from the Beyond. You need me there in case she is in a similar situation."

Farrow said, "Best to do a two-prong, maybe even a three-prong attack. Make a diversion to draw them out of their rathole." He pointed his finger at the barn doors. "This is where I saw men posted. They also had men on top of the building. We could use Marcus and his rooftop monkeys up there."

Tristan shook his head. "We cannot risk children to save another child."

"My crew wouldn't be at risk," asserted Marcus. "We'll use 'crackers. Street poppers. Cause that distraction you need. None of us would be close enough for them to catch us."

Tristan crossed his arms. "Fireworks would only work for a short time. Anyone with a brain will know it's a tactic to pull the men away from where the real action is happening."

I disagreed. "You're judging these men by your intelligence. In the heat of the moment, would they reason that out?"

"My men could do a frontal attack," said Farrow. "While you go under and enter from the sea, with a boat."

Fabien and Luis exchanged silent glances before nodding. Fabien said, "We'll help. When Claude told us a girl he knew had been taken, it made our blood boil. What's been going on in our city needs to be stopped. It's not decent."

Luis gave his contribution. "We can get a boat for you. Take you through the harbor side."

Claude added, "We'll need tackle, a saw, some other things. I can get those."

The plan worried me. "Would they harm Twyla if they feel under attack?"

"Not unless the inner circle is breached," was Tristan's summary. "They will move her once they feel really threatened, so we must find her swiftly once the action begins. If we can't get in and out quickly, we have bigger problems."

Chapter Fifteen

Where were all the ghosts?

"Is that odd?" Tristan asked.

"Yes, it is decidedly odd."

We were standing in one of the back alleys close to the wharf, just a block from a popular tavern. The safe house was only a couple of miles from the harbor, and getting here had not demanded strenuous maneuvers.

Standing in the shadows of the alley, you could hear the waves slapping against the ships and the wharf, and smell the rich, fishy scent of the sea. The masts of the sea-traveling ships were black skeletons against the moonlit sky. Occasionally you could hear the shouts of sailors or the ringing of a bell as they continued their work into the evening.

Here we would meet Claude and his fellow sailors and begin our watery journey into the Hollow Works. Tristan and I were dressed in dark clothes. I in a black dress and he in a sweater and laborer's trousers.

I told him, "I don't want to talk about ghosts when the sailors get here. They are notoriously superstitious. But the lack of spirits here worries me. It's odd."

The shipyard and wharf area should be filled with ghosts. The docks were part of the oldest part of the city, continuously inhabited since its founding. It was a place where death would not have been uncommon given its history. More recently, street fights or domestic tirades ending with a knifing or a beating also were common where there was drink and poverty.

A large black shape came down the street and turned into where we stood. It was Farrow. He had gone to scout the area again and see if the man he'd left watching the place had any new information for us.

"Anything new to report?" Tristan asked.

"A newcomer came by about twenty minutes ago. Must be a boss for they all deferred to him when he walked through the front door."

I couldn't help myself. "Did he limp?"

"Now that you mention it, yes, he did."

"Barbier," I told Tristan. "He must be here."

"Our fox hunt might be more successful than we planned," was Tristan's only comment as he flashed me a grim smile.

Behind Farrow, a smaller man appeared. Claude Draper. "Fabien and Luis have brought the boats. Are you to ready to ship out?"

"Yes. Farrow, give us an hour before you signal to Marcus to begin the show." Tristan gave Farrow a handshake. As I passed my bodyguard, he patted my shoulder and whispered, "You'll do fine."

Claude led us to a row boat alongside the next pier, where Fabian sat, his hands on the oars. Tristan lowered me into it and it rocked under my feet, so I was thankful for his steadying hand. Tristan and Claude followed more gracefully. There were piles of rope and a canvas tarp that made it a bit awkward for the four of us to find a space.

"Where's Luis?" asked Tristan.

Claude nodded out toward the water. "Here he comes."

Luis was guiding a little tugboat around a larger ship, and

brought it parallel to us. Fabian dug in with his oars, sending our little craft out to greet him. They maneuvered, so the tugboat was between us and the shore, shielding our rowboat from anyone on the dock.

Claude warned us in a low voice, "Don't speak. Voices here carry easily over the water. Luis will hide our rowboat with his tugboat. He'll make it obvious where he is and any eyes will be on him. His engine will also cover the sound of our oars. Now, I'm afraid that everyone needs to get under this oilcloth, for I'd rather if they do see us, it's nothing but a couple of old sailors."

Draped under the canvas, my nose filled with the smell of mildew and fish. Tristan had taken the bottom position, so I lay on top of his chest while his back rested on the coils of ropes. I heard the dip-splash of the oars and the chug-chug of the tugboat. My heart was racing, and I forced myself to take even breaths. What would happen if they discovered us? Would they start shooting? *Don't think of that. All will be fine.*

As if he could read my thoughts, Tristan gave a pat on my back.

It seemed to take forever, or just a moment, before Claude removed the tarp that covered us. "We're under the Hollow Works now."

The two men had brought lanterns, but they kept the flaps closed so only a weak light was emitted. I sat up, grimacing at a cramp in my calf, and took stock of our surroundings.

It was as if we had entered a dark cave. At the entrance I could see the harbor water, the waves flickering with light from ship lanterns or the lighthouse. But where our boat rested under the wreck of the building, the water slapping against our rowboat was pitch-black. Eerie shadows rose from the water. The landscape was foreboding.

"The timbers from the old docks," said Claude, explaining what I was seeing.

The sailors were right; it would be impossible to swim through here safely. You would quickly become lost or tangled with what lay below the water. As it was, Fabian was having to maneuver around the debris and you could hear some of it scrape against the bottom of our boat. Above us, the timbers and metal creaked and groaned.

"Where do you want me?" asked Fabian.

"We need to go in further, until we find a hatch above our heads."

Fabian rowed the boat deeper into the cave-like cavity that the building over the water created. It was not a pleasant place, even for a Ghost Talker.

Finally, they were satisfied, and he stopped the boat, slipping rope around one of the half-sunk pillars that stretched above our heads. Claude opened the lantern's swing door to gain more light. He raised it over his head, it illuminated the metal girders. Fabian pulled out a grappling hook and uncoiled the rope attached to it. When he tossed it upward, it sounded incredibly loud as it hit metal and wood before splashing into the water.

"I bet you two beers at the Anchor you can't get it on the next throw," said Claude.

The hook caught on the next attempt. Fabian shot him a grin. "I'll collect tomorrow, so you'd best have the coin."

In a flash, Fabian was climbing up the long rope, grabbing and pulling himself up in that smooth, effortless way of sailors. There was a whistle before a tumble of rope dropped to us. Claude caught it before it struck the boat or the water, and as he unfurled it, I realized it was a rope ladder.

"Didn't think madame could shimmy up like we could," murmured Claude.

Fabian must have taken a block and tackle, for Claude tied a rope around the handle of a handsaw, and that of a lantern. They were sent up to where Fabian sat on a steel beam, his feet dangling at least eighty feet over our heads.

Claude put one foot on the ladder and told us, "Wait until I tug, and then come up."

After some conversation we could not hear and some hand gestures we could barely see, the two got to work. As time passed, I wondered how much we had used of that hour.

The rope ladder jerked twice. Tristan indicated that I should go first. I was glad that I had found stout boots in the house we were staying at, and that it was dark, for I didn't want to think of how high up we would be going.

As I stepped up the first couple of rungs, the ladder swung away from the boat and over the water. I froze in place.

Below me, Tristan said in a low voice, "I enjoy seeing your swaying hips, Elinor, but don't move from side to side as much. Think straight up."

I did as he suggested and, while nothing could stop the thing from shifting since it wasn't anchored below, I managed. I thought only of getting to the top. Finally a hand touched my shoulder. It was Claude. His legs were wrapped around the metal girder, and he was hanging upside down like a bat.

"Fabian's cutting us a way through the boards. Luckily, most are rotten, so it won't be long before we'll have a way through."

A few moments later, we had some natural moonlight from above as Fabian removed the last board and placed it inside the building on the floor. He lifted himself up, Claude swung over and went next. Both men took my arms and lifted me up as easily as a feather. Tristan came last and without assistance.

"Fabian will stay with the boat, but I'm coming with you," explained Claude.

"See you soon," said Fabian, before dropping through the hole with such suddenness it made me catch my breath and close my eyes for a second in fear.

There was some wan moonlight coming through broken windows located high on the wall, so I could make out some of where we were. The floor might have been solid long ago, but it wasn't now. It sloped.

Bulky machinery stood like silent sentinels, those who had

worked it long gone. It must have been left behind when the building had become unstable. The warehouse was vast, and slim metal poles were evenly spaced out to support a spiderweb of girders that supported the next floor. It gave me an odd feeling of familiarity, but it was a poor man's copy of Parnell's palace in the Beyond, which had been made from imaginary marble and granite.

Claude had dimmed his lantern, and carried a coil of rope over his shoulder. Tristan gestured to us and we started making our way around the bulky giants smelling of oil and grease. We climbed up the tilted floor, our path taking us under a staircase made from raw decking boards.

"No one on this floor," Tristan said. He pulled out a pocket watch. "We won't have much more time before the show begins."

I barely heard him, distracted by seeing my first ghost of the evening. It was a slim shadow moving between the machines, coming closer to our position. Before I could summon it, the spirit saw me, and in a blink of an eye, it was standing next to us.

Neither Claude nor Tristan reacted, for I was the only one who saw the skinny teen who wore the coat, trousers, and neckerchief of a dockworker.

He asked me, "Are you here to take them away?"

Chapter Sixteen

Even as I asked him who he meant, I could feel them. The severed Ghastly souls were making a humming vibration to my attuned senses. I couldn't see any of them, but they must have been close, as the long scar on my forearm was aching.

"Have you found a ghost?" asked Tristan. At his question to me, Claude startled, looking quickly around, but obviously not seeing what I did. Claude knew what I did for a living and I hoped he'd be more open minded then his brethren.

"Yes. It's a boy who says the Ghastly soul-ghosts are here."

"Not the Ghastlies themselves?"

After discussing it with the boy, I told Tristan, "He describes them as strange ghosts, so I think they are the souls from the bodies the city has been burning. They are trapped here, still unable to cross to the Afterlife, despite the loss of their corporeal tether."

"She's glowing," whispered Claude, his eyes growing huge as he stared at me.

The souls of the girls Parnell had trapped in the Beyond had joined with mine and given me the power to sunder Vonn from all three planes of existence. But they were gone: Frida Korver, who had guided the Ghastly souls at the Luminary to the Afterlife; Sergeant Dupont's half-sister, Meike Roord, who'd gain the guardia a final peace; and Louisa Bonnet, who protected me when the possessed Dupont had attacked me at my father's workshop.

Only Renee Bassett was left. The girl who had never visited her country relatives. The Ghastly humming was now paired with the sound of her flute. She was ready to help these poor creatures, and I felt regret and sadness at the thought of another goodbye.

"You were right, Elinor, as always. It looks like we will be needing you for this. Does your new friend know if Twyla is here?"

The boy was still able to reason, so he must have died in the last twenty years or so. "There is only one living girl here. She's on the next floor up, but I don't know her name. All she does is sleep as those things suck on her soul." The last was said wistfully as if he'd like to be draining a young girl of her life.

"She is alive, though?" I asked urgently.

"Yes."

"Tell me where she is and who else is there. Are there machines like these up there?"

He told me there were two men with Twyla. Most of Barbier's men were guarding entrances, the areas that Farrow had already noticed. It was only nine people according to the ghost.

"No reason to waste more guards on someone who is sleeping," said Tristan. "He's probably spread thin, and that works in our favor."

The main problem was that this building was built large, and it had few interior walls so there would be less cover. Some machines were up there, but not as many as on this floor, along with some wood shipping crates.

Claude spoke hesitantly for the first time since the ghost had appeared. "What do those soul ghosts want? Can they hurt us? Kill us? Steal our souls?" His voice had genuine fear in it.

I was quick to reassure him. "They can't hurt you or take your soul. What they are doing to Twyla is because Barbier has drugged her and made her helpless. If she was awake, without that poison in her system, she'd be able to shoo them away like we do flies. They can do nothing to you. Leave them to me."

And if they tried, we'd stop them. Renee Bassett was glowing stronger as I spoke, and I felt an urgency from her. She'd have to wait until we worked out a plan so the living among us wouldn't be shot.

"My concern is the two men guarding Twyla." I went on. "The boy says they have weapons."

Tristan asked, "Has he seen a man who limps?"

"He's on the roof."

"We should move quickly before their leader comes back down. It's always easier to confuse foot soldiers when the commander isn't around."

"Will you help us?"

He looked hesitant. "Those things are scary."

"I won't let them harm you. And if you help me, they will be gone soon." I held up my hand, palm towards him, and let my last gold-girl Renee Bassett make my hand glow. "I promise we will protect you. And afterward you will have Hollow Works to yourself, or if you wish, I will help you transition to the Afterlife."

He gazed mesmerized at my hand and nodded. "I'll help."

"What do you think?" Tristan asked Claude. "Can you climb up overhead?"

He nodded. "There are ladders next to the stair that take you to the girders. I'll use that to get up. What do you have in mind?"

Tristan told us how a sailor, a ghost, and a girl with two souls would save Twyla.

～

Hollow Works had a brooding atmosphere. My mind was uneasy. The tilting of the floor, the looming rafters, the water that produced strange echoes, and the smell of decay made you peer into the shadows.

Objects moved by the unseen always scares people.

We came up the stairs, stepping as softly as we could. At the top, was the ladder, and Claude saluted us before starting upward. When he reached the roof, he moved like a spider, hand-over-hand across the girders.

Tristan went into the room next, using the shadows of the crates to hide behind. There was a light further ahead, and he peered around the corner of a hulking machine, then turned and whispered to me, "There's two of them, like the ghost said. Sitting on chairs. There's a mattress on the ground with someone lying under some blankets."

Carefully, I took a peek. A pool of light was cast around them from two lanterns as they played cards without a care in the world. *Huh! We'll make them care!*

Noise Ghosts love to set the stage for their dramatics. I had coached ours on what he could do and gave him enough energy to make it happen.

First, the temperature rapidly dropped. While it was a summer night and we were near water, the radical temperature difference could not be accounted for by anything natural. It took a few moments before Barbier's men recognized the change.

"This hellhole is freezing," said one.

"Take that up with the boss. I just do what I'm told."

Next, a lantern blew out. The one who had complained of the cold cursed as he tried to get the lantern's wick to flame again. Of course, it did not. He grew more frantic, but each match he struck blew out before he could set it to the lantern wick.

People need fire and light. Without them we paint the darkness with monsters. It helped that when the second lantern blew out, a ghostly wailing started. It was Claude in the rafters, mimicking a howling noise that he said monkeys in Perino could make. It didn't sound human and both of them jumped from their seats, looking around as if they could discover in the darkness what was making the sound.

There was a faint pop next, making me jump. *What was that?*

Tristan reminded me. "Marcus. On the roof." I had forgotten.

Using mind pictures and hoping she would understand, I asked Renee Bassett to make the Ghastlies visible to us all. She must have figured out my request, for the lost souls shimmered into human-shaped outlines on the earthly plane.

Ghastly souls flickered into being and filled the warehouse. Fifty, no, at least a hundred, stood around us. Men and women. Even teens. They glowed with that strange fluorescence of sickly gray that all Ghastlies had, and their faces were twisted in pain. Parnell or Barbier had convinced many of those desperate to live to take the drug that promised them a longer life.

It was quite terrifying to see their numbers standing next to Twyla's prone body, pulling at her hair and clothes, crying for her help. The red ribbon that attached her soul to her body was being pulled and tangled by their fingers.

One of the guards must have been sensitive to spirits, for he screamed and ran blindly towards us. The distant noise of the fireworks was getting louder, and it covered the noise of Tristan's weapon as it winged him. The man fell groaning, and Tristan and I started running to Twyla, as Claude shimmied down a rope he had tied to a beam.

Each time I stepped through a Ghastly soul, I felt an electric jolt throughout my body and my left arm became numb.

Tristan's fist brought down the second man. I barely paid them any attention, going straight to where Twyla rested on the straw mattress. The girl was pale, utterly limp in my arms, but feeling her neck, I found a pulse.

As I held her, Renee Bassett materialized next to me in a column of gold.

She was the last of the four, and the most gentle for she pulled herself away from me slowly and carefully. Perhaps she had learned from the other three how it had torn me to let them go, for this was done so softly, so kindly, that I did not feel that horrible physical pain in my heart. Or perhaps it was because she was older. Her features showed maturity around the jaw and forehead, lacking in the other girls, who had been in their teens or early twenties.

Renee turned her head, looking down at us from blind golden eyes, before she turned back to the Ghastly souls. She raised her hands as if addressing them, and they stopped their cries for help. One pressed closer, and as Renee touched its hand, the Ghastly disappeared. Another approached, and the same thing happened.

The crowd of Ghastlies, seeing salvation, started pushing forward at a more rapid pace and went back to screaming. "Save us! Save our souls!" Instinctively, I pulled back, throwing up my arm to shield my face, but none reached us.

Each vanished as they came close to Renee. As they did so, they let go of Twyla's soul cord. I grabbed that red ribbon and bringing her hand over her left breast, where her heart lay, I fed it back into her.

As Renee swallowed the souls, her gold form grew taller until she was reaching the rafters. I felt it in my flesh, that goodbye. There was a great whoosh, and a spray of rainbow light shot through the roof. In a blink she was gone, and with her, all the Ghastly souls.

The emptiness she left behind made me hollow. How had I existed before they had shared my heart? And how would I exist now that they were all gone?

Chapter Seventeen

Tristan's hand fell on my shoulder.

"How is the girl?"

"She's not conscious, but she lives."

"We need to leave." Tristan bent and picked Twyla up, slinging her over his shoulder so he could keep his hands free. "We cannot count on Marcus and Farrow keeping all of Barbier's men distracted for much longer."

Claude grabbed a lantern but discarded his rope. From the pace he set he seemed ready to leave. We returned to the lower floor at a faster clip, knowing what would be ahead, and the downward slant of the floor made us all rush forward, forcing Tristan to re-balance Twyla over his shoulder. The ghost boy did not make an appearance, so I hoped he was satisfied with what we had done.

At the hole, Tristan laid Twyla gently on the ground while Claude scrambled down the rope ladder. When he reached the boat and Fabian, he jerked twice on the ladder to let our friend below know we were back.

Tristan was next, but he handed me his weapon first. "Keep watch."

Using the block and tackle, Fabian and Claude sent up a rope made into a loop so it could work as a harness. Tristan put it around Twyla's limp weight, making sure she was securely fastened.

I thought I heard footsteps, but said nothing for I didn't want to rush the careful work of getting Twyla safely into the rowboat. Pulling back the hammer on the pistol, I waited.

The rope jerked as Tristan slipped down it, traveling beside Twyla to keep the body harness steady.

The hatch was perhaps two dozen feet from a trio of the machines grouped together, which gave someone a good place to hide. In the darkness, they loomed. The tilt of the floor made my imagination think they were moving, sliding towards me. I blinked to readjust my vision.

The sound of uneven boot-steps came closer. Suddenly, a white sleeve flashed from around the corner of one hulk, firing. It hit a metal pole right behind my shoulder, sending out a ringing note. I barely felt the burn the bullet had made as it skimmed my shoulder.

"Elinor! Get down here!"

I followed Tristan's advice and lowered myself halfway into the hole to provide a smaller target. On my belly, dress hitching, feet dangling, my toes tried to find purchase on the rope ladder. Bracing my elbows on the floor, using my training, I opened all my senses for feeling energy.

Feeling reckless, and wanting to provoke him, I yelled, "How could you betray me?!"

The figure came out from hiding. His shot rang high for he wasn't expecting me to be on the ground. Mine took him in the chest.

Tristan's gun was heavier than mine and it kicked in my hand, causing me to lose my grip on it. Because of the floor's slant, it slid out of reach. Below me, Tristan was shouting, but I ignored him, trying to reach his gun.

The man struggled to his feet, his weapon in hand. "You bitch!"

The man I had taken to be Barbier was Lord Jansen Buckard. "Damn."

From below Tristan grabbed my ankle; above, Buckard grabbed my arm. His face was inches from mine — curly blond hair, brown eyes filled with hate, his handsome features twisted with rage. Even injured, he was powerful, and his grip started to drag me out of the hatch. My free hand came within reach of Tristan's pistol.

"You interfering piece of sh—" As his hand raised his weapon, I fired mine. This close, the stench of gunpowder burned my nostrils. The second round took him in the stomach, and he fell forward, his gun falling as he clasped me me in a blood-soaked embrace.

Tristan hauled me down by my ankles. Held in a death-grip, Buckard slithered after me. As I cleared the hole, Buckard's weight pushed me down too fast, and I started falling, the dark water far below me rushing up.

Suddenly, Tristan released my ankles, and I was in freefall for a second before he grabbed me hard around the waist. His movement made the rope ladder swing backward, causing Buckard's body to pivot in front of us, breaking his grip on me. Buckard flailed, trying to grab a hold of me, but I twisted away.

He dropped past us, screaming. Below me was a large splash and then silence.

I was in Tristan's arms. Safe.

"I've lost your gun," I told him inanely.

"And it was a matching set," he told me. "Damn you, Elinor. This blood — are you shot?"

"My shoulder's grazed. But most of this is Buckard's."

From below, Claude shouted, "Are you two coming down? I think we should get out of here."

Tristan looked up, but there was no one else. The harness hung empty beside him, and he showed me how to put the loop under my bottom and where to grip the rope. "Take her down, boys," he shouted to the sailors. In moments I was in the rowboat; Tristan wasn't as fast as Claude, but he made good time.

There was no sign of Lord Buckard in the murky water. I didn't ask after him. Instead, I spent my time chafing Twyla's hands, which were ice cold.

"Please wake up," I begged her. *Considering all the times I had wanted her to be quiet, I would have given my right arm to hear her prattle.*

Tristan was holding her, half lying in his lap. His hand was on her throat. "Her pulse is strong," he reassured me. "She's young, Elinor. Now that we have her, I'm sure she will recover." I couldn't stop thinking of Ebbe Losendahl. Yes, I had *brought* her back, but the Baron's daughter had never been the same since her time in the Beyond, drugged and used by Parnell Lafayette.

"We need Charlotte. Dr. LaRue. She looked after me and we need her expertise."

Tristan did not dispute that. "Let us get her to the safe house and we shall send for your friend."

～

It was disorienting seeing Charlotte, looking and acting the same as always. Nothing seemed to have changed since our last meeting, yet so much had.

"Hello, Elinor, I hear you have another patient for me?" She stood there, tall, and rather gawky in her masculine trousers and bobbed hair. Farrow, playing butler, had brought her in through the front door. She was peeling off a wet overcoat, for a downpour had begun after we had reached the house.

Hearing the front door, I had raced to the stairs. "Up here, Charlotte!"

"I'm coming. I'm coming," she told me, handing Farrow her

dripping coat. When she reached the top of the stairs, I showed her the spare bedroom where we had placed Twyla. Tristan, who was standing near the bedroom doorway, gave her a grave greeting. "Doctor, I hope you can help us."

Charlotte radiated such calm competence, that for the first time since finding Twyla unconscious, I felt some hope. She approached the bed, where Twyla was as still as a doll. I told her how we had found the girl.

"So whose is the blood?"

"It's Lord Jansen Buckard. I killed him."

Her eyebrows rose, but her only comment was, "Good riddance. The man was a nuisance to any decent society." She set her bag down on the nightstand and took out her stethoscope and watch. "This makes a break from dealing with the Ghastlies. My morgue is more a crematorium now than a place to explore the causes of death. Let's see what we are dealing with."

"I fear she's been drugged with the same elixir that Parnell used on me." I watched Charlotte's face, looking for any sign that would indicate her thoughts, but she gave nothing away. "What do you think? Will she recover?"

Charlotte didn't reply but calmly continued her examination, counting the girl's pulse to her watch and listening to her breathing. She bent over and pulled up Twyla's eyelid before examining her mouth. The gums were very pale.

"This is certainly the oddest experience I have ever had," said Twyla. Her spirit had materialized at the head of the bed to gaze down upon her corporal body.

"Twyla!" I exclaimed.

"Hello, madame. I'm sorry I couldn't get here earlier. Those stupid Ghastly souls kept me locked up with barely enough energy to stay alive, let alone go into the Beyond."

Used to my eccentric talents Charlotte showed no surprise at me talking to empty air. "If the girl is here in some manner, see if you can find out what they gave her."

Twyla could hear her, even though the doctor could not reciprocate. She started her explanation with her kidnapping from Madame Granger's. "Mysir Durant locked me in my room, and at first I was happy to see Inspector Barbier arrive. I thought you had sent him in response to my handkerchief in the window! He put something over my face that smelled sweet, but in a nasty way. Then I blacked out."

I told this to Charlotte.

"Chloroform, but that isn't what made these marks on her arm." She pulled up Twyla's sleeves to expose the needle-marks I had noticed when putting on her nightgown.

Twyla's soul-shade came over to look at what Charlotte indicated. "Well! I don't know what that is about, for I haven't been awake since they grabbed me. Every time I tried to manifest in the Beyond, all those dead Ghastly souls crowded around, preventing me. They thought I could help them! Idiots!"

After I had relayed Twyla's words, Charlotte said, "So Twyla can't explain this?"

"I'm afraid not. But I'm guessing it's the same formulation, or close to it, that we've been dealing with. The only reason I thought it something different was because I could not reach Twyla in the Beyond. However, that was because of the Ghastlies."

Charlotte gave a dissatisfied sound. "Well, best to take this slow and hope for the best."

"Is there anything we can do?" I felt helpless and wanted to contribute.

"Bring a bucket for her to vomit in, just in case. A warming bed pan if you can manage one. We don't want her chilled. Towels and a water pitcher filled with tepid water would be good."

Tristan nodded and left the room.

"Honestly, please tell me. What do you think of her chances, Charlotte?"

"I am here, you know!" said Twyla. "I'm not dead yet, and unlikely to be. I'm not feeling the pull of the Afterlife."

I didn't want to explain to her that perhaps that lack of pull was because she would become a ghost instead.

Charlotte always spoke plainly. "In your situation, you were given one dose, and it was oral. This looks to be several injections. I don't like it, but her heart is strong, and her lungs clear."

"She's been missing for about three days," I told her.

"Well, she's young, stubborn, and in good health. That can make a world of difference."

"Thank you," said Twyla. "I told you I'm not meant for the grave. A fortune teller told me once that I wouldn't die until I had white hair, and my hair is far from white!"

Despite Twyla's optimism, the night was horrid. Her soul often disappeared; and after this had happened twice, I realized it always preceded a convulsion when her body would grow agitated, fighting those who were trying to keep her still. She mumbled and spat out intelligible words as her fever climbed.

"Withdrawal from the drug," was Charlotte's medical guess.

A couple of upholstered chairs had been brought up from the parlor by Farrow, and Anne-Marie, pale-faced from worry, kept us supplied with pots of tea and coffee until we felt we would burst. Tristan came in a few times, but there was little he could contribute to the sickroom.

The next day, late in the afternoon, with Twyla's situation unchanged, I exited the room to stretch my legs. Tristan drew me into our room. "My lawyers have arranged a meeting with de Windt tomorrow. Do you feel up for that?"

What if Twyla was still running these high fevers? Still half out of her mind? Could I leave her? Well, the world would not stop for one lone girl, and Anne-Marie could relieve Charlotte. My friends were in danger as long as I was wanted for Josephine's murder. "Yes, but I want to wear something that fits."

"I will send Farrow and Anne-Marie to collect something from the Crown." His hand stopped my protest. "Don't worry, de Windt knows where we now reside. That was the trade I gave for him to meet my demands."

Probably it was my expression that caused Tristan to wrap me in a tight hug. He rested his chin on the top of my head. "Twyla will be all right. You'll see. She'll be back to plague you with her nattering until you'll beg me to take her back to the Hollow Works."

"I should never have allowed Madame Granger to take her. Or when she got back, I should have insisted she stay with me."

"Don't think that, Elinor. Barbier had us all fooled. If she had been with you, he would have found some other way to take her. As it is, he has lost his prize, and it seems, his Ghastly army, for things have been quiet the last forty-eight hours."

"You do not think he has retreated? Given up?"

"No. He will try something and we shall need to be quick on our feet to stop him."

From behind me, Twyla's spirit said, "Has he told you he loves you? You can't be in such a tight embrace with a man who hasn't."

"We're married, Twyla."

Her mouth shaped into an O, and she clapped her hands in glee. "Does Anne-Marie know?"

Which made me realize I hadn't told her or Charlotte all that had happened since I had seen them last. Before I could tell her anything more, Twyla made a crying moan. "Oh, my body wants me. This doesn't feel good at all!"

I broke from Tristan's arms and, taking him by the hand, led him back to the sickroom. Charlotte looked up as we entered. "Fever's broken, and her eyes are fluttering. I think she's coming around."

The first lucid thing Twyla said was, "I'm so hungry! I could eat five chickens!"

CHAPTER EIGHTEEN

When Twyla had some chicken soup and toast, I left the room with Tristan. He grabbed my wrist and pulled me into one of the empty bedrooms, closing the door behind us.

"Do you realize we haven't been alone together for forty-eight hours?"

"You must be jok—" I had no time to finish my thought because his mouth was covering mine and his chest pressed me backward, until I felt the wall against my back.

I had heard of such things, sudden passions taken quickly, but I had never experienced anything like it.

Tristan gave a throaty chuckle. "Am I embarrassing you? It is just us here. Husband and wife." His hand came down the front of my borrowed dress to cover my stomach. "How is our baby doing after all those gymnastics at the Hollow Works?"

"I'm sure it's fine," I said, a little breathless.

"You frightened me to death when you came down that hatch."

"I'm sorry. I didn't mean to."

"You never do." His hand was at my throat, unbuttoning my blouse.

"What about the others in the house?" I hissed, looking towards the door in fear it might open at any moment.

"Give me some credit. I locked it." His hand brushed over the psychic burn that my father's watch had left over my left breast, making it tingle slightly. One sleeve came off my shoulder, and then the next. Tristan kissed the bandage over where Buckard's bullet had taken a divot out of my skin. "I'd have murdered him if you didn't kill your enemies first."

"I didn't mean to kill him!" I retorted.

"Don't fire a gun unless you plan on killing someone, Elinor. That's the price of carrying one." He sounded absentminded, his attention instead on unbuttoning, unhooking, or untying all of my clothes.

"I just wanted to stop him," I said weakly. My skirt slipped to the floor, puddling around my feet.

"When this is over, I'm spiriting you away somewhere with some peace and quiet."

I bit my lip, suddenly unsure. "You are happy about the baby, aren't you?"

He swung me up in his arms, took me over to the bed. "Over the moon." He laid me down and slid up against me.

"I wondered if a baby might change things between us. Like Leona said."

He put his finger on my lips. "I am not Lucas Bridoux and you are not Leona Granger. I am very happy about you and our child. Do you want me to show you how happy I am?"

"Hm. Yes."

Since the news of Barbier's and Madame's betrayals, all my emotions were wounded and on the surface. I felt vulnerable. Add following an incident where I almost fell to my death, it was perhaps no surprise that our lovemaking was different. It was passionate and fierce, with little care or gentleness on either of our parts. I didn't wait. We took our joy from each other, panting and, at the end, laughing.

Afterward, we lay side-by-side, covered in sweat. Rolling on my side, I admired his profile. "What is the real reason you don't want to visit Chambaux?"

"I haven't been back since — since I did that." Frowning, I realized that the dream where I had seen him shoot Minette must have taken place at Chambaux. How stupid of me not to realize that. "Are you sure you shouldn't go back? To remove the power that memory has over you?"

"It doesn't have power over me," he told me. "That part of my life is done." Staying on his back, he turned his head towards me, making eye contact. "I won't sully my future with my past."

"Oh Tristan," I cried, my eyes tearing up. "But giving up Chambaux. Your childhood home where you had a pppp-ony." My lip blubbered. I was feeling very sentimental.

His hand reached over, and his fingers entwined with mine. "I have sacrificed nothing; I'm walking away willingly. There is a difference. It's a fact that you can't gain without giving something up."

"It's all because of me you have to give up anything!" I wailed. "You shouldn't have come after me. You've been dragged into all of my trouble."

He rolled to his side to face me, his hand coming up to tenderly move a lock of my hair out of my face. "I wasn't letting the woman I love be thrown in some cell. Barbier framed you for Josephine's murder. A day later, he grabbed Twyla. If I had set you aside and thought of the king first, duty first, where would you two be?"

"Dead."

"Most likely."

I was crying now. To have such loyalty touched me deeply. Especially as those who I had known the longest had betrayed me.

"What do you think we should name her?"

"Her? It will probably be a boy," I told him. "A little boy who looks like you and can sway me with a smile."

"No, definitely a girl who will kill anyone who disagrees with her."

"I really didn't mean to kill him! Only, like — wound him a little."

Tristan burst out laughing. Suddenly, there was a tap on the door. "Madame, are you in there? Twyla wants to know if she can have cake."

As someone told me long ago, it's a good idea to wear something that makes you feel beautiful every day. It also disgruntles your enemies when you show up looking wonderful, so I wore my best outfit when we left to meet de Windt to convince him I hadn't murdered Josephine Baudelaire.

We met Tristan's lawyers at their offices. They were fraternal twins, a man and woman named Van Heerden.

"Pleased to meet you at long last," said Mysir Van Heerden, a man in his mid-forties.

"And congratulations on your marriage," said Madame Van Heerden, who was as tall as her brother.

"Yes indeed! Congratulations," added Mysir Van Heerden.

"We should get some wine when we finish to make some toasts," said his sister.

"A fantastic idea. Especially if it is supplied by His Grace and bears the Chambaux label," agreed her brother.

They were very efficient at their duties, reminding me we were only clearing up a misunderstanding. I was informed that I should only answer the questions I wanted. They would stop the meeting if they thought it was necessary.

We all went to de Windt's government office in the same carriage. Tristan gave me little advice on what I should say. "It's best you come unprepared, Elinor. If we rehearsed, your answers would come out stiff. Trust me, love, all will be well."

I believed him because he was utterly relaxed. He joked with the siblings about their father, another Van Heerden, who seemed to have ill-luck at trout fishing.

"Of course, Father fell in," Madame Van Heerden was saying. Her twin added to the story. "Like he always does! Thank goodness we insisted on him learning how to swim, otherwise mother would be a widower a dozen times over by now."

De Windt's offices were in a public building with an anonymous looking front to it. The interior was utilitarian with no ornamentation, like the royal residence and offices for parliament. We were shown into a room with a battered conference table and eight chairs. The place was one step above a gendarmes' cell. It made me think of when Tristan had held me at Barbier's station after I'd realized that the dead body in the morgue was related to the king. Hopefully, I wasn't going to be held under another house arrest. Or worse.

De Windt entered the room with his clerk, who seemed to know the Van Heerden's. They exchanged handshakes and briefly discussed a recent case. The clerk barely looked at me, and when he did he seemed very nervous, dropping his pen.

His superior was as pompous as ever. He was wearing his black uniform with cuffs of scarlet and had set on the table his flat cap with its gold braid. Older than Tristan by a good ten years, de Windt's black hair was thinning, and the age marks around his mouth and eyes were settling into place. He cast me a suspicious look but did not voice his thoughts, probably because I had two lawyers and Tristan with me.

"My clerk will be taking notes about this interview," he informed us.

"We will like a copy of those notes, and a chance to amend them on the public record," said Madame Van Heerden cheerfully.

I felt her unfazed, sunny disposition would have seen a man hanged with the same smile.

De Windt's mouth tightened, but he did not disagree, only nodding to his clerk to make a note of the request. "Madame Chalamet—"

"Lady Fontaine, if you please," interrupted Tristan. "That is now her legal title as we are married."

The sour look on de Windt's face deepened. "Lady Fontaine, tell me of your relationship with Lady Josephine Baudelaire."

"We had no relationship. It was merely an acquaintanceship, for I barely knew her."

"That is not what our witness says, but let us proceed discussing this acquaintanceship. How did you meet?"

I told de Windt about the dinner party at Hartwood over a year ago. "Before that, I had never met her or heard her name."

"A Hartwood housemaid testifies to an animosity existing between you."

Despite his serene posture, I could tell that Tristan alerted on that remark.

"Not on my part. I merely made a remark about a necklace she wore. My father was a famous jeweler and I have some experience in appraising jewelry, you understand? She was wearing a replica with fake stones. That is common, as some do not want to risk their jewelry to theft or loss. Lady Baudelaire seemed irritated that I knew. Since she is dead and cannot be asked about the state of her feelings, I am only guessing."

"A good point, Lady Fontaine. Since her corpse is missing her eyes and tongue, she cannot be questioned by a Ghost Talker. How convenient for you." I did not respond. I was not here to discuss my skill with talking to the dead.

"There seems to have been another thing she was displeased with: you had set your sights upon the Duke de Archambeau, the host of this party and her longtime friend." He tapped his finger on the clerk's paper. "Be sure to note that."

"I was his guest at Hartwood until a case involving a cousin of the king could be resolved. She misconstrued the reason for my presence there. However, you can ask Lady Valentina Fontaine or the Duchesse de Chambaux, whom I met when I was there. For why I was there, ask the king."

De Windt's eyes narrowed as he realized I had scored a point. The king trumped any house servant. "When did you see her next?"

"I was invited by Lord and Lady Montaine, to their home, Hightower."

De Windt's eyes glittered. He had arrived at the Montaines' in order to accuse Tristan of treason over the theft of the king's letters. Letters that Josephine had acquired and had asked Valentina to plant among her brother's things. Luckily, I had returned them myself, as well as stopping Josephine's blackmail scheme.

"You do seem to have highly placed friends, Lady Fontaine. Do you think they will lie for you?"

"There is nothing to lie about. I did not know Lady Baudelaire would be at Hightower."

De Windt looked down on some of his papers as if to find information there. I doubted that. He was well-rehearsed. "Speaking of Hightower, tell me how you gained His Majesty's letters."

Lady Valentina would not have snitched on that sensitive topic. Tristan obviously had not. That left only King Guénard.

"Lady Baudelaire had them from the king's mistress and thought it best they be returned to His Majesty. She asked me to return them."

De Windt threw his hands up in a got-you moment. "I thought you barely knew her! Why would she give you such a delicate mission?"

"Embarrassment? I cannot speak to Lady Baudelaire's reasoning except that she wanted them out of her hands." *How far could the truth be bent?* I was determined not to involve Lady Valentina in this mess. No one needed to know about Josephine's blackmail attempt or her devious plan of getting Tristan into trouble. "The letters were given to me during a beach party that Lady Montaine arranged."

"Why would Lady Baudelaire give letters to a rival?"

I expressed surprise. "Rival? I never considered her to be mine. She was already married."

"When did you see her again?" De Windt showed a peevish anger.

"Not until the night at the Luminary."

"We have witnesses to that." He tapped his finger on top of his stack of papers. "Sworn affidavits that you two were seen arguing."

"She seemed out of sorts that evening. I don't know why."

"You have a smooth answer to all of my questions."

"I can only tell you what I did, saw, or thought. I apologize if it doesn't please you. Answering these snide accusations doesn't please me." I let some of my frustration show.

"I have a witness that states you were the last person seen with Lady Baudelaire."

"I have a witness that puts me in a completely different place when you say I entered that carriage with her," I countered.

The lawyers had not interfered with the interrogation, so far but they had been taking notes, and nodding at me encouragingly. Now, Mysir Van Heerden finally spoke up. "When we interviewed the neighbors of Lady Baudelaire, all they could describe was a lady in black, heavily veiled. A description that could fit probably a hundred women in Alenbonné."

Madame Van Heerden said in her perpetually amused voice, "Why, it could have been a description of myself!"

"You are hardly a small woman, Madame Van Heerden," her brother reminded her, to which she laughed. "Indeed!"

De Windt's temper flared. "Were a hundred women found

with the dead Lady Josephine Baudelaire? No, it was your client! And with the corpse mutilated to prevent any questioning of her!"

Chapter Nineteen

That was the sticking point. Under the table, my fingers gripped each other tightly, while my face remained a mask.

"Did you find her eyes and tongue in the room? A knife to commit the act in this locked room?"

To Tristan's quiet question, de Windt evidently had no answer.

"Has it ever occurred to you, de Windt, that Elinor is also a victim? What I see is an obvious attack upon her. She barely knew Josephine; I knew her far longer and would have a much better reason to see her dead."

De Windt seized upon his words. "That being?"

"She was part of a criminal network that I've been investigating for at least two years. Her theft of His Majesty's letters was probably on order from her master, so I would be incriminated and removed from an investigation that was gaining momentum. Do you seriously think that Elinor would gouge someone's eyes out and remove her tongue? Those mutilations speak of hardened criminals willing to do whatever it took to protect themselves."

"A mystery gang that I've never heard of?" scoffed de Windt.

"It is the same gang that was smuggling those guns into Sarnesse, and you know the leader of it rather well. Inspector Marcellus Barbier."

Tristan had certainly captured de Windt's attention, for that information dropped like rock into a still pond.

"Evidence?"

"Barbier kidnapped Elinor's apprentice, Mys Twyla Andricksson, who will make a statement about how she was forcibly removed from her mentor's home, that of Madame Leona Granger. During her kidnapping, Madame Granger's manservant was murdered and his body left in the house's foyer. I think you have found that body?"

As if mesmerized, De Windt nodded slowly. The two lawyers were equally enraptured, as if Tristan were a storyteller speaking about a pirate's lost treasure.

"His plan was to use Mys Andricksson to control people that had used a mind-altering drug developed by Parnell Lafayette of the Morpheus Society. A man who seduced women to their deaths. The city's coroner, Madame Charlotte LaRue, can testify to the drug and how it alters people who are near to dying. The crowd of rioters who tried to burn down the Luminary were some of their kind, what Dr. LaRue calls Ghastlies. They are the bodies being found throughout Alenbonné.

"Barbier used blackmail against members of le beau idéal in order to gain information and money to fund his ambitions. I believe that Lady Baudelaire was one of his minions. Blackmailed, or perhaps through her own inclinations, she was convinced to assist him. My wife, Lady Fontaine, pointed out that Lady Baudelaire's precious family jewels were false, which probably made her think that her connection to Barbier was known for the man has been dealing a brisk trade in collecting jewels from the wealthy to fund his enterprise."

That certainly made sense with what we knew now.

"Lord Jansen Buckard was also one of his lackeys. He moved

among the fringes of society, looking for women he could prey upon."

"A fantasy story to protect your lover! Where is your proof?!" demanded de Windt, his fist coming down on the table. It startled his clerk, who had been furiously writing everything down.

Tristan said in his I-am-always-right-and-you-are-an-idiot voice, "The proof is self-evident: Barbier has vanished. Go and ask the gendarmes where he is. They do not know, and some of his confederates in the force are also gone. His quarters are vacant. He has disappeared like a wisp of smoke while you play games here, accusing an innocent lamb."

De Windt stood up and rushed for the door. Cracking it open, I could see other men gathered outside, and the crown prosecutor called to them. I heard Barbier's name mentioned several times, but I was feeling so light-headed, as if I had just outrun some horrible danger, that I didn't follow most of the conversation.

Tristan slipped his hand under the cover of the table to pat mine before returning it to rest on the tabletop.

De Windt came back, his face flushed and his eyes passionate with fury.

"You will tell me everything about this!"

"Certainly. First, I want to question this servant at Hartwood, who you say testified against my wife. For it was from Hartwood that Elinor was snatched, and that means I have a traitor living under my sister's roof. You can see why I would want that threat addressed immediately."

She must have been waiting for us, for we were immediately greeted by Valentina when we arrived at Hartwood.

"Elinor, congratulations on your marriage to my brother." Her hands sought mine, and she gave them a squeeze, kissing me on each cheek. Her face was pale with shadows under the eyes, but she still kept the upright carriage and grace of a noblewoman.

Before I could respond, she moved swiftly to her brother.

"Tristan." She kissed him also and clasped his upper shoulders in a brief hug.

While it was a grand foyer, the space was becoming small with everyone crowding in. Tristan's two lawyers were apparently known to Valentina as she greeted them by name; de Windt and his clerk, the latter holding a wooden traveling writing desk which contained paper and ink; and standing behind us, stiffly at attention, were two Crown enforcers (thankfully, not Jacques Moreau). Four others had been left outside to guard all the exits.

Valentina invited us all to adjourn to the sitting room, the place where the Duchess de Chambaux had once interrogated me about my intentions. The room with the painting on the wall concealing a hidden passage, which probably had been used to remove me after Dr. Armand Devereaux had been struck from behind. And which had allowed Anne-Marie's escape.

We found other guests already here: Lady Maryegold Talleyrand, Dr. Devereaux himself, and Charlotte. Charlotte was standing near a table loaded with coffee, tea, and sandwiches. She was filling a plate and gave me a nod. I wasn't sure what Valentina was expecting, but she evidently thought we all needed to be fed.

More greetings were exchanged, and since our marriage announcement had been published in the gossip section of the newspaper, everyone also offered congratulations on our recent union. I wasn't sure anyone was sincere, but I nodded and shook hands.

The footmen brought extra chairs and when his back was turned to the others, Ruben gave me a wink. Tristan placed me between the Van Heerdens while he remained standing. De Windt took a seat next to Lady Talleyrand and Valentina. Dr. Devereaux rose from his seat to stand next to Charlotte, who urged him to take a sandwich from her plate.

A chair in the middle was left empty.

Tristan began to lay out his case.

"Last week, Elinor was in this room with Dr. Devereaux when they were attacked."

Dr. Devereaux nodded, giving me an apologetic look. "It was mid-morning, and Lady Fontaine and His Grace were not at home. Madame Chalamet, I mean Lady Elinor Fontaine, and I were discussing my work."

Tristan interjected. "Yes, I was already at the Parliament building. Valentina?"

"I had a meeting with a few ladies to discuss an upcoming party." De Windt looked away from her steely gaze.

"So would it be around ten that you paid your call?" Devereaux nodded. "Several things were happening at once. Lord and Lady Bridoux were accosted at the park and shot. At my home, Dr. Devereaux was attacked, and Elinor abducted. When did Lady Josephine Baudelaire die, Dr. LaRue?"

"When I examined her, she was already in a state of decay. I would put her death the night before. Although the mutilation of the eyes and the tongue were done postmortem."

Anyone who had a plate of food lowered it to their lap at this pronouncement.

"And the day before, Elinor was at Hartwood, always with another such as myself, my sister, or her personal maid, Anne-Marie." A sigh seemed to go around the room; I know my shoulders let go of tension I had been holding.

"Then who murdered Lady Baudelaire?" demanded de Windt.

"I am sure it was under the order of Inspector Marcellus Barbier, formerly of the gendarmes. It is my belief that she was becoming a liability to him. She told Elinor the only reason she had wanted my attention was because she needed my protection. Something I did not give."

Lady Talleyrand gave a small start at the inspector's name, but quickly recovered herself. It made me wonder why she was here. The others were witnesses or family.

"Who told you where I could be found?" I asked de Windt.

He became flustered. "An anonymous tip was delivered to the inspector."

"A note I very much doubt was 'delivered.'" Tristan said dryly, "Who in this house accused Elinor of having a rivalry with Lady Baudelaire?"

Lady Valentina set aside her teacup and smoothed the silk of her dress. "It was Madeline Cossart."

I could see that Tristan was surprised. "Are you sure, Valentina? Madeline? Mother's servant?"

His sister nodded. "I'm sorry, Tristan. I was also surprised at this disloyalty. She is still in the house, under protection of one of Mysir de Windt's men. Should I send a note to Mother at Chambaux about it? She's still there for the summer."

"Let us see what she has to say first."

Madame Van Heerden leaned over to me and whispered in my ear. "An old family retainer. Her line has served the Chambaux family for at least five generations."

"I wish to question her."

De Windt only shrugged. "Go ahead, but do not browbeat the woman, for I won't stand for that. It was brave of her to speak up against a family with your power."

When she was brought into the room by one of de Windt's men, I dimly recognized Madeline Cossart as the servant who had brought the Duchesse tea the day she had questioned me about my forced residence at Hartwood when we were investigating Giles Monet's death by the tiara dragon.

I wished Anne-Marie was here to give me the servant's view of her, but she was with Twyla.

Madeline Cossart had an anonymous face that would be easy to forget. It was round and soft, with small eyes and mouth, and her hair was a mousy dark blond transitioning to dull gray.

Nothing about her features, her way of moving, or how she talked stood out in one's memory.

From her appearance she was a hard worker (chapped hands, and a worn spot on her dress from kneeling, although her dress was less than a year old); unmarried (no ring, or evidence she'd ever worn one), and her eyes showed a stubborn intelligence, though unimaginative.

De Windt immediately reassured her as he guided her to the empty chair. "His Grace has a few questions for you, Madame Cossart, but do not worry. I will not let him bully you."

Lady Valentina said, "It's best to be completely honest in all your answers, Madeline. I promise no one will hurt you, no matter what you tell us."

She looked straight at me, defiant contempt in those tiny eyes. And hatred. Oh yes, there was hatred. It made me uneasy, for I did not know what I had done to deserve it.

"Tell us a bit about yourself. Who you are, your family, and what type of work you do for my family," said Tristan. He would have made a fine lawyer.

She was ready to tell us. At first her voice was soft and you had to strain to hear it, but as emotions overtook her, it grew louder and more strident, shrill even as she explained why she had betrayed the Chambaux family.

Madeline Cossart's story:

My father worked for the Chambaux family as the head footman. My grandmother was a Chambaux housemaid. And my great-grandfather was their carriage driver. It's in my blood to be with them.

When His Grace's first wife passed, I knew his mother was concerned. She was determined to find the best bride for him. She would not be as pretty as Lady Minette, but she needed to be of quality breeding to continue the line. I knew that was her wish, for she often told me so when I cleaned her rooms or helped her maid dress her.

When SHE was brought into this house, it was obvious what she wanted. Her plan was to have him, and she would use her tricks to get him.

When SHE left the house, I breathed a sigh of relief. Her Grace told Lady Valentina that she had commanded her son to stay away from the girl. The matter seemed finished. We had survived the storm.

But Luca returned from the Winter Revels and told us all of some sort of night mischief between the two of them. In and out of bedrooms in the middle of the night. Oh yes, she had her hooks in him.

I tried to warn Lady Valentina, but she told me it was her brother's business and we had to trust him to make the right decisions. Ha! A man being beguiled isn't thinking!

I considered talking to Her Grace about the problem, but there was a crisis at Chambaux which required her immediate attention and I didn't know when she would return.

One afternoon, Lady Baudelaire was here visiting Lady Valentina. She returned for her forgotten gloves and noticed my distress. She told me about HER. Imagine! Only the daughter of a tradesman who was murdered!

Her maid servant was no better! A girl from the docks, her father a sailor and her mother a washerwoman? The servant reflects the inner heart of the mistress. I've always know that to be true. Both low-class, and grasping at things they shouldn't have. Both should have stayed at their grand hotel, mucking about with the dead, instead of coming here to turn our lives all upside down.

A week later, on my day off, Lady Baudelaire found me by chance in the park. She asked after events in the house and I shared my concerns. She told me some men get it bad when they want a young woman who is no good. Pardon me, Your Grace but she told me that you being a widower for some years, you would be easy to bespell. A conniving woman with her eye on his grand estate would have him like clay in her hands.

She believed His Grace was about to disgrace his name if we didn't step in to prevent it. When she asked if I would help save the family name from such a defilement, I told her, of course I would! Wasn't my family loyal to the Chambaux line? I swore to her I would do anything she asked.

When Lady Baudelaire visited next, I shared that His Grace and sister had left for Hightower, and that SHE was there too. Lady Baudelaire promised me she would take care of it. But a few months later SHE was back in the house, in *his* bed. Injured, he said. It was all an act. To gain his pity and sympathy. Oh, yes, I saw what was going on.

Perhaps it was a presumption, but I sent a note to Lady Baude-laire about it. She never responded so I didn't know what to do.

One of the oldest noble families was becoming the joke of idle market place gossip. Servants from other houses, knew I took pride in who I served, so they mocked me, making His Grace and his lover a joke.

The Chambaux name was suffering because this barnacle who had latched on to him! My ancestors were crying out to me in my dreams, demanding I do something. Was I going to let our name be dragged through the gutter by someone like her?

Then I got a note from Lady Baudelaire. We met in a little tea shop on my day off. She was so sympathetic and understanding! She knew exactly how I felt, so she suggested that we would play a good joke on the little madame.

If I could get them access to the house, they'd remove her. Not harm her, but leave her passed-out drunk at Fontaine Park to be found in the morning. Her reputation would never survive it and she would be out of our lives altogether, forever.

Chapter Twenty

Madeline Cossart spouted this evil drivel in a low, unending stream. Several times Tristan made as if he was going to interrupt her, but he controlled himself. I could feel my face going hot or coldly pale, depending on which insulting accusation she threw at me.

Everything between Tristan and me had been twisted and misconstrued. I sat there in shock, trying to digest such needless hatred.

Lady Valentina said, in her clear, well-enunciated voice, "I'm afraid that you shall need to leave this house and the Chambaux employment, Madame Cossart. I do not condone your actions or your beliefs. To make such claims against Lady Elinor is disgusting and foul. She's a brave woman, even putting herself in danger to protect me and my brother."

Valentina stood up, proud as a queen. "Come with me, Elinor. We will let Tristan deal with this matter."

I got to my feet, my legs feeling weak. She tucked her hand in my elbow and we walked to the door; me trying my best to emulate Valentina's upright and graceful carriage despite my trembling legs.

In a serene voice, she asked me, "Will you want the wallpaper and the drapes changed in your rooms? I've always thought Tristan had too many paintings of horses in his. Surely you might want something more picturesque? Some landscapes, or would you like a still life with flowers or fruit?"

Up the stairs we went. Valentina brought me to Tristan's room. Luca, Tristan's valet, exited the attached dressed room, and stopped, surprised to see us.

"Bring up some coffee for us. Thank you."

After he left, I sat down on the bed, my hand reaching up to touch one of the supporting bed posts. Valentina went to a wardrobe and opened it. "I brought a second one in here for all your things. Anne-Marie helped me move them over from the Crown. She should be back soon on a second trip."

When I said nothing, she came to me and put her hand on my knee. "You cannot give any credence to servant's gossip. It is tittle-tattle best ignored."

"But you would not have wanted me to marry your brother."

"At one point I was against it, but now? Truthfully? I cannot imagine him marrying anyone else. I am sure he told you I did not like Minette. Tristan wants to believe it's because I was jealous of her being the mistress of Hartwood, but— well, I never thought she would support him. Fully support him. There was something about her that was false. She would smile to your face, and the next day you'd discover she had told a dozen different hurtful stories about you to everyone at the dinner party. But they were married, and Mother, who had pushed the match, would hear nothing against Minette."

Valentina ended with a sigh. There was a knock on the door and Luca entered with a tray.

"Come to the table, Elinor."

I rose reluctantly and sat opposite at a little round table she had cleared off so Tristan's valet could set down the coffee and cups.

Luca made as if to leave, but Valentina told him to wait. "It's my understanding, Luca, that there has been some malicious gossip in the servants' quarters about my brother's relationship with Lady Elinor."

The man gave a guilty start. "I'm sorry to hear that, milady."

"It seems Madeline Cossart conspired with Lady Baudelaire to remove my sister-in-law by force from this house last week. She was laboring under the misapprehension that something untoward had happened between His Grace and Elinor. Unfortunately, that means I have had to release Madame Cossart from her position here. Most likely, she will be facing criminal charges."

Luca's face underwent several interesting changes as he listened to Valentina and the last phrase left him very pale.

"I cannot abide having such disloyalty around me. Anyone displeased about Lady Elinor's presence here, or her maid's, will be moved to Chambaux where they can rusticate among the vines. I'm sure living out their serving years under the guidance of my mother would suit them far better, do you not agree?"

"Yes, milady."

"Thank you for the coffee. You are dismissed."

She poured me a cup.

"I'm usually a tea drinker," I said.

Valentina smiled and went to the other wardrobe. Open, it revealed all of Tristan's coats, shirts, and trousers. She pushed them aside and groped for something in the back of the closet.

"Aha!" She turned to show me a glass bottle with a short neck that held a deep amber liquid. "Coffee is much more palatable with a dash of this, along with plenty of cream."

By the time Tristan arrived we were both tipsy and the best of friends.

Hands on hips, he towered over us as we sat on the floor, our backs against the bed. "That's imported! Do you know how old that is?"

"I'm welcoming your new bride, brother dear," said Valentina, raising her cup as a salute to him and giving me a broad wink.

I giggled and raised my cup in reply. "And I'm welcoming my new sister-in-law." I ended it with a hiccup that caused Valentina and me to burst out laughing.

He frowned at us for a moment before giving in. "Fine, let me get a glass out of the bathroom and you can pour me some. It's been absolute hell downstairs these last few hours."

~

The next morning, Tristan found my hangover extremely funny. Still, he did get me an ice-pack for my throbbing head and a tomato-based drink that he called the hair of the dog.

I was in a morose mood. "How can I stay here knowing all the servants are against us being together?"

"One servant does not equal all," said Tristan calmly. He tossed his robe on the chair and started getting dressed. I took a moment to enjoy watching him. When he started tying his cravat in the mirror, I said, "Why do something that complicated? You could wear a knotted tie. They are becoming all the fashion."

"Because it takes concentration and care. And it strikes fear into those who can't do it." Done with his knot, he admired it briefly before turning from the mirror and giving me his full attention. "Cossart was a rotten apple that has been removed."

"It's just as I feared though — everyone hates us together."

"Is that what Valentina said yesterday?"

"No."

"You're unaccustomed to being disliked. When you have had a decade of people hating you for being born the Duke de Archambeau, you learn how to ignore it."

"Oh, Tristan!" The towel holding the ice pack slipped off my head as I moved forward, extending my hand. I grabbed it before it hit the floor.

He came to sit on the bed and took my hand. "All that matters is that we are together and living our lives the way we want them."

"What about your mother?"

"She had her say once before. Never again." He stood up and dragged me forward by my wrist. "Time to face the world. I've got to go with de Windt and meet His Majesty. And later I want to take my bride to shop for jewelry."

He knew what to say to catch my interest. "What will we be looking for?"

"A wedding ring, silly girl."

It didn't help to worry about what King Guénard would say, or so Tristan said as he kissed me goodbye to go meet him. While I waited, I decided to find some work to occupy myself, such as reviewing the ledgers belonging to my father we had found in his workshop.

Because of the woman-hating Noise Ghost in his office area, I settled at Tristan's desk in his personal library. Lost in my work, I was surprised to find Ruben bringing me tea. He stood at attention while I poured out. "Yes?"

"If I may say so, Lady Fontaine, many of us below stairs are thrilled that His Grace has found happiness."

"Thank you, Ruben. I imagine that Lady Valentina's threat to sack anyone who wasn't happy produced such an encouraging result."

"Not at all," he told me stoutly. "Those of us who experienced life under his first wife know how things were. Most of us know the difference." He looked awkward for a moment, shifting his feet. "Madeline had a fancy for His Grace, but we never thought she would do anything to harm you." He explained hastily when I rose my eyebrows in surprise. "Not in a lover's way. She felt an ownership of His Grace, in a possessive way, like a doting aunt or mother. Proud of his accomplishments."

"I see. Well, I appreciate you telling me." He gave a brief bow and left.

With tea flavored with lemon and a few delicious biscuits, I continued reading through the stack of ledgers. Going through them, I became lost once more in childhood memories of all the necklaces, bracelets, pendants, rings and brooches my father had designed.

"Oh, I remember this one! I wonder where it is now?" I exclaimed, seeing a sketch of a brooch with the stern profile of a lady. She must have been well-loved for someone to commission a portrait of that uncomely face. Later, I found a bracelet design that sparked a memory of my father showing it to me, dangling it so the light would spark green fire from emeralds, one of his favorite stones.

Unconsciously, my hand went up to touch the area over my heart, where his watch had marked me after Marcus returned it to me. I had had no time to discuss with Twyla her theory of my father being a guardian. The girl was still at the safe house, recovering well, but weak. After delivering my clothes, Anne-Marie had returned to nurse her under Charlotte's instructions.

When Tristan had told me about the gold light and hearing the bells, it made me wonder. Had my father somehow given him guidance that day I needed his help? Guardians were a mystery, as there was little evidence of their existence. When Twyla had first told me of the possibility I was sure she was wrong but now?

They were attached to stories of intuition. Such as not taking a carriage that is later in an accident, or feeling a need to check on a family member and thus being able to stop a disastrous elopement. Luck. The chance of escaping death merely by making a different choice. Family stories about omens and vague impressions of presences.

Crossroad moments, when your life depends on a chance decision.

Being arrested for murder surely was a crossroads moment.

Why hadn't I been warned about Madeline Cossart?

Because you do not listen.

Startled, I looked around the room, but of course there was no one. Not even a ghost. "Are you here?" When nothing replied, I sighed. I needed to continue that discussion with Dr. Devereaux about that block in my mind. Especially as it was done by Madame Granger.

Thumbing through Father's books, I jotted down some notes which, when I reviewed them, seemed to show a pattern. A month before his death, he had met with at least a dozen nobles, and twice as many clients from the merchant class. From his notations, I deduced the type of commissions and the cost of the items.

Merchants and tradespeople who could afford his work went for simple pieces such as rings with small stones, lockets that would house a portrait, earrings, and men's tie pins.

These were what he called his bread-and-butter pieces because they could be cast from a mold he had on hand and quickly turned around.

The custom pieces brought in more money, but you couldn't rely upon a noble paying you on time. In a few rare instances, some were never retrieved. Then, Father sold them at a loss or melted down the metal, re-using the stones in other designs.

While my father had been known as the king's jeweler, in reality, he had been one of several the king might choose for a commission. For example, he was one of three who had reviewed the dowry of the king's bride, who had died shortly after the marriage from a stillbirth. King Guénard had never married again, much to the ire of his courtiers.

I made a list of the people Father had seen during the last three months prior to his death. Some were repeating clients and old friends; these I lightly crossed out. If Tristan's theory was correct, it would be a new client or someone he had seen only a few times. According to Leona, it had been a woman who had confided to my father about Barbier's blackmail.

Because Father used a code to write down his commissions, it took me some time to finally cross reference the client lists. My eyes widened when I saw a name I knew: Lady Maryegold Talleyrand, necklace, emeralds and diamonds, to be repaired in whole.

Lady Talleyrand had never mentioned that she had known my father. Or that she had brought in a piece to be 'repaired in whole,' my father's phrase for making a replica.

Lady Talleyrand who, with Lady Valentina, was about to host a dinner where opposing factions would discuss how to save a kingdom.

CHAPTER TWENTY-ONE

Lady Maryegold Talleyrand appeared as serene as ever, even though I had just accused her of being in league with Marcellus Barbier and the murder of my father.

Tristan sat opposite her in his library. He was behind his desk, the ledgers close at hand, and I sat in a chair next to hers so I could watch her profile. After I had found the revelation of her connection to my father, I had immediately told Tristan upon his return. He had arranged this meeting the next day.

Her face in profile showed her white hair professionally styled to form a well-groomed coif of fixed waves, deeply set eyes with eyebrows still showing the dark blond of her original hair color, and a shapely nose with a slight bulge similar to His Majesty's.

Tristan rephrased what I had said, as she had not answered. "Do you deny that you were a client of Augustus Chalamet's right before his murder?"

A muscle jumped in her jaw and was the only betraying sign of tension in an otherwise serene countenance. "We always think we can evade our past. However, the older we get, the more our past misdeeds come home to haunt us."

"So you don't deny it?" said Tristan. "That you commissioned

Augustus Chalamet to make a replica of a necklace so you could use the original to pay off Marcellus Barbier's blackmail?"

"No." Her shoulders relaxed. It seemed having this incriminating piece of news in the open almost gave her relief. But her hands, resting in her lap were still restless.

"Explain how it all came about," I said.

She licked her lips before beginning.

"I was a young girl and made mistakes." She gave a grim laugh. "How many times have young girls made mistakes? Too many! But he was handsome, and I was foolish. It was my débutante year, and all appeared to be at my feet. You can't understand how it all went to my head. I thought myself invulnerable! Emotions when you are young are so much more powerful. You live in the moment—think only of the moment. The bright shining happiness to be the one selected for a dance by the man you admire, or the horrible devastation when your favorite dress gets a torn hem. It is a maelstrom of high drama."

I barely stopped myself from screaming at her that, no, I didn't understand. As a young girl I had been mourning my father. There were no balls with young men dancing attendance upon me. Instead, I had been sleeping in a house talking to the dead under the guidance of a woman whose son had cut my father's throat.

Distantly, I heard her continue speaking, but I felt as if I was in a dream, a nightmare, watching her from afar.

"Looking back, I wonder how many suitors paid me attention because of my kinship with a king who had no heir. Perhaps I am being cynical?" Truthfully, it was probably a mix of the two, for she was an elegant lady. When we gave her no supportive response, she continued.

"I was chaperoned, but any girl with determination and intelligence can fool their elders. We made a game of sneaking around under the eyes of society." She gave another grim laugh. "How naïve I was, thinking we were the only ones playing such games! I only learned much later that he paid for my maid to turn a blind eye and ignore our absences or those stories that didn't match with the facts of where I had been."

I wondered what Tristan was making of this story for Lady Talleyrand's story of duplicity could have been Minette's tale. Lady Talleyrand had fooled her parents; Minette had deceived her husband. All games. Casting him a sideways glance, I saw only a stony profile that expressed no emotion over Lady Talleyrand's youthful indiscretions.

"Oh, he was so handsome, and he had a honeyed tongue. Perhaps his words about my being so different from the other girls were true? I certainly believed them!"

"Who was he?" I finally asked.

"No one my family would countenance! A man with little money or position. A third son with mediocre bloodlines and no title. Their expectations were far higher!"

She looked down at her hands, memories turning down a dark path.

"The story is an old one. Naturally, I became pregnant. You cannot meet for an entire season and there not be consequences. Those who could have advised me on what precautions I should have taken did not know the risks I was running. I will give him credit, when I told my lover, he immediately visited my father and asked for my hand. But he was forbidden the house."

Perhaps I should have felt sympathy for a fellow woman in the position I was now in, but I couldn't. Something was cold in me and I watched her cynically. I would never be able to figure the part she played in my father's death.

"True panic set in when I received a threatening note demanding that I pay a certain sum or my condition would be revealed in the society gossip column. Who had revealed my secret? I do not think it was my lover. He was merely foolish and naively optimistic, like I was. My maid, who may have noticed that I no longer had my monthlies? My dressmaker when my waist measurements changed? Or was it simply someone who had observed our trysts and made a lucky guess? I never discovered who it was."

"It was an exorbitant sum and one that, I, as a young girl still under a guardianship, couldn't pay unless my parents helped. If you had known them, you would understand why that was not an option. They were selling my virginity on the open market, and the humiliation— they would not have been understanding. I was their only daughter, and it was expected that I would make a brilliant match, which would fill them with pride and increase their bank account."

Their's was a cruel world. It made me glad that I had signed away Tristan's wealth. My child would never be constrained in such a way.

"How did you receive the note?" Tristan asked.

"A street urchin ran up to me when I was out shopping and gave it to me."

"How were you to make arrangements to pay for it?"

"At a certain time and day, I was to leave the money wrapped in a parcel near the mermaid statue in Fountain Park."

I became impatient. "So to pay it, you brought your necklace to my father?"

"Yes. When I told a girlfriend I needed a large sum to pay off a gambling debt from playing cards, she suggested him. I thought I could use an emerald or diamond from it, pay him off, and later replace it after my marriage with no one knowing."

She gave me a weary smile. "I liked your father so much, Elinor. He was a gentle man and very kind to me, a scared and uncertain girl."

She did not need to tell me about the type of man my father was. I knew. What she needed to speak about was how she had gotten him killed. Tristan's eyes swiveled in my direction and returned to Lady Talleyrand. "What happened between you and Mysir Chalamet?"

"My parents were fine with him making a facsimile piece. Especially when traveling, one does not want to risk real gems getting stolen or lost. But when he was discussing the work, I made the mistake of saying I just wanted one emerald replaced instead of getting the entire piece done. It was stupid of me, but I wasn't thinking clearly. Of course, he knew immediately that I was in some sort of trouble. Your father was so sympathetic and I ended up crying and telling him all."

Father had been soft. Womanly tears would have moved him when money would not.

"How surprised I was when Mysir Chalamet told me I wasn't the first with a tale of woe. Clients had been begging him to change their jewelry so they could pay off debts. That year, he had had at least a dozen such requests and it struck him as unusual. It disturbed him. As in my case, he was always given a plausible story, but he didn't feel it was the real one. Frightened, I confessed to him about the blackmail."

"He had suspected something nefarious for some time, as he mentioned some in his profession were seeing an increase in stolen gems on the market."

That rang a bell. Father had changed his gem-seller that year and when I had asked why, he'd replied that some were not as honest as others.

"Mysir Chalamet said people highly placed would look into the matter for him. He promised he would not mention my name, but that this was too important to ignore. Before I could see him again, I read in the paper that he had been murdered."

I looked away from her, my eyes welling up. Yes, my father had probably thought he could help the vulnerable, but it had cost him at the end.

Her shoulders heaved with a sigh. "I had left my necklace with him. It was returned anonymously to me with one emerald missing, and a note that it was for payment. Since it had been with Mysir Chalamet, I knew the man was connected to the jeweler's death."

Even after all these years, Lady Talleyrand paled as she remembered it all.

"Did you keep paying?" asked Tristan.

She said abruptly, "No. I miscarried. There was no longer any proof of my dalliance. I had committed nothing in writing to my lover, only shared pages of poetry torn from books."

"Did you know who was blackmailing you?"

"Not until you exposed it." She shook her head. "It shocked me to the core, for I had never suspected it would be someone in the gendarmes. I think you saw my surprise the other day, Elinor, when Madame Cossart was questioned."

I nodded slowly. Lady Talleyrand had given us a plausible tale, so why was I so suspicious of it all? "Then you married and became a confidante of the king."

"Yes."

"And you were never contacted again by Marcellus Barbier?" asked Tristan.

"No! I wasn't. I told you."

Tristan stared at her, weighing what she had said. "You still wish for this diplomatic dinner to go ahead?"

"Of course! We must quell this civil unrest. Those Ghastly creatures may be gone, but that doesn't remove the threat of anarchy."

Tristan's face retreated behind its wall of politeness, making it hard to read even for me. "Then the party must take place, of course."

CHAPTER TWENTY-TWO

De Windt and Tristan worked together on the security for the party. Their raised voices echoed through Hartwood, more headache-inducing than the liquor Tristan hid in the back of his wardrobe.

Trying to find a quiet spot was difficult, as there were few in supply. Valentina and Lady Talleyrand were making lists about food, choosing plate ware, and debating on whether they should have someone to play music during the periods before and after dinner. Would the gentlemen retreat to Tristan's study? Or should they all adjourn to the music room for dessert and coffee? What would be the most relaxing option to encourage genteel conversation?

It was far too complicated. I would rather sit in a cemetery and commune with ghosts.

With Tristan's reluctant permission, I left the house to visit Charlotte and Twyla. Farrow accompanied me as guard and we took an unmarked carriage. It had been about ten days since the Ghastlies had dramatically collapsed. Driving through the city, things seemed calmer to me; as if Alenbonné had stopped holding its breath, waiting for another disaster.

Tristan had said that the speeches in the student quarter had calmed down, probably because Theodoor Vischeer's friends were preparing for Valentina's dinner. The university district no longer had roadblocks, and it was expected that classes would resume the following week.

The gendarmes only kept roadblocks and checkpoints around government offices, and any nobles who requested protection. Lord Bridoux's murder was still a hot topic in the newspapers, but public concern had shifted to reporting on his wife. She had survived, but her health hovered on a knife's edge.

The reporter's wording of the assassination was also subtly changed, implying that it seemed to have resulted from a personal, not government, matter. Probably because de Windt had notified the papers that any more stories implying nobles were a target would be met with penalties and arrests.

Or perhaps it was simply the weather. A brisk wind from the sea had blown away the smoky smells from the cremation of the Ghastlies. The dense fog lifted, and we could see blue sky and the sun now. This was when summer would show its best before the weather began to change.

As soon as I entered the safe house, Twyla rushed to embrace me. "I can't leave the house. Isn't that ridiculous? Would you tell Dr. LaRue I'm recovered? I'm completely healthy. Oh! Where did this ring come from? Is it from the duke? How much did he pay for it? Was it one of your father's pieces?"

I was actually glad to hear this onslaught as it reassured me she was indeed recovering from her misadventure, despite her pallor that made the freckles sprinkled over her cheeks stand out even more.

"Why don't we sit down and I'll tell you all about it?"

Charlotte appeared at the top of the stairs and, seeing me, started down. She was in her usual trousers and men's shirt with a vest, but wasn't wearing a coat. "Is my patient telling you she is ready to be unleashed upon an unsuspecting world?"

I waited for her in the foyer and asked when she gained the bottom step, "Has she even thanked you yet?"

"Of course not!"

Anne-Marie was running an errand, but she had left stores in the kitchen. We assembled a tray of biscuits and slices of a cake she had baked. While I sorted some plates, cups and saucers, with forks, Twyla demanded again, "The ring! Tell us about the ring!"

Charlotte turned from the stove where she had placed the kettle, and I held up my hand to show the one Tristan and I chosen yesterday.

"Very nice," Charlotte said sedately. "Glad you picked a sturdy setting, given your adventures."

"How did he ask you to marry him? Did he shake you? Did you cry?"

"There was no shaking," I told her.

"But what did he look like? Where were you? Did you know he was going to ask you? Did you scream? Or did you swoon into his arms?"

"Twyla, I think you have an odd idea of how adults behave."

"Not at all! I've made a study of His Grace. He gets physical when he is emotional."

I took the food tray while Charlotte brought another one with the teapot and cups to the parlor. When we all found a seat, I poured out, as Twyla kept up her monologue. "Did you know he was going to ask you? Anne-Marie and I thought he would, but she said you'd refuse him. I thought you might be stubborn, but give in at the end."

To Charlotte, I said, "It seems I continue to be the subject of idle servant gossip."

She only smirked over her teacup. Twyla was not to be contained. "You two are an example of the modern way of doing things. Marrying for love and not position or money. The aristocracy cannot continue inbreeding with their small numbers, and the merchant and trades class is where the money is being amassed. Your marriage makes for sound economic principals."

"Even better! Now I'm a model on how wealth should be distributed. I didn't know you had such an eye on socio-politics."

"It's all just common sense, really." Somehow, despite all her talking, Twyla had worked herself through one piece of cake and was halfway through a second. "But you still didn't tell us how he asked you! Was the sun setting behind you? Did he get on bended knee? Give you flowers? What was the kiss like? I'm sure there was kissing."

"Well, I shall tell you if you give me a moment."

She made an exaggerated motion of sealing her lips, which didn't quite work as she immediately opened them again to take in a forkful of cake.

"Much like yourself, Twyla, I was kidnapped from Hartwood House." I began to tell her of Madeline Cossart's decision that I wasn't good enough to marry into the Chambaux family and how she had helped with me being snatched away. How I had awoken next to the dead body of Josephine Baudelaire. That left Twyla speechless, so I could easily continue my tale, skipping who exactly had kidnapped me and why. I would address that later.

"The Crown prosecutor, Mysir de Windt—" Twyla interrupted me with a *boo*. "They were about to arrest me when Tristan appeared with Farrow." I told them how Farrow had dismounted a cavalry officer, given Tristan the horse, and how my dear friend Jacques stopped us from being shot to death.

Twyla's eyes widened, and she even forgot her food, hanging on my every word as I described being married over the anvil, insisting upon a morganatic marriage so I would not inherit Tristan's ancestral wealth. This was the only time Charlotte interrupted my narrative.

"Hurrah! That will silence the critics. Well done, Elinor!"

"But you gave up everything! What's the point of marriage without sharing in his belongings?"

I didn't bother answering such a complex question. She would figure it out one day when she fell in love. "We fled the city using a wagon filled with horse manure!"

Charlotte laughed, but Twyla was not pleased. "That isn't romantic!"

"The romantic part was the rescue. And being on the narrowboat."

"What boat?!"

By the time I had finished and answered every one of her questions, Twyla was exhausted. Seeing her sagging and clutching a cushion, I told her gently, "I do think it's time for you to get some rest. We shall talk more later."

She only protested mildly before agreeing. We took her upstairs, got her settled, and returned downstairs. Adjourning to the kitchen, I started making some soapy water for washing the dishes. It was easier to talk about difficult subjects when my hands were busy. Halfway through the washing up, I finally asked what had been preying on my mind.

"Did you know, Charlotte? What Marcellus was doing?"

Charlotte neither showed surprise nor grief at my question. Of course, she had heard at Hartwood that Barbier was the master criminal behind the Ghastlies, and my and Twyla's abductions.

"I didn't know, nor was I part of it. Looking back, there were signs I ignored." As she talked, her circling wipes with the towel on the rinsed dishes I had handed her slowed. "It's not unusual for a guardia to be on the take or to work in a morally gray area. You deal with criminals and violence all day, week in and out. Sometimes you have to grease wheels where you'd rather have taken the wheels off. If you had asked me last year, I would have said that was all it was."

"But you think something changed?"

"With hindsight, what I ignored or thought was something else comes into focus."

I was done with soaping, so dipped my hands into the rinse bucket and dried them. "What incidents?"

Charlotte shrugged. "He became harder. He seemed less concerned with victims. A few comments he made in the morgue struck me as rather brutal. It's easy to grow cynical in this work, as dead bodies can all start to look the same. Why, I've seen that callousness with my own students during postmortems who make tasteless jokes, mocking the deceased. They are trying to separate themselves from the fear of their own mortality."

"You sound like a mind-doctor!"

She laughed. "Far from that. No, I'll leave that to Devereaux to sort out. But back to Barbier. I saw a few arguments between him and his commander that showed he was not above bending things to suit him. And I knew he had nothing but contempt for the nobility, even the king. It felt personal, but I never asked him to explain his dislike. Don't we all have a story about some uppity noble ruining our day? That's all I thought it was. I was as shocked as you were to find out what he had been doing."

We were both done with dishes and, having put them away, returned to the comfort of the parlor.

"There is so much I need to tell you." I related what had happened to Sergeant Dupont. How his soul had been separated from its body, and his corporeal self had been used like a puppet by Barbier. This time her face did express shock.

"How terrible for our poor sergeant! Although, from a scientific point of view, I admit to feeling a horrible fascination on wanting to know how that was done."

"My guess is possession. It's the only thing that makes sense. Some ghost with a foul disposition possessed him when his soul was removed."

"Possession? Like what happened to Archambeau at the café?"

"Yes. But Tristan was possessed by a ghost that had a strong attachment to the early plane because of his desire to communicate with his lost love. Once that was resolved, he transitioned to the

Afterlife. Usually, the living person dominates the ghost; human desires and needs will always rule over the dead. But I think Dupont was an experiment by Parnell."

"Why do you think that?"

"I remember overhearing him telling Dupont he was surprised to see that he was still around. What Parnell wanted was ghosts to manifest as flesh on the earthly plane, and for the living to dwell in the Beyond in a physical form."

"Doesn't Twyla already do that?"

"Yes, but she's an anomaly. And when we were being chased by Vonn in the Beyond, she tired and needed to return to the earthly plane rather quickly."

"So Dupont was a failed experiment? A test run?"

I nodded. "Our sergeant was getting too close to Barbier's schemes. When I found Dupont in the Beyond, he was looking for his lost sister, a woman who worked for Forrest Boutin, a man smuggling for Barbier. Boutin was later killed to prevent him from talking. Would Parnell and Barbier leave the sergeant to speak of his suspicions? I think Parnell cut Dupont's soul loose from his body using that drug, and later filled his body with another spirit. A nasty one."

Hannah Wahl, brutalized by a man before being murdered by Vonn. Parnell at the bottom of the stairs, supposedly from a jump to his death. Eyes watching me from the room above my father's workshop, and later Dupont appearing to attack me.

Charlotte shook her head in dismay. "I swear to you, Elinor, I knew nothing about this."

"I believe you." I didn't add that if she had, Barbier would probably have had her killed. Her ignorance was part of what had kept her safe. In the silence that followed, you could hear the traffic of horses and carriages outside, the shout of a newsboy. Yes, Alenbonné was returning to itself.

"I remember when Barbier first brought you into my morgue. He always struck me as a hard-headed man, feet firmly on the ground, but here he was bringing this slip of a girl to me to see my corpses! I thought he had gone mad."

Smiling, I set aside my grief over his betrayal for the present. "Oh, how you barked at him to get me out and leave your morgue."

"Barking is what I do best. It weeds out those students who think they can be doctors, but don't have the stomach for it. But you, you were something else. Souls and spirits didn't concern me at all; it was the flesh that mattered, and you challenged my every belief."

"Do you still think that?"

She laughed. "If I put thought into saving souls, I wouldn't get any work done. It would be far too distracting. We both work with the dead, just with different approaches."

"We make a good team." I felt a sharp twinge thinking of Barbier, who once had been a part of it.

"You were still wet behind the ears when you showed up, carrying your case and determined to help solve crimes. It only took a year before you stopped gagging at the corpses. Another five to get really good at crime detection. Most gendarmes I deal with have a worse track record."

"Charlotte!" I cried out in mock offense.

She reached out and took my hand, the one with the ring, in hers. "I truly wish you and Archambeau every happiness in the world."

My eyes misted, and my hand came to rest on my stomach. "I have one last thing to tell you."

"What?!" cried Twyla.

We swiveled in surprise to find her sitting on the stairs; her face pressed against the balustrades, watching us. At our astonished faces, she defended herself.

"With all this excitement, you didn't think I was going meekly to bed, did you?"

Charlotte and I exchanged looks before we burst out laughing.

Chapter Twenty-Three

The next day the Morpheus Society invaded Hartwood, requesting my help. Their revered leader, Leona Granger, was dead. One of their star members, Parnell Lafayette, was not only dead but disgraced. De Windt's men were serving royal search warrants to all the senior members, some of whom had retreated to the countryside during the chaos.

The Society had relied upon forceful personalities instead of true skills to lead them, and now they were a bunch of lost sheep. I was not interested in being their shepherd.

Valentina was going over her household accounts while I was reading a book. We were both in the drawing room when Ruben entered and presented me with a silver tray upon which a cream card sat. Ignoring it, I told him, "Just put it with the others."

Valentina held up a hand to stop him. "Their cards are piling up, Elinor. Perhaps you should see at least one of them."

"The Morpheus Society betrayed me," I told her, closing my book to return her stare.

"Not the Society. People within its organization did. Perhaps others might be feeling as hurt as you are?"

I wanted to throw my book at her. *Hurt? Hurt like I am?* The woman I'd viewed as a second mother had taken me in so her son wouldn't be arrested for my father's murder. No one else was as betrayed as I was!

"When your nostrils flare like an angry horse, you oddly remind me of my brother."

"I am nothing like him!" I stated. Grabbing the card off the salver, I looked at the name *Madame Claire Vogel*. "I don't know her."

To Ruben, Valentina said, "Show her in." To me, she asked, "Do you want me to stay or go?"

"It matters not a whit to me," I assured her.

She arched her eyebrows, and then rose from her chair at the desk, to come sit in one of the armchairs arranged for conversation.

Claire Vogel entered the room hesitantly, stopped, and then rushed over to us. She addressed Valentina first with "Madame Chalamet," only for Tristan's sister to indicate that I was the person she needed to address.

"Madame Chalamet," she repeated, only for me to correct her. "You may not have seen my marriage announcement, but I am now Lady Fontaine."

This only flustered her more. She looked between the two of us, and Valentina took pity on her. "I am Lady Valentina Fontaine, brother to Tristan Fontaine. This is his wife, Elinor Fontaine, formerly known as Madame Chalamet. Please, have a seat."

She gave a gulp of understanding, bobbing her head and dipping her body in some hybrid of a bow and curtsy. Examining her with detachment, I could see she was in a nervous frenzy. From the material and style of her dress, and the plain band on her hand, she was probably from the tradesman class. Yes, that profusion of exotic feathers on her hat, which she probably could not afford to buy, pointed towards a husband who was involved in the import trade.

Considering her middle years, most likely she had joined the Society because of the close death of a loved one. *Oh.* The other hand bore a ring in a particular style: a centered, semi-precious stone, framed by two small diamonds. A ring often chosen by women to honor a child. Married with at least one child, deceased. I thought other offspring were unlikely. Her scuffed shoes, and a thread coming unraveled on her glove, showed a lack of attention by household staff. Doubtful there was anyone at home to supervise children in the middle of a weekday.

"I am with the Morpheus Society." The lily pin on her dress and her card ad told me that. When I remained silent at this pronouncement, she took a deep breath and pressed forward. "We need your help."

Perhaps a year ago I would have jumped at the chance, but I had been battered, bruised, and betrayed. Where had been the Society when Parnell was conducting his twisted ghost parties? When Leona conspired with a criminal? When I needed help as an accused criminal? Hiding under their beds. All of them.

"We are besieged, Lady Fontaine. Besieged!"

When I still did not respond, Valentina looked at me and then our guest. "How so, Madame Vogel?"

"Our members have had their houses and offices ransacked. Some have even been arrested!"

"Do you need a lawyer? I highly recommend the Van Heerdens." I picked up my book, placing it meaningfully in my lap.

Her nervousness grew. "We thought with your connections —?" Her hands flapped helplessly in the air. "You might gain the king's ear. Put a stop to this persecution."

"A persecution implies that it is unwarranted. From where I sit, the Society is culpable for several crimes. After all, some of our members actually helped Parnell Lafayette with his parties, which helped him to develop that soul-altering drug."

Perhaps there was some steel in her somewhere. "Not all of us. Mysir Lafayette paid the ultimate price for his crimes, and we have cooperated with the gendarmes on that investigation."

"Let me guess? The guardia investigating Parnell was Inspector Marcellus Barbier?"

"How did you know? He promised us that the evidence would show that the organization did not condone the actions of Mysir Lafayette. Indeed, only a handful of us were aware of these morbid parties, and we immediately gave him a list of the chemists who concocted that terrible potion. That's all the inspector required. Now we have to deal with this de Windt fellow!"

That answered the question of how Barbier had gotten a hold of the drug after Parnell's death. Something cold inside me pulled me away from being involved in this imbroglio. "My advice is to comply with whatever Sven de Windt wants. He's the Crown prosecutor, and he can make things very unpleasant for you if you do not."

Madame Vogel tried another tactic. "Madame Granger was your mentor and with her loss, we are sadly at sea. We thought she could rally us, but with her gone—"

"Trust me, the Society is better off without her guidance," I said sharply.

"A sensitive topic," warned Valentina in a low voice.

Stopped at every turn, Madame Vogel sagged from the top of her head to her toes. The wrinkles on her face deepened and her shoulders slumped, and her hands fell to her side to hang like dead fish.

"I very much doubt Elinor could have stopped the searches or the arrests. The Crown controls that. Perhaps it would be best to simply wait out the storm?" suggested Valentina, who was being suspiciously pleasant to a woman she wouldn't normally greet on the street. "Cannot some senior member serve? Perhaps yourself?"

"They are all quarreling! They fear that if they stand forward, it will make them a target. We lack leadership."

"Cowards," I said, my fingers starting to drum on the cover of my book.

"I, and a few others, have put together this appeal to you." She handed me a tube of rolled up papers tied with a ribbon that she had brought in with her. When I did not reach out to take it, she set it softly on the little table near her chair. "Perhaps you will read it when you have time?"

"Perhaps." I stood up, forcing her to do the same. "Good day, Madame Vogel. And good luck."

Chapter Twenty-Four

I was still extremely nervous about the dinner party. "The guns that Barbier brought into the city. Surely he means to do something with them?"

We were in our room, putting the last finishing touches to our attire. Anne-Marie had helped me dress and put up my hair, and Luca had made sure that everything Tristan wore was starched and creased to perfection.

Tristan said, "Those wooden crates we saw there looked new, and I was proved right. De Windt found at least one stockpile at the Hollow Works. It's only a guess, but I think Barbier planned on using the Ghastlies as his army."

"But you think the Ghastlies are finished?"

He came and gave me a kiss on my forehead, each hand on one of my shoulders. "You have been too close to this. Consider this. The Ghastlies collapsed about the same time Leona Granger died."

I gasped, horrified, earning myself a look of pity. "Yes, my dear, I think Madame Granger was working them like puppets to help her son succeed. Only her natural death foiled the plan. You'd be surprised to know that often happens in war. A message gets lost, which turns the battle. Or rain makes the field so sloppy with mud, that artillery can't be moved. Fate can hinge on tiny things."

"That she would do such a thing? I can't believe it!" But yes, she would, and probably had. She'd raised me, taken me as an apprentice, hiding her true motives all the time. Leona and Barbier had in common their art of duplicity and a desire for secrecy.

"We need to find him. Before he hatches some other plan," I said, nibbling on a nail.

"Agreed. But let's see through this dinner first."

"Aren't you worried that he might show up at this party?"

"Concerned? Yes. But I have my men and de Windt has his all in place. If Barbier is foolhardy enough to risk coming here, he will be caught, so I don't expect him. He's a careful man."

His words did not quite reassure me. Perhaps I was merely worried about meeting people in a social setting and having to be pleasant. If it wasn't so important, I'd beg off with a headache, stay in my room reading a book and eating biscuits.

"I have something for you."

His words brought me out of my distraction. He was holding a velvet jewelry case. Opening it, it revealed a beautiful diamond necklace made in the latest style.

"I was hesitant to buy you something without your approval. I hope you like it."

My finger reached out to touch it. The necklace was made from platinum in an openwork bib style, showcasing delicate diamonds. The geometric pattern of lacework combined old-styled cut leaves and round stones.

When I said nothing, Tristan added, "It's platinum. Would you have preferred gold?"

"My father never worked with it." I picked it up, feeling how light and delicate the work was. A master had made it. "It's beautiful."

"May I put it on?"

I nodded, overcome. His hands touched the nape of my neck,

and I shivered as the cool metal slid down over my throat and collarbones.

"You do like it?"

Hugging him, I reached up and kissed him. "I like it very much."

Downstairs, we found Valentina with Lady Maryegold Talleyrand. The two ladies were checking the table settings and making sure the flowers in the silver vases were perfectly arranged. Seeing Lady Talleyrand increased my uneasiness. I didn't trust her and never would, for she would always be connected in my mind with my father's murder.

Tristan felt my mood as we walked into the drawing room where a woman was tuning her harp. "Relax, Elinor. You are wound tighter than a clock." At my frown, he added, "I do have some news that I think will please you."

"What? You know where he is?"

He shook his head. "Not that type of good news. No. I received a letter from my mother about our marriage, which she discovered in the newspapers before mine could reach her."

"Oh." What could be good about that?

"She has had a nasty fall from a ladder. If I know her, she was probably inspecting someone's work so she could better criticize it. She's been told by her doctor not to travel, so we shall be spared her presence."

"I'm sorry about your mother, but was it awful?" Even the relief of knowing I wouldn't have to face down his mother right away, was not enough to remove the tension I felt.

"I'm used to her tongue-lashings. After I glance through her letters for any actual news, I consign them to the fireplace."

I heard Ruben in the foyer opening the door and greeting guests. One of the first was Jacques Moreau in his military dress.

For a moment it gave me déjà vu, remembering the first time I had attended a dinner party at Hartwood.

Tristan bent forward so he could tell me privately, "I thought you might like to see him after our adventure, and de Windt wanted someone on the inside he could trust." I wondered once more if Tristan knew that Jacques had had an affair with his wife. He hadn't mentioned any such connection, and I wasn't about to inquire. I thought not since he seemed sincere in his invitation.

With Jacques was Lady Tulip Langenberg. She was dressed in a pale pink silk that shimmered as she moved. In place of jewelry, she wore a choker with one fresh flower, and more matching flowers were woven into her hair instead of a tiara. She looked very fresh and young.

Her accompanying Jacques surprised me, as I had thought she would come with Mysir Theodoor Vischeer. But no, Vischeer arrived with his friend from the park, Olivier Maillard, who had given such a rousing speech that the gendarmes felt it best we should all run away. Both men were wearing their best coat and tails. The only difference was that Vischeer had a white cummerbund, and Maillard a gray.

Someone must have helped Olivier tone down his eccentric style for him to be wearing something so de rigueur for the occasion. His brown hair was brushed into place, and his mustache trimmed and freshly waxed. He was far better dressed than that horrid plaid outfit he had worn in the park when preaching revolt to the masses.

Vischeer intrigued me. I had already noticed that he wore plain clothes with little ornamentation. The suit he wore tonight was most likely the same as the one he had used during the dinners at the Winter Revels. He had a fresh flower in his buttonhole, and his cufflinks were silver and ónyx. He wore no rings. His eyes were examining everything in the room with intelligent interest; whereas Olivier focused on the people.

"Lady Fontaine, I hear you caught one of my speeches," he

said to me after our formal introductions. Olivier had a magnetic smile, which revealed a dimple in his cheek. I wouldn't have called him a handsome man, but he had something more valuable: charm.

"It was quite entertaining. I wish I could have heard it all."

"The establishment never cares for truth," was his reply. Turning to my partner, he congratulated Tristan on his marriage. "Stealing away one of our best, I do believe. Your union will inspire an equality in our society, I hope. First, we change the home, then our government."

It hadn't been my plan for our marriage to be a model for anything, but a duke marrying a commoner would make chins wag whether I wanted it to or not.

"Is it comfortable being lauded as a pioneer to change the world?" asked Vischeer, cynically. Yes, Olivier may have the charm and carry the day with his words, but Vischeer was the intellectual who found the world a place to laugh at.

"A marriage change the world? I doubt mine will do that."

"The populace is far more influenced by romance. What is more romantic than a noble of le beau idéal stooping to lift a commoner from the mud?"

Tristan mused, "I didn't realize you were in the mud, my dear, when we met."

"Neither did I. As I remember, we met over a rotting corpse in the city morgue."

"That's a tale I'd like to hear!" said Olivier.

Tristan made it into a funny story about the dramatic fakery of Madame Nyght, but of course he removed the fact the body had been related to the king, for that would have put a damper on the mood.

Valentina and Lady Talleyrand were in the hall talking with guests who were arriving. The newcomers were three older men, two with their wives, and the third with his daughter. Government representatives were carefully selected as the most influential and possibly open-minded enough to increase the seats in the House of Commons.

As all assembled in the drawing room, Tristan released my arm. A married couple hanging onto each other was considered bad form. We were expected to mingle and pretend we didn't want to be together.

Eventually, what I had been trying to avoid happened, and I was left alone with Jacques. We were both drinking white wine, standing in a corner, withdrawn only slightly from the group of men who were already discussing politics. Lady Talleyrand was in the thick of it.

"I saw the announcement in the paper. I guess congratulations are in order."

"Thank you for the wedding gift of stopping us from being shot."

He produced his first honest smile of the evening. "It's Giles' fault he couldn't ride and thus lost his mount. His horse shouldn't suffer a bullet because of his poor horsemanship."

The air between us grew more comfortable as we tentatively eased back into the brother-sister teasing that we had long enjoyed.

"Shall you be happy, Elinor?"

I gave him a serious answer. "I think so. We understand each other. Tristan respects me for what I am and bears with what I am."

His gaze moved around the room and settled on Tristan talking to Olivier and one of the government nobles. "If you care for him, I must have done him a disservice. Your eyes see people clearly."

"That's all in the past," I told him firmly. It was clear that Minette had milked secrets from him and had used him like she had many others. But what could be helped by discussing that foolishness? Nothing.

I changed subjects. "Has de Windt revealed to you who is at the root of this chaos in the city?"

"Yes," he said shortly. "I couldn't believe it! How hurt you must feel by this betrayal! There's someone I'd like to shoot! At least now I can stop being jealous of him."

"Jealous?" I exclaimed.

"Because I thought you cared more for him, than you did for me. It hurt at the time seeing the two of you with your heads together, solving crimes, making me feel like a third wheel."

Tucking my hand inside the crook of his elbow, I gently bumped his upper arm, chastising him. "There's only one surrogate brother." I gave a lopsided smile, for I couldn't pretend that I found the situation of Barbier's betrayal amusing. Maybe a decade from now, or perhaps two, I would be able to laugh over my stupidity in trusting him.

"But you've given me someone else to feel envious about." Jacques stared at my husband across the room, now chatting with the wives of the two lords.

Not sure what to say, I mumbled, "I'm sorry."

"It's the second time he's possessed someone I love."

I tried a jest. "Come now, Jacques. You never loved me in that way. We were like siblings."

His eyes burned into mine. "I could have loved you in another way if given the chance."

I did not want to have this conversation. What response could I give? I had never viewed Jacques as a possible romantic partner.

"Elinor—"

Thankfully for me, before he could complete his thought, Ruben arrived in some haste to the doorway to announce an unexpected guest: His Majesty, King Trygve Guénard.

CHAPTER TWENTY-FIVE

Like a toddler, King Guénard had found a way to cause the most inconvenience. His arrival prevented the purpose of the party. Discussing anything in a casual manner was off the table.

He was looking more like an egg than ever. An egg that surveyed the room with a smug expression as we gave our bows and curtsies. Emotion swept through the guests, most of it being dismay. The corners of Tristan's mouth conveyed deep irritation. The reactions of Theodoor Vischeer and Olivier Maillard were probably the most complex: surprise, perhaps even some awe, and with Vischeer, sardonic humor.

Lady Talleyrand couldn't hide her expression upon this unexpected arrival, but she quickly recovered. She came forward and started touring with him through the group, introducing him to everyone, one-on-one.

With the king's presence, the energy in the room shifted. What had been congenial and casual was now becoming formal and tense. What we could discuss behind the king's back was not the same as what could be said in his presence.

At some point, Valentina excused herself. I imagined she was busy rearranging the seating, for when dinner was announced, it placed King Guénard at the head of the table, the seat of honors, while she took the opposite end as hostess of the house.

Lady Talleyrand sat at the king's left while the rest of us were sprinkled down, alternating the sexes. I was seated midway down next to Jacques, for it was another rule that husbands and wives could not be seated together; being seated by a stranger would encourage conversation.

Tristan was on the king's right, opposite Lady Talleyrand. Olivier Maillard was paired with Lady Tulip, and Theodoor Vischeer with one of the older ladies, a wife of one of the government nobles.

The trouble started with the first course. As the soup was brought out and the footmen filled our glasses with sherry, the guests started tentative conversations with their neighbors. There was an uneasy atmosphere and the three government men glanced often at where the king sat.

From what I overheard, most were discussing ordinary things: the latest offering at the theater, a music performance by a promising newcomer, or whether the fashion for mutton chops on men was returning. Everyone was studiously avoiding discussing the recent troubles. Except for the king.

"Have you taken care of those creatures, Tristan?"

Light conversation stuttered to a stop, and all eyes swiveled to Tristan. He took it in stride, showing no aggravation or ill-temper. "I am cautiously optimistic, though we may have a few more to deal with."

"Good. Good."

Sherry was drained, and the soup bowls cleared. Now a few began to share recent experiences with the Ghastlies. None mentioned the disgusting part of them collapsing into heaps of bone and flesh, for that would have spoiled the meal. Two of the government wives had servants who had been Ghastlies. That couldn't be a coincidence. I wondered if Tristan noted that tidbit, but his face was stoic and unrevealing. It almost made me want to throw a dinner roll at his head.

For the fish course, Lady Valentina had selected roasted trout wrapped in bacon. It made me think of Tristan's lawyers, the Van Heerdens, and their father who fell in creeks and rivers trying to catch them.

"What makes you smile?" asked Jacques.

"Thoughts about fish," I replied, not wanting to explain about the Van Heerdens. "This is delicious."

The woman on the other side of Jacques was a lord's daughter. Her brother had recently joined a regiment, so she asked him several questions about his training. On my other side was Theodoor Vischeer. We compared the meal to the one we had shared at Lindengaard during the Winter Revels.

The next course was a flaky open-topped pastry, the vol-auvent. It was stuffed with chicken in a cream sauce. I had to admit that Madame Darly, the Hartwood chef, was certainly providing us with a superb meal.

"Lord Tassin, do you think Parliament will open next Tuesday?" Lady Tulip asked the man sitting across from her. Before he could answer, Guénard interjected loudly, "Of course we shall do so."

"Is that wise, with things still in disarray?" Lady Tulip's concern was answered with another breezy declaration by the king. "The Duke de Archambeau says the problem has been taken care of, so we shall proceed with confidence. The government must open. There are tariff matters to be approved, and ships to be financed."

The man whom Lady Tulip had tried to ask patted his mustache clean before responding. "It would require a quorum, Your Majesty. I am not sure there are enough nobles in Alenbonné to meet that number. We may need another week so others can return from their estates."

Beside me Vischeer leaned forward so everyone down the table could see him. "The House of Commons could make a quorum if you give the Alliance the additional seats we've been asking for."

There it was. Out in the open. Right at the start of the meat course. Despite market prices and shortages, Valentina was serving a roast joint with carrots and peas for the relevé. Glasses were changed out as we were poured a red wine, another selected from Chambaux.

Lady Talleyrand waded in, calming those who were grumbling strenuously against awarding the seats and gently encouraging those who appeared neutral or open to the idea. "Hasn't the number been increased before?"

"Over sixty years ago. After the Battle of 08, seats were added when our boundaries expanded," said Tristan.

"Not an act to be undertaken lightly," stated Lord Tassin. One wife nodded, but the two other gentlemen said nothing.

Vischeer made another move in his chess game. "The seats in the House of Lords were determined by property owned by a ranking noble. Alenbonné has doubled in population after sixty years. As the seat of His Majesty, and his primary residence, it should have more representation."

As if on cue, Lady Tulip said innocently, "Are you saying that the lords outnumber those who live here?" *Well played, Lady Tulip.* It dawned on me why she had come separately from Vischeer; she couldn't appear to be aiding him to reach his goal.

"Alenbonné always supports His Majesty's interest. Because our interests are the same: the best trade deals for Sarnesse," said Vischeer. "That can't always be said of a lord sitting safely in the countryside, surrounded by sheep."

King Guénard had been closely following this exchange. He was not stupid, only selfish. "How does increasing the seats in the House of Commons benefit me?"

Maillard put on his most charming smile. "Merchants stayed while lords abandoned the city upon the first sign of trouble."

"Here now!" said Lord Tassin, offended.

Maillard ignored the outrage, raising his voice over the din, "Only consider, Your Majesty, the vote on the city taxes. Country property tax is less than half of what is collected from Alenbonné, although the houses of the nobility and their land are far larger. Why? Because the nobility does not wish to pay their fair share."

That's put the cat among the pigeons!

Jacques leaned closer to me. "Are you not enjoying yourself? You've hardly tasted anything."

Perhaps it was the tension at the table, a week of murder and accusations, or simply the baby was making itself known, but for the first time I found my stomach to be queasy. "The food tonight is very rich."

"Rich? I've never known that to slow you down." Jacques became persistent in wanting to know what was wrong, while the conversation around us grew more fraught with arguments. So many were talking it was beginning to give me a headache.

"I tell you I'm fine."

"You can't hide from me, Elinor. There's something you aren't telling me."

Petulant, the king shouted. "I will give seats in parliament if I want to!"

The party became quiet after his majesty's outburst, causing my response to Jacques to be heard by all. "Since you insist on knowing, I'm pregnant."

I stared at Tristan but he only smiled, quirking an eyebrow. No help there. As everyone stared at my blushing face, the game course arrived: wild duck with game chips, potatoes so thinly sliced you could see through them. Diplomatically, Valentina raised her glass and said, "May I propose a toast to my brother and his new bride?"

My face flushed as red as the wine as glasses were raised. Women didn't talk about stomachs or their womanly parts in public. I wanted to sink under the table.

Tristan took it all in stride, probably because he had proved his manhood by getting me enceinte so quickly. He raised his glass to the guests and then to me, straight-faced. "To my beautiful bride."

At least I had provided a distraction from the heated discussion. Everyone was back to being pleasant to each other by the time the entremêts arrived: the sardines and cheese, an aspic jelly, and finally the savarin, a ring-shaped cake with flavored syrup, whipped cream, and peaches.

I picked at my food while Jacques apologized very, very quietly.

"You're always pushing at me. Can you please stop?"

"Is that why you married him? The baby?"

Can a woman not enjoy her damn dessert in peace?

"No. I married him because I love him. Does that satisfy you?"

Abandoning Jacques, I asked the opinion of the lord sitting across the table, about the additional seats as he had remained quiet during the fracas.

"I am not against the idea. However, the number needs to be carefully decided and I fear that His Majesty, facing opposition from Lord Tassin, has just dramatically veered in the other direction. Thus he will provide too many. He's always been easy to manipulate."

"So you think King Guénard was maneuvered?"

"Outgunned and boxed in," was his response, as he set his fork down on his empty plate. "Knowing him, he will draft something by tomorrow and be in a hurry to sign it before Tuesday."

Vischeer who had been speaking with Lady Tulip looked as pleased as punch. Maillard was euphoric, either from the king's concession or from all the wine he had drunk during the eleven courses.

"I've never had a more excellent meal, Lady Fontaine," announced King Guénard, as the dessert plates were cleared away.

From down the table, Tristan raised a sardonic eyebrow.

Chapter Twenty-Six

Barbier had vanished so successfully that none of Tristan's connections or de Windt's men could find him. With that problem preying on my mind, I woke up the morning after the dinner party with an idea.

"I know a way," I told Tristan.

"Mm-hm." Tristan's nose was snuggled into my shoulder, his eyes closed, and his arm covered my stomach in a protective pose that he had adopted after learning I was carrying his child. One eye opened a slit. He had such long eyelashes! "What time is it?"

"Four o'clock. Remember the cemetery at Hightower? Where we met the first one buried in it? The one who knew I was carrying the souls of Parnell's victims?"

"Mmm-hm."

"We should go to the Alenbonné cemetery and ask the *Premier Esprit,* the first spirit for help. The guardian there is called Angelien. Ghosts are everywhere. Surely one of them might have seen something, know where Barbier is."

One sleepy eye opened fully. "I thought the ghost protector couldn't leave its cemetery."

"They couldn't until the Gray Lady's curse was lifted. That

doesn't apply here. She's different— unique, special. Everyone in the Morpheus Society knows of her."

Both of his eyes opened, and cognitive thought started replacing the sleepy haze. "We keep coming up empty. If he's in the city, he's hidden well. Better than what I could have done. How would we do this?"

"Go to the cemetery tonight when it is deserted and ask her for aid."

"Seems simple enough, but since it involves you, I do not think it will be."

Of course, Tristan was right.

While Alenbonné had many cemeteries, the largest and oldest was fitted snugly between the government offices and the market square. It was a rambling, zig-zagging lot of over five acres. Every Morpheus apprentice knew the grounds, for it was here we were tested before being allowing to become a full-fledged member of the Society.

Everyone in the Society also knew of a hidden entrance, while the public did not. The cemetery provided training to mediums during their apprenticeship and entering at night, without being detected, and handling a multitude of spirits was a rite of passage. One day, I would bring Twyla here so she could show her skills and graduate into a full-fledged, independent member. If that was still her wish, after all that had happened.

"I don't want to do anything illegal and add to our problems," protested Madame Claire Vogel, my new acquaintance of the Morpheus Society.

Personally, I felt that breaking into a cemetery was a minor offense considering the others the Society was guilty of. It wasn't like we were grave-robbing, as in days of old.

We had picked up Madame Vogel in Tristan's anonymous

black carriage, and on the drive over, I shared my plan on contacting the cemetery's first spirit, its Premier Esprit. We passed the high ornamental iron fence on its boundaries and the stone house at the formal front entrance, where a gatekeeper paid by the city lived. I did not plan on entering through that gate, and the carriage rolled past.

"Mysir de Windt is searching for one man, and once he is found, the pressure on the Society will be lifted," I promised her.

It irritated me that she looked to the only man in our trio for affirmation. Tristan said, "His Majesty is aware of the need."

Namedropping, the king seemed to reassure her. I added a carrot. "I reviewed your group's proposal, and some of it has merit."

She sighed. "All right. Let us go. Though I doubt you will be successful. Angelien has not been seen in decades. Some are beginning to think she was a myth."

I knew it was a gamble, but I wanted to try. Tristan had exhausted his own contacts. Let me try mine.

We exited the carriage as quietly as we could. Tristan signaled to his driver to walk the horses. He warned Davis not to wander off as he had done at my father's house when I was confronted by Dupont.

It being the new moon, there would be no illumination revealing our position, making it a good night to prowl a graveyard. A breeze blew in from the ocean and the night air was cooler than usual for summer, making me glad that I was wearing my cycling outfit, made of thick wool tweed with a divided skirt and coat. Instead of bringing my case, I had stuffed my pockets, and a few of Tristan's, with things I thought we might need. One of them was the small bottle of Eyesbright that I hoped would give Tristan the vision needed to see any spirits.

Nervous, Madame Vogel scurried away. We followed, although I knew where we were going. The Society owned a house near the cemetery, but it was the yard that was important. She unlocked the first gate, and we slipped inside. This fence was made of solid wooden panels to discourage snooping. Any view from a second-story window would be obscured by a couple of trees and a tool shed.

The building was a dingy thing with peeling red paint and a dirty opaque window. That was all part of its disguise. She unlocked the shed padlock and pulled it open, and as we entered, Tristan was surprised. "Clever."

The back of the building was gone. All you could see was the cemetery fence, mostly covered with an aggressive vine that climbed from the ornamental iron over the shed's roof, providing further cover of our activities.

Probably from nervousness, Madame Vogel dropped her key ring, which Tristan picked it up for her. "Oh, thank you," she said, practically gibbering as his fingers touched hers. How she could work with the dead and be this anxious was beyond me.

When the fence swung open, it didn't squeak, as it was kept well oiled. I knew the gravel paths from memory, so I didn't hesitate in the darkness. To help Tristan navigate, I took his hand in mine.

Because of the city's low sea level, a series of floods had once caused coffins to be swept up and float down the watery streets. To prevent this from happening again, bodies were now placed in crypts or their graves covered with heavy slabs. We passed the rows, all the graves tightly packed together. Some tombstones were leaning, and others had words too worn from the salty sea air to be read. It was an ancient home to the city's dead.

Saturating the air was the rich, sweet smell of the flowering vine. Rest My Love, a favorite in cemeteries. Even in the dark, one landmark could be seen: a row of tall, pencil-thin cedars which marked the tomb Maarten, a past mayor of Alenbonné. The trees and his tomb, with its sculpture of a ship in full sail on its roof, was a guide for anyone wanting to find their direction among the labyrinthine graveled paths.

"Here we are." After making her declaration, Madame Vogel drew back, allowing us to see the marker.

"It's small. And no words?" noted Tristan.

"It's the oldest. The first," I said with reverence.

Yes, it looked insignificant, overwhelmed by the carved ladies with wings; or statues of mermen holding tritons that marked graves of sailors, but this one was the most important. The deathbed of the First Spirit, known as Angelien.

After using it myself, I handed the bottle of Eyesbright to Tristan.

"You gave this to me at the Montaine's cemetery?"

"Yes."

He unstopped the bottle and dosed his eyes. Madame Vogel refused when he held it out to her. "I don't need it." *Ah.* That explained why she was with the Society. She was a natural, someone who saw spirits unaided, more like Twyla.

Before I began, I explained my purpose, not because Tristan didn't know already, but it cleared the mind and helped it to focus. "I will be asking Angelien if she can use the spirits of Alenbonné to aid us in locating the man, Marcellus Barbier."

"Petitioning her rarely ends well," cautioned Madame Vogel.

"Desperate measures for desperate times," was Tristan's reply.

The Premier Esprit, or First Spirit, of a cemetery was usually the first one buried there. Their spirit was tied to the place forever. It was rumored that some individuals were even murdered, sacrificed to hold that position. How she had gotten here, or what her life had been on the earthly plane was unknown. Only that Angelien was the first in this oldest and most famous cemetery of Alenbonné.

What her real name had been, no one knew either, but in the early encounters with our founder, Lady Alouette Sarte, she'd become known as Angelien. Her powers were not those of a mere mortal sacrificed to guard holy ground. She was something more, for it was believed that when Maarten had asked her to stop the Great Fire, she'd gifted a downpour of rain that lasted ten days.

A ghost who had ascended into something else, a protector of the city. She could not be summoned like any spirit. There was more need for ceremony and respect.

From my pockets, I pulled black candles, matches, and a small knife. I scored a pattern into the wax, symbols of protection but also summoning. Finished, I dug a hole at the base of the grave and wiggled a candle into it. I lit it, and using its flame, caught the wick of two other candles, handing one to each of my companions.

Slitting my finger, I held it over the grave, letting my blood soak into the dirt, as I started to chant a summoning.

Mother and father,
Sister and brother,
Hear my call
Of welcome.
Your advice to guide us,
Your wisdom to teach us,
We need your counsel,
O Ancestor.
We invite your spirit,
With our blood's life
To appear.
Open the door.
We invite you.
We need your counsel.
We welcome you
Sister, brother,
mother, father,
Hear my call.

Perhaps the wind picked up, but otherwise nothing happened.

It was sometime well after midnight and the city around us was quiet. To my irritation, Madame Vogel said, "Can we leave now?"

"Tristan, your hand." He gave it without hesitation and I slit his finger, bringing the blood down on top of where mine had gone. Male and female energies; the balance of opposites. I hoped it would be enough, for we didn't have a child and crone to complete the traditional four points of balance.

The wind gained speed, swirling around us, and lifting the tendrils of hair from my neck. Madame Vogel clutched the top of her hat with one hand while her candle was snuffed out. Mine and Tristan's held their bright and steady flames.

I repeated my call, putting more energy into the summoning. The mark above my breast started to burn, and a trembling vibration came up from the ground through the soles of my feet, climbing up my legs, racing up my spine, until it hit my brain with a cold, shocking numbness.

"I have come."

The manifestation rose from her grave, floating high enough that she could look down on us. Like most ghosts she appeared as solid and real as the living. Angelien's form was that of a thin child, perhaps of about ten with knobbly elbows and knees; her face was shadowed with emaciation. Her dark hair was lank and thin, making her ears prominent. Her winding-clothes, her shroud, fell past her feet, trailing into the ground, rooting her almost like a string to a kite.

The word that sprung to mind was 'eldritch.'

Like many bound spirits she could be capricious, spiteful and angry, or magnanimous and inclined to give a blessing. In the last few years there had been no sightings reported but I blamed that on drunk apprentices wanting to test their powers by calling her.

As if reading my mind, she said, "The last person who summoned me was Leopold Maarten during the Great Fire. His body is laid out over there." Her pointed chin gave a nod past us to our right.

"Thank you. Thank you for gracing us," gibbered Madame Vogel. She had drawn closer, her eyes round and an expression of worship on her face. Angelien ignored her.

"Renee Bassett, Louisa Bonnet, Meike Roord, Frida Korver." With each name she spoke there was the sound of a distant bell. "Anyone who dies in my city, I know. Even if their souls are separated from their bodies, it is the flesh I care for. Dust to dust, they return to the earth that gave the life."

I spoke softly but firmly. "I am here about a man who threatens Alenbonné and its monarch."

"There have been many threats to our grand city." Her high-pitched child's voice sounded hollow and inhuman. "Yet, we still stand."

"He deprived you of the Alenbonné dying, suspending those near death to serve his needs."

The vague gaze she had been giving upon me turned sharp, and her voice became arrogant. "That puppet-master overstepped herself, denying me my due, and thus I cut her mortal thread. When her body sinks into my soil, I shall curse her soul."

I blinked. So, my mentor's death had not resulted from natural aging. Truly, Angelien was no mere spirit. She was the protector of the city itself, and death was her domain.

"Madame Granger was only part of a greater conspiracy. We seek her son, and hoped for your answer on where he is hiding." Tristan added, "He has weapons, new and powerful. We fear that he might assassinate King Guénard or bring violence to the city."

We waited while she considered our request.

"Nothing is given without something being taken. It is the nature of such aid. Leopold Maarten was a true patriot, thinking of the city first, a rare individual."

Before I could stop him, Tristan stepped forward. "I have spent most of my life protecting Alenbonné. I am the king's man."

She drifted down so her eyes were almost level with us. This close, you could see she lacked both iris and pupil, what was under her lids was marble white. Her expression was inhuman. "I have my champion, better than any king's man. But he needs a host in order to leave my boundary."

Not good. I tugged on Tristan's arm, but his body was a brick wall. I was regretting this impulse. Angelien could not be easily manipulated or reasoned with. What faced us was more ambiguous and disconcerting than what I had imagined.

"By host, are you speaking of possession?"

"Yes."

"Does your champion kill or subvert the will of its host?"

"Not purposely, but in conducting the act of vengeance, sometimes the unforeseen happens. He is not always careful with the bodies he inhabits."

"He leaves once the task is completed?"

"Yes. He returns to me, for he is my liege-man. My avenger. Vassal and vessel of retribution and punishment."

"I have been possessed before."

I cried, "No! This is not a good idea."

For all the attention he gave my warning, Tristan might as well have patted my head. He spoke only to Angelien. "I'm willing. Your champion will find Marcellus Barbier and leave once we have taken care of him."

"Behold. For he is here."

Chapter Twenty-Seven

Stubborn men are intractable once they set their course.

"No, Tristan," I said again. "The king is not worth this sacrifice."

"I'll be fine, Elinor. I've been possessed before and survived it."

That had been an ordinary spirit. This would not be some love-sick fool.

"My champion," declared Angelien.

When a figure appeared behind Madame Vogel, she cried out and scuttled to place herself behind Tristan and me.

The spectral form was a knight wearing the old-fashioned armor of about 800 years ago. With his visor lowered, anything human about him was concealed. His armor, the leathers, and the surcoat in Alenbonne's colors of red and white didn't make a sound. Not a creak of metal or a snap of cloth moved by the wind; he was as immobile as a statue.

"What is your name?" asked Tristan, but the silver-plated form did not answer. Its silence only added to its foreboding presence.

"He is too old for a name. You may call him Le Bourreau, for he is my executioner. Know him as a force, the essence of valor and boldness. He will not stop, nor stand aside, until justice is done."

No. No. No. "Tristan, please do not do this. We will find Barbier ourselves. I wish I had never thought of this."

"Calm down, Elinor. Your Angelien has outlined the deal, except she has not named the price."

"Augustus Chalamet's watch."

"What? Why?" At her request, my hand instinctively went to the pocket that held it. As I pulled it out, I found it warm in my hand.

"You have a guardian. I am curious about him, so he shall stay in exchange for the use of my champion."

"I don't have a guardian," I said automatically. *She means Father.*

"Give me the watch and you may use my champion. That is my price. I will not take any other."

"Never mind, Elinor. She wants too much." A moment ago I hadn't wanted Tristan to sacrifice himself, but if the watch would gain us the location of Marcellus Barbier, shouldn't I also contribute to this venture? "Will you return it when we bring back your champion?"

"No."

Every impulse rebelled! I couldn't lose one of my last links to him. Even as I drew back, ready to put the watch away, it twitched in my hand. When I closed my hand over it, it stung me, forcing my fingers open. Like a magnet it pulled my hand towards Angelien.

Release me.

Before I could think about it any further, I laid it upon the granite slab that marked her grave.

Angelien drifted down. When she touched it, something pulled deeply at my heart and my body spasmed. "Oh yes. This is fascinating." Without any warning, she severed the tie between me and my father's watch.

The wrench was sharp, like someone withdrawing a thorn. With the watch gone, so went the painful mark above my breast.

I felt lighter, like a burden had been lifted. My grief, the ever-present heavy sadness of losing my father, was gone. Startled, I probed the space it left, and found no pain. There was a dull ache, but nothing like the constant sorrow I had felt for over a decade.

"Are you all right?" Tristan asked.

"Yes. Only a little light-headed."

"You have twenty-four hours to find your man."

Angelien vanished, leaving us with three burned out candles and knightly figure that did not speak.

"Are you sure you are all right?"

"Yes." Now was not the time to discuss my thoughts and feelings.

Madame Vogel spoke up. "Can we leave now?"

"I think we must deal with Angelien's executioner first." My voice was stronger, and I shook off Tristan's grip. "Are you sure? It won't be like before."

"We don't know what it's going to be like, but I find myself curious." Tristan gave le bourreau a measuring look up and down. "How do we make this happen?"

He stepped closer to the figure, his hand came up to lift the helm, revealing nothing. He turned away, a question on his face, while behind him an inky blackness glided out of the helm.

"Tristan." I stepped forward, but the inky smoke was already covering his face, entering his nostrils, ears, and mouth. I bit my lip, wanting to scream. Instead I grabbed him, holding him tight as a powerful tremble shook his limbs. In a moment he stilled again and I stepped back. "Tristan?"

In his eyes, what I saw was not entirely my dear love. "Let us go."

"Finally!" said Madame Vogel.

With nothing else to gain we left.

Tristan strode in front of us like a marching soldier. He said nothing and barely waited for us to finish locking the gates behind us. At the curb I waved, and Davis brought the carriage down to meet us.

Without waiting for the ladies, Tristan entered, letting the door fall loose behind. I caught it and let Madame Vogel enter next. To Davis, I gave directions to return to Madame Vogel's residence, where we would drop her off, and then he was to proceed to Hartwood.

The ride would have been silent, except that Madame Vogel's nervousness would not let her remain quiet. "I never would have thought. We actually met Angelien. *Angelien.*" She shook her head. "I can hardly believe it. It must be fortuitous. A sign that the Morpheus Society will recover."

Tristan and I were seated across from her, but she directed her conversation towards me, her eyes sometimes skittering nervously towards Tristan. I did not blame her. He radiated a dangerous energy that was impossible to ignore.

At her house, when she gained the curb, she turned back to me. "I know you don't want my advice, but be careful, my dear. Gifts from the dead are not always trustworthy."

"I understand."

Davis whipped the horses, and we were moving along again, this time to Hartwood.

Free of Madame Vogel's presence, I asked, "How are you feeling, Tristan?"

"Possessed. Unlike Bastiaan Hagen, I know this one is here. He is in every thought— every pore." I reached out and took his hand in mine. It was icy. "He wants one thing: Marcellus Barbier. He's so cold. Frozen. His only passion is for vengeance."

I squeezed his hand, causing him to look my way. "Stay with me, Elinor."

"Of course I shall!"

"No. Don't leave me alone with it. It would consume me, take everything that is mine. Its thinking is alien, inhuman. You make me feel alive, Elinor." Abruptly, he grabbed me by my throat. His grip was so tight, I could barely breathe.

Silly girl, this is Tristan. He wouldn't harm you. And something else.

He kissed me so hard that his teeth cut my lip. Feeling the salty taste of blood in my mouth, I wrapped my arms tightly around him. "I love you, Tristan Fontaine."

"Never let me forget that," he muttered.

"I won't let you. Nor will I let you go. We have twenty-four hours, and you'll be yourself again."

"If my mind survives this."

By the time we got to Hartwood, my fear was growing. Tristan's mood veered from being excited to morose. It was so unlike his usual rectitude that it frightened me. How much control was he able to exert over this ghost? As the carriage stopped in front of his residence, remembering how shaky he had been during his first possession, I asked, "Can you make it to the door?"

"Yes," he said through gritted teeth. He told Davis we would need him again, and to just walk the horses.

Thankfully, we met no one inside. Tristan stalked to his study, and I hurried after. He was opening a cabinet, where he pulled a case out that contained a set of pistols. He showed me how to load and fire them.

"What is the plan?"

"You were right, Elinor. The ghosts know every living thing that resides within the city's boundaries. This creature— he's like a homing pigeon. No. More like a falcon high above who looks down and spots the vole trying to hide itself. I know where Barbier is."

"Where?"

"The ruins of that burned down theater, that's near the Luminary."

"The Royale?"

"Yes." Tristan gave a laugh as if he was finding it hard to

breathe. "It's funny because Barbier's in the tunnels. Do you understand? He's *underground*. Child's play for a spirit to find him *in his living grave*."

His laugh continued, verging on hysterical. I gripped both of his hands hard. "Control him! You are the master, not this Le Bourreau!"

I could see the effort it took him to bring his breathing back to normal. "Yes. He is eager to slip the leash, like a dog getting a whiff of the fox."

"Shall we get de Windt? His men?"

"No," Tristan said sharply. "I have the distinct feeling it would be best if no one else witnesses what happens."

I tried reminding him of all the times I had rushed in alone and got myself into trouble. Wouldn't it be better to bring some armed men? But he wasn't listening to me.

"You are letting the possession take control." The hardness that had cast his face into stone did not change. I tried again. "What if Barbier has others with him? We could be stopped by his men and never reach him."

"He's alone."

There was nothing to gain in arguing. Tristan had made his decision and could not be moved.

Dawn was about to break, and only the early morning staff were about. In the foyer, under the startled eyes of a housemaid carrying her coal scuttle, Tristan handed me one of his two pistols.

"This is my second-best pair. Don't lose this one like you did the other. And this time, shoot to kill. It's more humane than letting a man fall to his death."

Chapter Twenty-Eight

As we traveled to the theater district, I asked for details. I felt it was better to keep Tristan's mind occupied. "How could he be hiding there? It's a burned-out shell of a place."

He said, his voice deep and rough, "Theaters use a basement to store costumes and backdrops. It runs under the stage. Cable systems lift pieces of the stage and bring heavier backdrops up to stage level." He flashed me a familiar smirk. "I see you're imagining some romance with a dancer or actress. No. After a magic act that baffled me, I asked for a tour. He had used a cleverly concealed trap door to disappear."

"So your — companion knows he is there?"

"Yes."

"Does he know how to get in?" He didn't answer. "Tristan?"

The carriage was rolling to a stop, and he jumped out, leaving me behind. I stepped down more carefully and told Davis to wait further down the street where he wouldn't be seen. "We will let you know when we need you."

Tristan had abandoned me to prowl through the burnt wreck

of the Royale. The remaining stone steps now led to a hollowed out shell instead of the grand old theater. I placed my hand on a column, one of several that formed a row across the front. The roof was missing, revealing the peculiar pre-dawn color of the sky.

Tristan had already shoved away the doors, which were barely hanging on their hinges. One of them cracked and the upper part fell away, hitting the wall. The structure shook from the force of its assault. A powdery fall of burnt bits and brick dust showered us both. He ignored it. Stepping over a downed beam, he disappeared into the dark interior, hidden from my view. I followed more carefully.

Inside the lobby, the smoky smell of charcoal was stronger. The solid exterior walls of red brick had survived, but the wall-paper was scorched halfway up to the ceiling and the tattered remains of velvet curtains fluttered above us like banners that had experienced cannon fire. In the foyer, the solid wood of the ticket counter was blackened, and beside it were heaps of paper rubbish. Perhaps playbills and tickets?

Cloaks and coats discarded in the rush to flee the blaze looked like flattened bodies. I stepped over a glove, incongruously white among the black smutty rubble. It bespoke a sad tale. The panicked audience had fled the fire caused when a lamp on stage fell and lit the curtains. How lucky that we had prevented such a horror at the Luminary!

Tristan entered through the next set of doors, the ones that would lead you to the seating area for the audience. The fire must have burned very hot, as the rows of seats were burned lumps showing only shreds of red velvet and gold braid, hinting at the Royale's former grandeur. Restoring the theater would require a substantial investment, which was why it remained a shell.

This area still retained its roof, and it made the interior gloomy. I pulled out my matches and lit the two lanterns we had brought. He took his without a word, his face barely registering me. His dog was scouting for the fox and had no time for petty conversation.

He started down the aisle, approaching the stage. Before the stage he stepped over the railing, before jumping into the orchestra pit. He did not wait for me as I awkwardly clambered down, trying to hold my lantern and keep ahold of my pistol.

Music stands made skeletal trees and my foot landed on the remains of a cello, half burned away. It made a loud crunch and as I struggled to free my foot, Tristan grunted, "Here," and vanished from sight. Following him, I found another doorway and a step. Entering it put us in the underground warren under the Royale.

Surprisingly, the air in the warren was fresh, so there must be another entrance or some ventilation to outside. Up ahead bobbed Tristan's flickering lantern, and I hurried after him. The floor slanted downward unexpectedly, and I pitched forward, almost falling into Tristan's back. My hand went to the wall to steady myself, and I felt rough stone. Feeling it, I brought my lantern closer.

"This is quarried stone," I said, surprised.

"The Royale sits on top of the original fortifications of the city." In the dark, his voice sounded disembodied. "Only when the canals were formed did the buildings stop sinking into what had been a marsh."

"Can you reach the palace from here? Perhaps Barbier means to gain access to the king that way?"

"Unlikely. Those tunnels on our end were bricked up long ago to prevent that very thing."

Holding the lantern in one hand and gun in the other, he continued. My own weapon I kept pointed downward. I didn't need to accidentally shoot him if startled. Besides, it was heavier than my man-stopper and my arm was growing tired.

We found offices along the way. These chambers had minor damage to them; I supposed the fire which had started on stage must have used the fuel of curtains, wallpaper, and timbers, to move upward. There was a dim smell of charcoal and smoke, but the stronger scent was of mildew and the presence of rodents.

"Costumes," he said.

Dresses on racks resembled people in the dark. A dressmaker's dummy almost got shot when I saw it out of the corner of my eye, reflected in a mirror that cast odd shadows as we passed it.

In the center of the room was a worktable with the tools of the dressmaking trade: pins, chalk, and scissors. The scissors were as sharp as the day they'd been made, and on one blade was etched the initials, B.V. Someone's favorite pair, probably marked to prevent them from being lost or stolen.

"Come along," Tristan said from the doorway before he disappeared. I grabbed up the pistol. Being in a hurry I spilled hot wax on my hand causing me to grimace.

With his long legs, Tristan had put distance between us. He turned left and entered another storeroom. Chairs, tables, lamps, a coat-rack, urns that looked like plaster but were made of light-weight wood. Ah. These were the props used on stage.

"Where is he?" I whispered to Tristan as he passed me, returning to the doorway.

"It's like a scent trail; I know he's been here. We are getting closer." In a rush to find his quarry, Tristan increased the distance between us, loping down the hallway.

"Tristan! Wait!" No one answered me. Before I could go after him, I stepped in something sticky. Stopping, I brought my lantern down for a closer look. My finger touched it, and bringing it to my nose, I smelled honey. Suddenly, there was a large clanging noise. A metal grill dropped in front of me, blocking my way. I jumped back in surprise and hit a second grill coming down behind me.

A disembodied voice echoed around me. "I wish you had not come, Elinor."

~

Marcellus Barbier had imprisoned me with a portcullis, the gates used in castles. The corridor of stone had a dropped gate in front of me and another behind. I was trapped. My hand on my pistol tightened, but I had nowhere to aim it.

"They used these corridors to trap invaders. The slits in the wall were for swords and arrows to hit their quarry. But don't worry, Elinor, I have no intention of dealing with you in that manner. You'll be safe here while I see about his lordship."

"Barbier!" When he didn't reply, I shouted, "Marcellus! Tell me—"

"Make it quick, Elinor. I have other matters to attend to."

"After you murdered my father, did you enjoy my begging for you to help me?" My voice cracked. But even as I felt the desire to shoot him, I worried where Tristan was. He wouldn't know I was trapped here; and I couldn't go to him if he needed me.

"Chalamet shouldn't have stuck his nose in my business."

"Didn't you feel any guilt? Were you salving your conscience, or did you want me kept under guard? You knew I'd never give up on looking for who killed my father."

I wanted to keep him talking as my eyes examined the slitted holes that he said had been used for arrows. If I saw any movement in one could I get off a shot? It seemed unlikely.

"So many questions." I was sure he was hiding behind the walls. It was probably a corridor that ran parallel to mine. Something like the passageway set up at Lindengaard that the count had shown me. "I don't kill children. You were young. Lost. So I arranged a safe place for you. I don't regret your father. It had to be done."

"Parnell Lafayette. How did you get involved with him?" I had blown out my lantern, not wishing to give him light. Running my hand along the stone, I could feel the grooves and the arrow slit holes he had described. However, no shadows or lights from his side helped me pinpoint him.

"That's the irony, Elinor. He came to my office to complain about you working with the police. I saw quickly that he'd be a useful tool. His potion made people witless and thus easy to control. He gave me an army."

"Not anymore! Your mother died, and you lost them."

"They served their purpose. The city was in turmoil, the populace scared and angry. A perfect brew for panic."

"But your real goal is to become your father's rightful heir. Be the next Lord Bridoux." There was a scraped behind the wall. A footstep, perhaps?

"How did you—? Oh. My mother's ghost. You must have spoken with her."

"We did have a chat after her death."

"I never believed in spirits until I met you. Even Leona never convinced me of their existence. She was a master manipulator, and I figured this was just another one of her tricks. Until you came to the morgue, revealing the secrets of corpses."

I had hoped Tristan would realize I wasn't with him and return. But I feared that Angelien's executioner had a one-track mind. "Please give up this plan. It will never work."

"Oh, Elinor," he said with pity. "My little do-gooder. Of course it will work. When Parliament meets on Tuesday, I plan on giving them an explosive surprise. With so many of their number dead, they will be desperate to have anyone claim a title so they can keep their seats. There will be few who will wonder where I came from if my paperwork is order."

Paperwork?

"Let me guess, you'll produce a marriage certificate."

"Clever, Elinor. Lady Bridoux will soon be dead and no one will be around to contest that my father had an earlier marriage. After all nobility marrying Ghost Talkers seems to be the rage this season."

Shaking the portcullis with my hands, I found it far too strong and heavy to budge or break. "Your crimes bring you wealth. Why be a lord?"

"I will have my birthright. No one will deny me what is rightfully mine," He said it grimly. "Now, goodbye, Elinor. I need to take care of your partner."

"What about me?" Barbier said nothing. I shouted, "Tristan!"

But no one answered.

Chapter Twenty-Nine

It was time to get out of here.

Upon entering the confines of the Royale, I'd found the atmosphere had the gritty texture of many ghosts. How many had perished in the fire? Most of the cast and some of the audience. Others had been crushed to death, running down the aisle.

The dramatic allure of such a tragic death would attract lost souls. It was this ghostly concentration that probably had given Barbier's location away to Angelien's agent, her executioner. Anyone who had died in Alenbonné was a part of her.

I summoned Bartel Kingma, an actor who had died in the Royale's fire. The one who had agreed to fool Annabel van den Berg at her birthday party so I could convince her that a ghost had pushed her down the Hartwood stairs, not tripping over a piano wire set by Valentina and Josephine.

Ever since the soul-sisters had entered me, I had found my medium abilities enhanced. Although they were gone, I felt a new power inside me, and my summoning was answered promptly.

He was a tall, handsome man of middle years dressed in evening clothes. A rose, as fresh as the day he had died, was in his buttonhole. In a rich baritone, he said, "Elinor Chalamet. What a surprise."

"Mysir Kingma, thank you for answering. I am in a bit of a pickle and could use your assistance. Have you ever considered being a Noise Ghost?"

"Madame, if there is an audience for it, I can perform it."

A Noise Ghost used the energy of the living in order to do their theatrics. It was why they frequented households with children and teenagers who had an overabundance of it. Somewhere behind the walls was a mechanism to move the grill of the portcullis. I wouldn't be able to reach it, but he should. I described what to look for and where it was probably located.

"Found it. But it's not budging."

"I can give you the power you need, but once I channel it to you, make it quick. The connection won't last long." Ghosts burned through human energy quickly; it was why Noise Ghosts specialized in throwing books, moving keys, and slamming doors. They were sprinters, not long-distance runners.

A scraping noise, and the metal grate started moving upwards. Putting the lantern and pistol aside, I placed my hands under the bottom of the portcullis and pushed up, trying to aid him.

The air was becoming so cold I could see my breath. Not trusting that Kingma could keep it going, when there was enough room, I squeezed through. It rose another six inches before it squealed and became stuck in a frozen position.

"Thank you, Mysir Kingma."

But his presence was gone. He'd exhausted his ability to sustain a presence on the earthly plane. Picking up gun and lantern, I staggered to my feet. Giving him so much energy had drained me, but I needed to find Tristan.

~

At one point I found the paths split; one choice was blocked by tumbled bits of furniture. Barbier was forcing the card, getting Tristan to go a route where some other trap would be sprung.

I pumped my arms, running harder, juggling the lantern and my gun, when I heard two gunshots, one after the other. The sound was ahead and to my right. It looked like the corridor opened to another room where a faint light was visible.

With my back to the corridor wall, I approached, but slower. Barbier was shouting something insulting. From Tristan there was nothing.

At the doorway, I set my lantern down. Holding Tristan's pistol in one hand, I peered around the corner. There were two points of light from two different lanterns. One, I assumed, was Tristan's.

We were in a forest. No, it was a painting of life-sized trees on a canvas backdrop. It took me a moment to realize that I was looking into a storage room for the theater's scenery. There were trees made of wood and plaster — a staircase that went up to a landing with a door that opened to no-where. A wood facade of a house with another door. They all made a maze of looming shadows that flickered against the walls from the lantern light. Plenty of places to hide.

A noise to the right. Shoes scuffling along the floor. There was the click of a door being shut or opened. Should I go in? Before I could make that decision, a shadow descended from the ceiling. Seeing a familiar silhouette, I gave a shout. Tristan ducked to the right, and the sandbag hurtling down towards his head hit his shoulder instead. He went down to one knee before ducking into a roll to hide behind a piece of hanging canvas.

Again it went quiet. I swore that I could hear heavy breathing, but I couldn't pinpoint from where. Now that my eyes had adjusted, I moved inside the room slowly. There were rolled canvases leaning against the wall and I sheltered behind them, wondering how I could best help. Probably by staying quiet and not confusing Tristan.

Something rolled across the floor, and there was another shot, with the smell of gunpowder in the air.

The two men said nothing, which I found disconcerting. It was a silent game of cat and mouse, but I wasn't sure who was the cat.

I wished I could read Tristan's mind, and know what to do.

A painted wooden wall of scenery came crashing down, and I found myself now under a lean-to. The fall had stopped short of from smashing me because of the angle where it had struck the wall.

I heard cursing, and emerged to see Tristan and Barbier in a tight grapple Using my weapon was out of the question and there was nothing I could pick up to strike Barbier with.

This wasn't a boxing match with a code of gentlemanly conduct. Barbier was using street fighting tactics, trying to knee him in the groin. Wrapping a foot around his ankle, he hooked Tristan's leg and in a half fall, he grabbed Barbier by the upper arm and pivoted his weight to stop his descent.

They swung around each other. Tristan got in a blow to the side of Barbier's head but that didn't seem to slow his opponent down. Barbier grabbed Tristan tightly around the waist and, ducking his head against his chest, ran him into another piece of scenery. The papier mâché tree toppled, the real tree branches which made its crown cracking and splintering as they hit the floor. Barbier, being on top, was struck in the face by a branch. He staggered backward, releasing Tristan, who immediately rolled off the tree trunk to gain his feet.

Before I could think, I raised my gun and took a shot. It went wide. Barbier threw himself under the staircase that climbed ended in space. It must have been on wheels, because the collision shoved it away. Before he could scramble for cover, Tristan had collared him.

Barbier tried using his head to slam into the side of Tristan's jaw and cheek, but Tristan reared back in time to avoid the full force of the blow. He threw a fist into the side of Barbier's neck, followed by a sideways punch to his ribs which lifted Barbier bricfly off his feet.

Barbier yelled in fury and tried once more to get Tristan in a wrestling grip. Tristan slammed the palms of his hands against Barbier's ears. The shock made Barbier relax his grip enough that Tristan could twist away. Facing him, Tristan said, "Surrender. It's over."

"Never."

This close I wouldn't miss. The bullet hit Barbier high on the shoulder and he went down. Tristan put his knee into his chest, holding him down. As I approached, pointing my weapon at Barbier's prone body, he cast me a sideways glance. "Where were you?"

"Barbier trapped me in a corridor using a portcullis. A ghost helped me out."

"Of course it did," muttered Tristan. His nose was dripping blood, he had a split lip, and his knuckles were raw.

"Are you all right?"

"Acceptable. Thanks for the warning on the sandbag drop."

"I figured if he trapped me, he had one for you."

"Get me that rope from the sandbag so I can tie him up."

I could barely stand Barbier as he spat out a long stream of poison about how we should work together, for old times' sake. Did I really trust this aristocrat? He was using me like they all did. He'd throw me away as soon as I was inconvenient.

I finally looked down at him. "Just shut up," I said wearily. Why didn't I feel triumphant? We had emerged victorious, but I didn't feel like I had won anything.

"What will happen now?"

"Well, Le Bourreau has several ideas. He thinks we should hang him right here. Use the stairs as a makeshift gallows."

I stared at Tristan, shocked. "You — you aren't serious?" His face held a sinister cast, and he didn't sound amused, nor did he smile or laugh. "He should be arrested and tried."

Tristan cocked his head and gave me a look, as if I had just spoken in a foreign language he didn't know. "Have you thought that through, Elinor? What proof do we have that he murdered your father? The evidence, if there was any, is long gone. Who would come forward to testify about his blackmailing scheme?"

"Lady Talleyrand—"

"Absolutely would *not* testify. It would destroy her reputation if it became known she was compromised. The king would never trust her again."

"His partners in crime—"

"The ones I questioned didn't know his name or face. He kept in the shadows. Perhaps Buckard could have identified him, but he's dead."

"He murdered Lady Baudelaire."

"I agree. But we have no proof of that either. Where he did it. How he moved her to that room where he put you."

Growing angry, I snapped, "He shot Lord Bridoux!"

"Only Bridoux's wife saw the assassin, and she is in a coma, unlikely to recover. His alliance with Parnell to create an army of the dying? That evidence was destroyed when Parnell died. Remember, someone cleaned out his records. Yes, you talked with Madame Granger, but a ghost's third hand testimony won't convict Barbier of his many misdeeds."

"He's planted explosives. That's what he told me when he held me trapped."

"Where?"

"He didn't say exactly, but somewhere in these tunnels, close to the Parliament building."

"Hm. My men will take care of that."

At the look he gave to the man bound at our feet, I said, "Tristan, you can't kill him."

In that aloof, impersonal voice, he mused, "Why not?"

"You told me you've shed enough blood for your king. Remember? Minette? You had other choices. If you kill him, you'll become a murderer twice over."

"But killing him would be so satisfying." At my horrified look, he smirked. "Le Bourreau has such fascinating ideas on justice. He isn't constrained by morals. Why should we be?"

Barbier tried again. "Elinor, your father spoke about you when he died. Let me go, and I'll tell you his last words."

Tristan gave him a swift kick to the head that spun it around. "Shut up, filth," said a deep baritone voice that wasn't my husband's.

Shaking, I forced myself to walk away. To give myself something to do, I found the other lantern and brought it back. "We are not going to kill him. I don't know how we will punish him, but it won't be by a rope in a dungeon. Now, can we go?"

Tristan jerked Barbier to his feet, and shoved him out the door, and we started the long way back. When we reached the portcullis, it took time to find where the controls were to lift the gates as Barbier didn't share the information and Kingma was long gone.

By the time they were up, I was leaning against the wall, my legs feeling like jelly. I avoided looking at Barbier, trying to pretend that the man I had spent over a decade hunting for was not standing right beside me. Would it bring me any pleasure to slap him? None. He disgusted me.

From there, we made good time as the passage was familiar and easy to traverse. Emerging from the orchestra pit was like rising from the grave or a deathbed. The world would never be the same. I took the lead, eager to get out to the fresh air, to see the sun, to smell the salt of the sea.

Walking up the aisle of the Royale, Barbier tried one last time. "Elinor, don't you want to know what your father said before he died?"

I didn't bother turning around. "No."

Chapter Thirty

Alenbonné
Two weeks later

D r. Armand Devereaux finished signing that day's paperwork and, setting it aside, rose from his desk. Locking his office, he was about to leave when a nurse approached him.

"It's about the new patient, doctor."

"Is he causing trouble?"

"Not anything we can't handle. We've had worse." The two started walking down the hall to the end gate, which had to be unlocked so they could exit the ward.

Armand gave a nod to the guard, who returned it. Everyone knew him, for there weren't many doctors who would come here to this place of violence and despair.

"I only wonder if it wouldn't be best to put him on a suicide watch."

"Ah. That would probably be wise. Sometimes it takes a while for them to adjust."

The nurse admired Dr. Devereaux for taking time from his

busy and lucrative private practice to visit the Institute for the Criminally Insane. Although, she did think he was eternally optimistic about who could be helped.

"Unless you can perform a miracle, doctor, I don't see this patient ever leaving. His delusions are deep-rooted. And he's violent. We've had to put him in Ward 5."

Dr. Devereaux tut-tutted. Ward 5 was reserved for the worst offenders. "Still believes he's a criminal mastermind? Has mounds of wealth? The only true son of Lord Bridoux and should be holding down his seat in Parliament?"

They both shared a knowing glance, having dealt with so many who falsely believed themselves of noble parentage. "I'm afraid so."

After going through another locked and guarded door the two exited to the outside where the air was fresher.

"Well, nurse, I fear you are probably right. I do believe Mysir B will be with us until his end."

Armand bade her goodbye and headed through the front gates of the charity hospital, breathing a sigh of relief that he wouldn't have to return for almost a week. He was a free man, and could look forward to the choice of going home to a warm supper, or enjoyable evening with genial companionship — unlike those poor souls forever lost in their minds.

My father's grave was in a cemetery outside of Alenbonné in a small town where he had been born. I went alone. It wasn't that Tristan hadn't offered; I simply had not asked him. This journey was for me alone.

Deep in thought, I barely noticed the passing streets and buildings out the window. Today, I felt hollow and perhaps a little lost, since the driving force of over a decade was no more. My father's killer was found and punished. I should have felt joy or relief, instead I was tired. Maybe it was the doubt over whether we had done the right thing.

As Angelien had promised, twenty-four hours after the visit to her grave, Tristan was once again himself, free from his possession. There was no fanfare, no smoke, he simply was himself.

Both of us were relieved.

I hadn't argued with his plans for Barbier. Was it fair? I wasn't sure. In the end, he would not stand trial. The publicity would be bad for the king and also for Sarnesse. Having the details of how close the country had come to anarchy exposed in open court could lead to far worse than dead Ghastlies.

Intellectually I understood the necessity of keeping many of the facts hidden, such as the criminal ring blackmailing the nobility and government officials at the highest levels, but was the bar for justice met?

Why did I not shoot to kill?

Wouldn't that have revenged my father? Life for life.

Barbier had trapped me at the Royale. He could have killed me. He had not, and I liked to think it was because in the end, he had cared for me. He had been part of my life for thirteen years, my father for seventeen. While Madame Granger had fostered me, Barbier had acted as uncle, brother, mentor, and later friend. We had shared late nights tracking criminals, sharing humor and food. He had championed me against his superiors and let me work in the morgue. Despite it all, I believed that in a way, Barbier had respected me.

I could not have shot him. A life ended was a one-way road. I knew better then most the finality of death. And I could not let Tristan take the blame for being relieving the king of a problem.

Barbier couldn't hurt anyone else where he was, and his future would not be pleasant. That would have to serve as punishment enough for my father's murder, and for Lord Lucas Bridoux. For Lady Baudelaire and Cédric Durant, Leona's manservant. Miraculously, Lord Bridoux's wife had rallied and she might eventually recover.

For all the mayhem Barbier had caused, was sitting in a cell sufficient justice?

From the train station, it was only a twenty-minute walk to the cemetery. The trees were still enjoying summer, and the grounds were park-like. Father's grave was near the top of a hill, which gave a view of the valley.

I set up the bouquets I had brought in the urns; one for Father, the others for Mother and my baby brother. Finding a tap, I filled the urns with water. Then, sitting on the soft grass, I started speaking out loud as I had done on so many other visits.

"Twyla says you are my guardian. Or maybe not, since I gave Angelien your watch. I'm sorry about that, but in the end, we got him. The man who did this." I found it hard to describe what that act had been. Murder. "He's put away forever and won't be able to harm anyone ever again."

White fluffy thunderheads overhead indicated the possibility of a storm later. The season was turning to fall.

"Things are changing. I'm married and expecting a baby in about four months. I wish you could be here to meet Tristan. To hold our child."

I knew graves didn't always hold the essence of a being, and I felt no presence. Souls preferred places familiar to them, not cemeteries. Still, it seemed only right to be here.

"Madame Granger, the woman who started training me as a medium, did something to my mind. It made me forget a lot. There's a doctor who's helping me recall those memories again. We don't know if I'll remember everything, but I'm hopeful."

Dr. Devereaux had given me exercises to do and a journal to write down my dreams. Little things were returning like the color of my mother's eyes, or the nickname my brother had used before he passed. Small treasures, more sweet than bitter.

It was through talks with the doctor that I had slowly realized why I'd joined the Society in the first place. Every time I had helped a grieving family, assisted someone in crossing over, or brought a ghost some peace, it was an attempt to lay my own dead to rest. Yes, it had brought me satisfaction helping others, but it had never done what I had hoped for — eased the pain of losing my father.

My hand went up to the lily pin on my lapel, given to every Morpheus Society member when they passed their initiation. I undid the clasp and slipped it off, holding the bronze pin in my hand.

"I've done what I wanted to accomplish. Found your killer. But I also found that two people I thought protected me were only using me. Not very smart, huh? Funny. I thought I was too clever to be deceived." I gave a heavy sigh. My thumb rubbed up and down the metal stems of the pin's lilies. "The Society whose principles I pledged my life to uphold has shown itself to be corrupt. They've asked for my assistance in re-organizing, but I ask myself why should I help? Perhaps we humans should just muddle through our grief on our own. What do you think, Father?"

Naturally, there was no answer. No guardian whispering in my ear.

The day was getting late, and the fluffy clouds had turned darker. I needed to go if I was to meet the train back into town. I rose from the grass and rested the pin on the top of his gravestone. I intended to leave it, but as I turned to go, I was interrupted. "Madame? Are you with the Morpheus Society? The people who talk with the dead?"

It was a man in his sixties, and the worry in his eyes forced me to answer honestly. "Yes, I'm a Ghost Talker. Can I help you with something?"

"I don't want to bother you." His eyes traveled to the graves that marked my family.

"I've finished with my loved ones. Was there something you needed?"

"It's my wife." He gestured behind him.

"Do you want me to talk with her?"

"If it's not too much trouble." He led me over to her grave. The stone was new, probably less than a year old. "I wanted to say goodbye."

"I don't have my equipment here," I said apologetically. "Do you have anything that was hers?"

He pulled off a ring from his pinkie. As I reached out to take it from him, my hand passed through his, and I realized that he was a ghost. Startled, I met his eyes, but his expression had not changed, and he seemed not to notice my inability to take the ring from him.

I studied the grave again. It was only hers. Where his body was I had no idea, and I expected he didn't know either, as he thought he was still among the living. Since I had only his wife's name, I used it, but nothing answered the call of summoning. There was that particular blank feel you get when a person had transitioned.

"I'm sorry, but she's moved on to the Afterlife. I can't reach her."

"Oh. Good." He nodded before giving me a wide smile. "She was so devoted to me, I didn't want her to stay here alone. You've been very helpful. He told me you would be, and asked me to make sure you missed your train."

In an eye-blink, he was gone.

By the time I returned to the train station, he was right. I had missed the three o'clock and would have to wait for the last one, coming in at five. The station master told me I could wait across the street at the only café the village offered. It was a simple place so I ordered tea and an omelet. Sitting at the window, I saw my reflection and realized that I had instinctively re-pinned the lily on my lapel.

It seemed I wasn't done with Ghost Talking yet.

My carriage back was not as quiet as the one that had brought me. A woman with two young boys entered my carriage. As her boys tried to climb the walls, open the window, play with sliding the door open and shut, she ignored them with the stoicism that only a hardened mother of boys could maintain amongst such unrelenting noise.

"I'm glad I missed that earlier train," she exclaimed with such relish that I knew she wanted to share a story.

Obviously, she wanted me to ask why, so I did.

"Horrible accident on the line. The conductor was just telling me about it. The three o'clock was switched on to the wrong line and collided with an outbound train from Alenbonné. Horrible loss of life," she said, her eyes gleaming with ghoulish satisfaction.

The hair on the back of my neck rose. *I should have been on that one.*

"Troy, give the conductor back his hat this very minute."

"But I wanted to play train!"

CHAPTER THIRTY-ONE

It was a month since Parliament had opened, and the additional seats for the Commons had been already added when we were both summoned by the king.

We were in the Throne Hall, and Guénard was sitting on his massive throne placed high on a dais that allowed him to tower over his subjects.

Having endured an hour of waiting, we were now scolded like children for two hours. His near death during the Winter Revels had marked the king's face, making it less jolly and more worn. As he ranted, it became redder and redder. This tantrum could end in his death, and a cynical part of me thought at least I could finally sit down if it did.

"Have you read the Beacon? The Monitor? The Observer-Times? They are mocking me for being a weak king who caves to commoners. It is your fault! You advised me to meet with them."

In his tirade, he neglected to mention how he'd gotten drunk and promised more than Lady Talleyrand or Tristan had ever wanted him to risk. If he had stayed away from the party, they would have negotiated far less.

How silly of me to think King Guénard would be satisfied

with all that we had done to save his city and crown. By the cynical gleam in Tristan's eyes and the twist at the corner of his mouth it looked as though he had anticipated this outcome.

I expected him to argue, give some defense, but he only said meekly, "I understand, Your Majesty. It was unforgivable."

"And where is Marye?! Retreated to the country, claiming her estate needs her attention, instead of being by my side to see me through this mess that you two created!"

No, she had retreated from public life because she feared being exposed as a victim of Marcellus Barbier's blackmail! Listening to this twaddle got my back up!

My expression of disgust was seen by our monarch.

"Do you have something to add, Madame Chalamet?" demanded the king. Perhaps he used my maiden name to rile me. Or had he simply forgotten I was now a Fontaine?

I had heard married couples often develop one mind, sharing thoughts. I knew Tristan did not want me speaking up, but the attacks on his honor infuriated me. "The last time I spoke with Lady Talleyrand, she was quite satisfied with what was accomplished on your behalf that evening."

Guénard's face expressed the confused fury of a maddened bull. He grabbed papers from the table beside him and angrily flipped through them. Realizing he needed his glasses, he threw them down in his lap, picked up his gold-rimmed spectacles and put them on. Reaching for the paper again, he read from it.

"His Majesty showed the depth of a thimble's worth in his negotiating strategy by forming nine seats in the House of Commons to be filled with an open election. What is next on His Majesty's list for reforming Sarnesse? Allowing women the vote?'"

He tossed the paper aside and grabbed another. "Noble households across Sarnesse are in an uproar after the king gave away nine seats to be determined by open election. Perhaps that is why people dropped dead in the streets last month? They couldn't bear the thought of being governed by street-sweepers and bottle collectors.'"

Neither of us laughed, but really, it was ludicrous. You would have thought it was the end of the world, considering all the drama being made over a few merchants gaining a chance to be involved in government.

"Don't you give me that look, madame!" King Guénard pointed a very pudgy finger my way. "My life hasn't been the same since I've met you. Attempts on my life! Having to bargain with *students*." He said the last word in a tone that housewives reserved for rats. "You are as much to blame for my predicament as he is!"

When the king had pointed at me, Tristan's eyes had narrowed on his stony face. Just what we didn't need right now was him rescuing me.

"I'm very sorry for that," I replied as humbly as I could.

"And nobles have been on my doorstep every day, demanding I retract what I promised. Lords, barons, viscounts, and whoever else pleading that their way of life is threatened by some merchants. They feel betrayed. They threaten to lower the rate I receive from their estates with a new bill!" He smashed his fist down on the arm of his chair. "They are baying for my blood. No thanks to you two!"

He spluttered to a stop, breathing heavily, his nostrils flared. There was a moment of silence, before Tristan spoke.

"I wish to relinquish my title, Your Majesty."

The room became so quiet, that I could hear the blood rushing to my head. Perhaps Guénard realized he had pushed Tristan too hard, for he sat stupefied as Tristan explained.

"You will need a scapegoat to appease the nobility for the concessions you made, and we all know that I am their favorite to blame. They will readily believe that I influenced you to accept this compromise from Vischeer and Maillard. My abdicating the Chambaux title should appease their hunger for someone's head."

Stunned, I whispered, "Tristan, no—"

He held a hand towards me, fingers spread, begging for me to be quiet.

"My peers have long held me in dislike because they believe I have an undue influence upon you." I almost snorted, but held it back behind tight lips. "If you were to blame me for why the seats have been signed into law, you will quickly gain support."

I couldn't help myself. "Just get rid of it. His Majesty signed it into law, he can take it back."

Tristan gave a small smile, shaking his head. "His Majesty can't nullify the law without losing credibility, and the backing of the merchants. It would not only return us to where we were before, but incite anger on one side, and disdain on the other."

King Guénard leaned to the side, right arm bent and resting on his throne's arm as he bit his forefinger in thought. "Yes. It would serve. You are a man who inspires extremes of feelings: loyalty or hatred. Your haughty manner unnerves them, and now this marriage to a commoner has set tongues to wagging."

"Blame my counsel. And in return, make them believe you punished me because of my bad advice. It should stop any criticism of Your Majesty's action."

I wanted to stomp my foot and pull my hair. What was he saying?! Tristan had done more than anyone to save His Majesty's throne. How could he give up so much because of this spoiled man?

For the first time since I'd known him, Guénard actually looked like a king as he contemplated Tristan's bowed head. "Is this truly your desire?"

"Yes. I've served Your Majesty the best I could during hard times, but my heart is no longer in the work. I would prefer to retire from public duties and that can never happen as long as I bear the title. The title is the man."

Tristan continued with preternatural calm as if he were planning his own funeral.

"I would like to pass my estate officially to my second cousin, who has been working hard at keeping Chambaux running properly these last few years. He is not involved with court matters and prefers an agricultural life. I would also request, if it pleases Your Majesty, that my mother retain her title until her death; that my sister keeps the address of lady, and that she be given the Hartwood property and another small holding I own. A dairy farm that produces a modest income."

Guénard and myself were in some kind of shock. He said quietly, "This is a serious step, Fontaine. I will need to think about it."

We were dismissed.

Outside the Throne Hall, Tristan put his head close to mine and said quickly, "Let us talk outside."

As we walked the long hall through the government building, I could feel the glares cast in our direction. I wanted to storm out, throwing things, smacking faces, and screaming. My emotions demanded melodrama, but they were left unsatisfied.

We emerged and started walking down to the street to Tristan's carriage, the one with his coat-of-arms emblazoned on the door. Seeing it made me want to weep.

His hand took mine as he helped me, cautioning me about the step as if I was a fragile thing.

The door had barely closed when I cried out, "Tristan, why?!"

He actually smiled. "He's a coward and would have sought the easy way out of trouble. Guénard could have canceled those seats, which would have been a disaster. This country needs this compromise. Without it, I fear we would be headed towards a civil war."

I froze, stunned. "Surely you aren't serious?"

He nodded. "The signs were there for social change, whether stiff-necked nobles wanted to admit it or not. Progress must happen if the country is to survive. Growth means expansion. If

Guénard does not compromise, he will not keep his throne. As it is, I doubt he has more than another ten years before we become a democracy."

"Surely not!" I could not imagine Sarnesse not having a reigning monarch.

"His popularity is not high; and he has no heir. If he died tomorrow, there are at least three cousins who would attempt to claim the throne. Sarnesse could become destabilized, and Perino would be quick to take advantage of us. Parliament must take a bigger role so we can avoid total chaos when that day comes."

Seeing my distress, he took one of my hands and gave it a gentle squeeze. "Barbier saw that and took advantage of that unrest. I am of the opinion that he meant to use the Ghastlies as a private army. If he had, I am not sure we would have been victorious. However, Madame Granger's death stopped those plans in its tracks."

I didn't want to talk about Barbier. All of my attention and concern was for Tristan. "But why did it need to be you?"

He squeezed my hand again. "Because my title is so high in the peerage that in being seen to punish me, Guénard looks strong. If he revokes the seats he's already signed into law, he'll be seen as capricious and weak. It would also anger the merchants. You can't give something and take it away. Much easier never to give it in the first place."

"I doubt Vischeer or Maillard will give you a medal for helping their cause." It all seemed unfair!

Tristan laughed. "Most likely they will throw a party to celebrate defeating another dastardly noble."

I reached over and touched his cheek. "Why do you seem so light-hearted? Why are you smiling at such a loss?"

"I know this may be hard for you to understand, but working for the king demanded my life. It may not seem like it on the surface, but with this move, I'm taking it back. I've been thinking about this for months. Since our time at Hightower, in fact, when I knew I wanted to spend the rest of my life with you."

"Don't say you did this for me! I don't think I can bear that responsibility." The loss of his childhood home. His title. Leaving behind his peers.

"I knew you'd take it this way, and that's why I didn't discuss it. That you'd see this as a sacrifice I was making on your part. It's true and it isn't."

"I don't understand!"

"Elinor, please listen. This is hard to tell you because it took me time to work it out myself. When you first declined my offer to be my mistress—"

I quickly inserted, "Not knowing you had offered."

"—it made me wonder what I could offer to convince you otherwise. Other than a title and wealth, both of which you ignored, I had very little."

Using my fingers, I ticked off potential benefits. "Good looks. An admirable method of tying your cravat. A cologne that smells delicious."

"I had more than I thought!" When he stopped laughing, Tristan continued with a more serious air. "How would I explain shooting my first wife? What justification of that act could I provide in my defense?"

I opened my mouth, but he covered it with his fingers.

"I murdered Minette because of honor. At the time I thought I had only two options: either bring her back to face trial for treason, or to fight a duel to give her a chance. Sometimes I thought it would have been best if she had won, and it was I who died that day." He heaved a sigh, his eyes contemplating a memory that still gave him nightmares.

"After I came to love you, I realized I had alternatives that day I faced Minette. I could have let her flee to another land. Or bring her back to Alenbonné and plead for clemency. Used my influence and lawyers to save her. Owing blind loyalty to the king prevented me from seeing them."

He shook his head.

"You were right to stop me from killing Barbier. Being possessed by Angeliene's executioner gave me an appalling insight. It was disconcerting how his purpose, his thinking, mirrored my old thinking. Blind loyalty, coupled with arrogance. I was repulsed by it, and all the things I once admired."

Tristan pulled me over to sit beside him, his hand going down to cover my stomach. "We have a future, Elinor. A family I want to be with and to protect. If I stay as the Duke de Archambeau, one day I will be forced to choose the king over you."

"Tristan!" I started crying again. Being pregnant played havoc with your emotions, and it didn't help having an idiot for a husband.

"You relinquished any right to my title and wealth when you married me. The least I could do is return the favor. Now our standing can be equal. Isn't that what you wanted?"

I wiped tears off my cheeks and lashes. "No! It's different for me. I didn't grow up with it. You said yourself— it's easier to not have something then to take away something you have."

He laughed again. "Well, I can't say I'll give up being an arrogant fool at times. Would it comfort you to know I do have a private fortune that isn't entailed with Chambaux? I might give up being a duke, but I am not willing to live without servants and the comfort of hot water at the turn of a tap!"

Still ranting, I barely heard him. "It's a horrible sacrifice, and for whom? A spoiled brat! Couldn't you have just stopped working for him and kept your title?"

"No, dearest. My name and title are synonymous with the king's dirty secrets. People I had to question, those he demanded I dispose of, people who were charged with crimes I had to make stick, regardless of the means. Ugly work, Elinor, that I have never shared with you, and which I will never speak of again once I step down."

He gave me his handkerchief, and I quickly made it damp. "It will be a rough time, my darling. They will sling a lot of filth and some of it will stick. I don't know if you might want to take a long trip away, perhaps to Perino or Zulskaya."

"Certainly not! I won't desert you. But what about your mother? Your sister? They won't be happy with this."

"Actually, I think Valentina will be relieved by my choice. She knows I've been unhappy for years. Mother? No. But I'm not living my life by her commands."

"Perhaps the king will refuse to do it."

"He will consult with his courtiers and realize what a great gift this is during these troubled times. Yes, I don't doubt that I'll be a humble mysir before the month is out."

Chapter Thirty-Two

The gossip after Tristan relinquished his title became viscous. The worst was that if you disputed it, no one believed you! People just shook their head, saying, "No smoke without fire."

It was Lady Valentina who shared the most disgusting rumors.

"Elinor, I hate to bring you such bad tidings, but there is something I must tell you. People are saying—"

I set my teacup aside. "Oh, I've been told a lot about what they are saying, Valentina. Do not think you can surprise me. According to the gossips, I'm a ghoul, one of those Ghastlies, draining Tristan. Or Tristan only married me because I knew he'd murdered his first wife."

Well, the last was true, but Valentina didn't need to know that.

"I'm afraid this one is about the baby," Valentina said in a low voice I strained to hear. She was sitting opposite me. By her walking gown and hat, she must have just returned from an outing.

"My baby?" My pregnancy had become known during the diplomatic dinner and unfortunately news of it had spread quickly among le beau idéal. "Is it the theory where I used my pregnancy to force Tristan to marry me?"

"No. It's worse than that one." Valentina was pale, her eyes shadowed. Tristan relinquishing his title had not been easy on her, as he had blithely assured me. Instead, she felt guilty for her involvement with Lady Baudelaire, and the fact that Hartwood and the farm would be hers once the lawyers completed the paperwork.

The duchesse had broken her leg, or she would have already been here. Instead, she was flooding her children with letters and telegrams. Neither of them spoke to me about what their contents, although from Tristan's grim expressions and Valentina's pale countenance I imagined they were very detailed missives that voiced her extreme displeasure about Tristan's choice to step down, as well as his marriage.

After receiving another one, Tristan had decided to visit Chambaux and had left yesterday by train. He'd denied needing my support, telling me the trip would be a dead bore and I should stay in town. Was it selfish to feel relieved that he hadn't demanded my presence?

I gestured for Valentina to continue. "Charlotte tells me the pregnancy is going well, so don't think your news will cause me to miscarry. Just tell me."

Valentina actually blushed as she told me hesitantly, "It's being said the baby is really King Guénard's."

My startled laughter made her blink. "The king's? They think I would lie down with that egg-shaped, pathetic knobhead?"

Valentina was taken aback by my mirth. "It's a serious rumor, Elinor. If the child is male and believed to be Guénard's, it may have a claim to the throne. It throws off the line of inheritance."

The whole thing was preposterous. Anyone with sense wouldn't believe it. "I didn't think Guénard could sire children. None of his mistresses ever had any."

"That's an entirely different rumor," said Valentina primly. "I hate to say this, as it seems disloyal, but from speaking with my friends, I've traced this slander back to the royal cabinet. It's coming directly from the king."

I remembered: *You certainly should be punished.*

"Hm. Yes. I see."

"It's vile. Men are boasting that it proves Guénard's virility." Valentina's face became rosier. "There have long been rumors that King Guénard is infertile, so this rumor makes him more appealing. It's disgusting."

I shook my head in disbelief. "It's just tittle-tattle. No one will believe this tripe."

"This speculation on why Tristan gave up his title, and who is the father, has eclipsed the fury over the additional seats."

"How convenient for him." The simmering anger I had been holding about Tristan being the king's scapegoat for adding seats to Parliament grew to a fury. Tristan had reassured me that relinquishing his title would allow us to move forward with our lives as private citizens. Obviously, the child-tyrant was too petty to let us go without one last slap.

King Guénard would pay.

A woman's voice sprang to mind: *Who could imagine me being swept off my feet by the Earl of Grimoard? A drip, my dear. A soggy drip.*

In my mind's eye I replayed that afternoon on the beach, a confidence shared between myself and Lady Madeleine Montaine about how she had fooled le beau idéal to accept her son as that of a higher noble. The farce she had used to win the day.

Yes, King Guénard would pay...

"Why do you suddenly look so pleased? You can't enjoy people thinking you were the king's mistress and that my brother is a—"

"A cuckold? But isn't this exactly what the le beau idéal admires?" I said sarcastically. "I've climbed the ladder of success and have gone from a duke to a king. Aren't you pleased?"

Valentina was shocked. "I cannot believe that you would betray my brother."

I quickly reassured her. "Of course not! These are lies the king is using to punish us while increasing his standing with his courtiers." — Who probably were enjoying humiliating Tristan, a noble they envied but had also feared when he was the king's man.

"The more I know of our king, the less I like him."

Well, well. Perhaps Valentina might be won over to the republic's side.

"If I were to deny it, more will believe it. Ridiculous, I know, but it's human nature. I don't care a snap what they say, except I've realized I can use it now to help us."

"How so?"

"When Tristan decided to step down from his title, he thought he'd be safe, but with this move, the king has shown that he doesn't care if Tristan is attacked. We are exposed to his enemies. De Windt might even feel bold enough to arrest him."

"De Windt? On what charges?" Valentina was outraged at the very notion.

"An imaginary one! Look at what happened after they found me with Josephine's body! Or something he did in the past for the king, which now His Majesty will deny responsibility for! I will not risk him. We've seen how his peers shun him for marrying me. The cards and invitations from your friends are few. I wonder if that is not part of why he has gone to Chambaux."

"Not at all!" said Valentina, defensively. "Tristan would never run away. He had to go because of Mother."

She was probably right. I was being too sensitive. I was now about five months along, and my emotions were easily triggered.

"But how can this rumor help?"

"Think! Valentina! This stupid lie oddly increases Tristan's status with his fellow nobles. His wife has secured a child whose father is the highest noble in the land! He will be congratulated for it. *Amour plus fort.*"

Valentina was beginning to understand. "Because you picked the *love that is stronger.* I see. It's the code of love that excuses affairs."

My mood was bitter. "Imagine I, a commoner, the daughter of a jeweler, conceiving a love-child with the king, the pinnacle of the noble's hierarchy. Think of the envy that must be created in the hearts of ladies everywhere."

"But Elinor, the child *is* Tristan's. None of this is true," protested Valentina.

She was getting stuck in thinking the truth mattered.

"These rumors he started will actually prevent King Guénard from retaliating against us. Tristan has already sacrificed his title and Chambaux, and the public believe it is a punishment for him 'convincing' the king to add those seats to parliament. The king should have been satisfied." I snarled that last word. "But no, he had to go further to humiliate us with these silly rumors."

I took a deep breath, seeking calm. "So if I embrace these foolish stories, the code of love stops the king making any further moves against Tristan. He'd be seen as being vindictive against his lover's husband! Not done, Valentina, not done. The higher-ranked lover can never punish the lower noble who has allowed their spouse free love, the stronger love. The *amour plus fort.*"

She was beginning to understand. "Yes, I see. He'd be laughed at. Despised."

"If King Guénard tried to arrest or imprison Tristan, it would be seen as being in the worst of taste. It would betray the very foundation of how the aristocracy builds alliances. Tristan would instantly win the support of the entire peerage."

"I do not know if Tristan will see the benefits of giving this lie credence. He can be very proud."

Which was why I wasn't going to write to him about my plan.

～

I brought Madame Van Heerden with me to meet the king. Not because she was a woman and might feel sympathetic, but because I knew her sense of humor would enjoy the farce.

Coming up from my curtsy, I deliberately stumbled, clutching my stomach. Madame Van Heerden helped me to rise with her hand under my elbow. "Chair!" she requested, and someone came forward and gave me one. I made a show of collapsing into it, my hand over my heart.

King Guénard said impatiently, "I've granted you an audience, although I've said all I want on the matter. Fontaine is stripped of his dukedom. If you are here to plead his case, you are too late."

"Oh, that is not why I'm here, Your Majesty," I said breathlessly. "It's about the child I carry."

The three other people in the room, courtiers and the closet intimates of His Majesty, exchanged knowing looks. Guénard gave them a nod, and they vanished out the door. Once they were gone, he said, "What about your child?"

Perhaps there was a trace of sheepish guilt in his voice? No matter. I would not be letting him off the hook.

"When you're pregnant, it makes one think of the past. Why, just last night, I was reminiscing about my time at Lindengaard during the Winter Revels."

He squirmed. *Good. Remember how my friend and I saved your life and didn't mention a word of it to anyone.* Back when I had still held some loyalty to the crown. I planned on him squirming far more before our conversation was done.

"Perhaps that is why some have assumed we are lovers." Hopefully, I wasn't overdoing this scatterbrained girlish twitter. "Of course, I was in your bedroom, very late at night, and someone might have seen me leaving it, wearing nothing but my dressing gown."

"I was ill!" he practically shouted. His face was becoming blotched with red spots over pallor, and sweat was starting to bead on his forehead. As I had suspected, he didn't like a frontal attack.

He'd prefer to slander a woman from the shadows, using his courtiers to do his dirty work.

Fluttering my eyelashes, I clasped my hands over my heart. "Sick with love; that is what people are saying. Apparently, we had quite a torrid love affair right under everyone's noses."

He was caught. He had ordered his court to spread this foul rumor, but couldn't admit that. Neither did Guénard want anyone to know a noble had made an attempt on his life that was only foiled because of Tristan Fontaine and his wife.

"People often believe stupid things," he said, practically twitching.

"Yes, they do. While it is flattering, I don't want to deny such a rumor and have everyone learn the *real* reason I was in your rooms at Lindengaard." I paused, letting him digest that. "Speaking of the Winter Revels, I was sad to hear that Count Westergaard has passed away, leaving his estate in shambles since he did not have a recognized heir."

"It has come to the Crown," he acknowledged.

Yes, another estate that you will gobble up if allowed to.

"I propose a plan that would benefit us both, at very little cost to you."

"Somehow, madame, I doubt that!" he snapped. I could tell he was in a cantankerous mood, but unlike Lady Talleyrand, I would not appease him with sugared words. It was time he learned that he should not have sent poison arrows after me.

"I've been reviewing the estate's tax papers, and it needs an infusion of money and wise management for at least a decade, maybe two. Truthfully, it is more of a liability than it is an asset. Or so says my lawyer."

I had come prepared with the balance sheets, all pulled from public record, in case he wanted to review them. Madame Van Heerden took her cue and murmured, "If you would care to examine the accounts, Your Majesty."

"No. I am quite aware of the state of things at Lindengaard."

He waved my lawyer and her papers back from approaching the throne. "Why are you so interested in the count's property?"

My smile may have been the reason the king started to look frightened.

"I propose that I sign a statement that my child will not seek any inheritance from Your Majesty in exchange for being given Lindengaard. This will only enhance the rumor that my child is yours. In exchange, the estate and its title will revert to myself as the owner. Perhaps an additional marriage gift of five years' freedom from taxation to give time for the estate to recover?"

He spluttered, both hands gripping the sides of his throne. "What a ridiculous idea! The child is not mine!"

I shrugged. "These pesky rumors say otherwise. Consider, Your Majesty, the value of your reputation if you were seen as its father. That value is far more than what Lindengaard could provide."

"I just took Fontaine's title!" cried King Guénard. "Now you seek to win him another?! I'd be seen as a fool!"

I let him rage for a while. It would do his ego good to think I was listening to him. When he sputtered to a stop, I laid out the rest of my proposal.

"Change the inheritance of the estate to pass through the female line. Matrilineality may be uncommon in Sarnesse, but in Perino it is standard. Tristan would only gain his title through his marriage to me, and he would lose it if he ever divorced me. That is how we shall draw up the papers for transferring the property."

I felt a grim satisfaction. Count Westergaard's family had lost a chance at the crown because of a female ancestor. Now a woman would seize it back from a greedy king.

"You are a cunning woman," King Guénard said with reluctant admiration, shaking his head in disbelief. "When Fontaine tires of you, if he tries to quit you, he'd lose all over again."

Let the king think my union with Tristan needed that coercion, I knew better.

He rang a hand bell from the table at his side and the doors opened. "I will consider your petition. You are dismissed."

Walking down the hall, I felt the weight of curious stares, but Madame Van Heerden was her usual jolly self and suggested we go to a very public place for lunch.

"Good to be seen out and about," she said. "Makes it harder for you to disappear." She laughed at her own witticism.

I had no plans on the king making me disappear. Instead, I was about to be more noticeable than ever.

As we climbed into Tristan's carriage, I asked her, "Have you ever lunched at the Crown hotel? They have a chef who makes meals to die for."

Chapter Thirty-Three

When I received the letter from the king telling me he was not interested in my plans for Lindengaard, I gave a grim smile. We would see about that. He had started this game; I would end it.

Three weeks later, I knew my plan to change his mind was working when Madame Vogel returned. This time she visited with two gentlemen. They made quite the noise in the hallway, insisting they must see me. I took pity and told Ruben to let them enter the drawing room.

I was curled up on the sofa wearing a loose robe dress tied at the waist, fit for receiving guests at home, when Madame Vogel came in. "You must help us!" The two gentlemen behind her added a chorus. "We need you!"

"What must I help you with? Leadership at the Society? I've already refused." I gestured for them to take seats.

"We have a situation," the older man said. He had a tired face well set into lines of long-held grief. He wore black, as I had done when working as a Ghost Talker. On his lapel was the Society's lily pin, on his finger a black ring band denoted that he was a determined widower, and his boutonnière was an inky rose. A man who wore his heart outside and who loved drama; a man after my own heart.

"We can't solve it," said his weak-chinned companion. He wore an ordinary tweed suit with a limp brown tie. The neck of his shirt was gray, and he had lost a cuff-link at some point this morning. Someone with no sense of style or even self-respect. He probably lived in a boarding house, certainly with no mother or sister who cared for him.

"If the great brains at the Morpheus Society can't solve it, I don't know what you expect me to do," I said cynically.

They exchanged looks. "Tell her," the younger man hissed at Madame Vogel.

"Our members are reporting a strange phenomenon with the Alenbonné ghosts. After recent experiences with the things—"

"You mean the Ghastlies."

She bobbed her head, assenting. "Yes, after those Ghastlies, it is easy for people to be frightened by anything supernatural. As you can imagine, our members have been in demand for reassurance and to answer questions. But every time they contact a spirit, it says only one thing before vanishing."

"What does it say? 'Leave me alone, I'm reading a good book and about to take some hot cocoa?'" My eyes traveled to the cup that was losing its steam. Of course my visitors had arrived just as the heroine in my book had found a mysterious locked door in her employer's castle.

Before she could tell me, the older man quoted in a deep baritone, "'The lion must give his cub what he owes.'"

I forced my eyes to widen in surprise. "How fascinating. And they all say the same thing?"

The younger man eagerly gave me the full details. "Yes. Every ghost, every time, says it. We have recorded at least thirty experiences of it from different mediums, in separate households. Ghosts who only moaned before or spoke of loss and yearning now say only this strange phrase."

"The lion must give his cub what he owes."

"Yes, André. I'm sure she heard it the first time," said Madame Vogel impatiently. "We have no idea what it means. We throw ourselves at your mercy, Lady Fontaine." I didn't correct the address, for I hoped to be a lady again very soon.

Perhaps sooner than I thought, for the footman announced, "His Majesty, King Guénard," as the roly-poly form of our sovereign entered the room. We all rose and sank into curtsies or deep bows.

I couldn't resist sharpening my knife.

"How unexpected, Your Majesty. Are you here to see Lady Valentina? She is out shopping for lace. Tristan? He is packing his things at Chambaux to prepare for leaving it forever."

"I am here to see you, madame!"

Someone, Madame Vogel or the weak chin, gave a sharp inhalation of awe.

"How pleasant. Do you wish for refreshment?"

"No, I do not! What I wish is for my ancestor to stop popping up all over the royal premises moaning about what I owe."

The older gentlemen said in a sonorous whisper, "The king's coat of arms is a lion."

So were those of many nobles, but yes, the monarch's did have a very prominent lion in its design. What a coincidence.

"Which ancestor do you mean, Your Majesty?"

"A very annoying one." He sat down heavily, the antique chair of the Fontaines' creaking under him. If he broke, I'd be sending him a bill. The king gestured at my trio of visitors. "Who are they?"

Madame Vogel was quick to introduce herself and her companions and the purpose of their visit. "We are also concerned, Your Majesty. It is very odd and disturbing behavior on behalf of these ghosts."

A well-loved voice from the doorway said, "If it's odd and disturbing, then you can lay a bet that my dear wife is involved up to her neck in it."

"Tristan! How pleasant to see you back!"

"Is it?" He cocked his head. "Because I find you in my house—"

"Your sister's house," I corrected him.

"—cavorting with your lover!"

"Oh, dear," I said, giving him a sad clown frown.

I wasn't sure Madame Vogel's mouth could gape any bigger.

Someone shoved into Tristan's back. Her journey from the foyer had probably been delayed because of her crutch. It was Tristan's mother, the Duchesse of Chambaux. "*Her lover?* She already has a lover? I'm not surprised! Her class can't remain loyal for long. Who is he?!"

The Duchesse of Chambaux was the very model of superior nobility. Her stiff, unbending carriage; the bold nose that no lesser woman could have carried with such a haughty flair; and the commanding eye that gave us all a basilisk stare, roaming the room, finally resting upon the king's graceless form trying to break her chair.

I told Ruben, "I expect Her Grace may need some refreshment after her long train journey."

Pointedly ignoring me, she limped over to the sofa. André leapt up to place a pillow behind her back, an act for which she did not thank him.

"Did you have a pleasant stay in Chambaux, my love?" I asked.

"It was memorable, dearest." Tristan took the sofa where I had been sitting, removing my open book from the cushion to set it on the table beside it. "Imagine my surprise when I ran into an old acquaintance on the train. He congratulated me for having — as he so indelicately put it — a bun in the oven, and the baker being no less than His Majesty!"

I couldn't decide which was more entertaining, the duchesse's face, or the king's. No one said a word.

Thankfully for everyone, the tea cart arrived. Nothing can change an atmosphere like food and drink. Proper behavior practically demanded a ceasefire.

Tristan's mother opted for imagining I wasn't there and started a conversation with His Majesty about mutual acquaintances. He politely discussed the arrival of a new little lordling, and what would be the proper gift for the birth. Through it all, his gaze avoided Tristan's.

The trio from the Morpheus Society exclaimed over the quality of the petites fours and the brand of tea. With a wave, I encouraged them to stuff themselves. I returned Tristan's glowering stare with a sunny smile.

However, even cake could not forestall a storm of this magnitude forever. Having worked her way through three petites fours, a stack of biscuits, and two cups of tea, Madame Vogel asked in a timid manner, "Do you think, Lady Fontaine, that the ghosts speak a warning? Or do you think it a prophecy?"

At her addressing me as 'Lady Fontaine', my mother-in-law almost broke the handle of her teacup with the force of her grip.

"Oh, certainly it's one of those."

"What are these ghosts saying?" asked Tristan. He had returned to being the suave noble, determined to ignore His Majesty as much as his mother was ignoring me. He looked so handsome, so above us all, in his traveling clothes, that I really wished everyone would just leave us so I could greet him properly, like a good wife.

Madame Vogel was pleased to have someone interested. I was sure it didn't hurt that he was the most handsome man in the room. "All the ghosts that have been contacted only say one phrase before vanishing: *the lion must give his cub what he owes.*"

I nibbled on the end of a biscuit, peeping coyly at my husband. "Whatever could it mean, I wonder?"

His stern glare tried to discomfort me. "It's almost like the city's ghosts have all been talking with one person."

Madame Vogel twittered. "Oh, Your Grace." No one dared to correct her about his title. "When a great event is about to happen, they do grow rather prophetic in their statements. It's as if they *know*. That's what is so concerning. Is Alenbonné heading towards another disaster?"

People will believe anything if a ghost tells it to them.

Trying to be the cleverest in the room, Weak Chin spoke his thoughts out loud. "It must be about someone closely connected to the king. A child of tender years. Hence cub."

"It's probably why your ancestor has been visiting you, Your Majesty," said André.

Bless their innocent souls! They would need the connection spelled out, it seemed.

"It does seem to be issuing a warning," I said. "Intelligent people do what the spirits advise. Do you remember that case, Madame Vogel, where the ship's captain ignored his ancestor's ghost that commanded him to keep a black cat on board at all times?"

"All hands lost," said André. It seemed he liked sad things, for he said this dramatically, with a sigh of woe, the ends of his mustache fluttering in sympathy. He really should hire himself out as a professional mourner.

"Or that woman who was told not to take that train to Isse-holf. When she did anyway, it was wrecked when the bridge collapsed. All aboard killed," said Weak Chin.

Madame Vogel was not going to be outdone. "The child spirit who appeared three times, telling the family to leave the house. They didn't. On the fourth night the poor souls all died in a fire because the house-maid toppled a lit candle in the nursery."

The king looked like a steam engine about ready to blow its whistle. He stood up, wiping away the crumbs left on his trousers.

With a flourish, he consulted a timepiece pulled from his vest pocket. "Duty calls."

We all rose when he did. Even the duchesse had struggled to her feet, with André hesitantly helping her. To me, King Guénard muttered, "That matter we discussed? I'll have the papers drawn up and sent over. Good day."

He didn't run from the room, but he set a good pace.

My new friends from the Society might have wished to linger, but the brooding presence of the duchesse discouraged it. Madame Vogel thanked me for the refreshments and once again asked if she could meet me to discuss the future.

"I'm sorry, but I'll be very busy setting up my new home."

"Oh." Her face fell, and I felt a bit of guilt over having used her to accomplish my agenda. "Leave your card again and I'll write to you when I can, but I don't think you need to worry about these ghostly statements anymore."

As I left, I heard her say to the older man, "The king visited her personally! The rumors must be true."

It left us three.

"Are you carrying the king's child?" demanded the duchesse. She didn't have her umbrella, so she reached over and poked me with the end of her crutch.

"No. I'm carrying your son's."

"And have lost him his title! And his lands!"

Tristan's roll of eyes and exasperated snort told me he had heard this many times.

"No, he lost those on his own." Standing, I collected my book and announced, "I shall go lie down for a nap, for I'm feeling rather tired."

As I left, her booming voice demanded of her son, "What exactly *is* your wife's relationship with King Guénard?"

Tristan must have also fled, for he was behind me by the time I made it to our bedroom. We entered together, and he locked the door behind us.

"Elinor, will you please explain what the hell is going on?"

Embracing him, I set my chin on his chest and looked up at him in delight. "I'm so glad you are home. I've missed you something terrible."

"Elinor?" He repeated in a warning voice.

Since it was all settled and unlikely to be reversed now, I told him how I had convinced the king to give me Lindengaard and the title of countess. "Of course, the baby is yours, but since no one would listen to me, and I quite dislike King Guénard, and I love Lindengaard, I thought this would suit. What a perfect place to raise our child. Plenty of fresh air and places to play. Room for a pony. Will you mind being a count?"

Tristan's expression was like when you've told the grocer to deliver apples but received potatoes. "You do realize that I just stepped away from a title?"

"Which you never should have! You did that without consulting me, so I have done this without consulting you."

I couldn't make out what he was thinking. Had I overplayed my hand?

"So you will leave Alenbonné?"

"We can keep a townhouse here for visiting."

"Elinor." He sounded exasperated.

"I don't care about titles or estates — I did it for you! You left yourself too vulnerable to these people," I cried, holding him tighter, for he had not embraced me back. "Even after your sacrifice, he wouldn't leave you alone. He started these rumors, trying to hurt you again. Now I've turned the game back on him. He cannot act against you ever again."

Unlike Valentina he immediately understood me. The gifting of Lindergaard would be an unofficial acknowledgment of the king and I having had an affair. Rules of society meant that he could never move against my husband. It just wasn't done.

"But your reputation?"

"He's already dragged it through the mud. Sadly, once he

started the gossip, there was no way to stop it. At least this way, I paid him back for it."

His arms came up around me. "What you need is a thorough spanking."

"But you missed me, didn't you? Missed me and all my chaos?"

"You are a devil, madame. An absolute devil."

EPILOGUE

Lindengaard
Five months later

When I went into labor, I still had far too much to do. "I've been told about this nesting instinct pregnant women feel, but aren't you taking this a bit too far?" asked Charlotte.

We were in the library at Lindengaard, and I was dusting books in between labor pains. Charlotte was sitting in one of the wing-backed leather chairs near the fire. Dressed in her usual trousers, she wore her shirtsleeves rolled up, and her vest unbuttoned. She was sipping a glass of wine from our cellars, and reading a book between checking the watch sitting on her thigh.

"The cleaning would go faster if you helped," I suggested.

Charlotte waved her hand. "No. No, thank you," she said. "Housekeeping? Not what I do. When this baby is ready, I will be too."

Even as my friend finished her sentence, a contraction started.

"Breathe, Elinor. It doesn't do to hold your breath." I forced myself not to grit my teeth against the pain. "Are you sure you don't want me to call for Tristan?"

"You told me it could take hours before we are getting close. I have no need for him to hold my hand while we wait." I took down a few books and started wiping their covers with my cleaning cloth.

"I really think you're taking this idea of keeping your independence too far," said Charlotte.

"You told me that most women don't have their husbands there for the birth," I reminded her.

"Tristan said he wanted to be here."

"Well, he is here! Dealing with the plumbing!"

Charlotte couldn't help but laugh. "If you had told me a year ago I'd see him with a wrench in his hand trying to fix a leaky pipe, I would have laughed."

"It's not my fault that Lindengaard is falling apart! Next time, I'll suggest the king give me an estate that is in better repair."

But I wouldn't. I'd fallen in love with Lindengaard the moment I stepped out of the carriage and saw it. It was perfection — despite crumbling plaster, leaky pipes, and bats in the attic.

Oh. Another contraction hit me, and I stopped talking.

Charlotte was by my side in a flash, taking my pulse and looking at her pocket watch. "I'm fine, I tell you."

"Your contractions are coming closer together. It's time to quit this house-cleaning, and let's—"

"What's happening?" The love of my life entered, sleeves rolled up, and his shirt wet, with a pipe wrench in his hand. If I wasn't in the middle of a contraction, I would have admired the delectable masculine picture he made.

"She needs to get to bed," was Charlotte's firm response.

Before I could reason with her, Tristan set aside the wrench and came over to pick me up.

"Tristan!"

"Elinor!" he returned, mockingly. He started up the stairs, me in his arms, and Charlotte behind him, carrying her medical bag.

"I'm the countess of Lindengaard. You can't be picking me up without my permission."

"You can dismiss me, milady, if I've overstepped my bounds, but considering how difficult it's been to get a plumber to come out here, you might consider that carefully."

A youthful voice floated up from downstairs. "Is it happening? Is the baby here? What name did you decide? I think Eduard is nice. Or maybe Jolene, if it's a girl."

We all shouted to Twyla at once.

"Tell Anne-Marie we need that boiling water up here," Charlotte instructed.

"Would you grab that book down on the table I was reading?" I told her.

"Leave the book, and get the water and towels," ordered Tristan.

By the time we were at our bedroom door, I was hit by two other contractions.

"They seem— more intense," I told Charlotte.

"It's your body getting itself ready. Perfectly normal. Right now, lie back and let me check on how things are progressing."

Tristan made a mountain of pillows. He sat beside me, holding my hand. I clenched his rather tightly as Charlotte 'checked things.'

It might seem strange that I had asked Charlotte to attend me instead of a midwife, but I had utter faith in her. Especially as she had told me she knew all the ways a woman could die from childbirth; corpses of pregnant women were highly sought after by the University's medical college.

Morbid. Don't think of that now.

Suddenly, the room filled with people. Cook brought up a pot full of steaming water. Anne-Marie was quick to warn her. "No! Don't put that on that wooden table. It will scorch the wood!"

Melody, the servant I had met so long ago at Lindengaard, laid a thick towel down on the tabletop, and Cook plopped the pot down on top. I breathed a sigh of relief. Anne-Marie was right. We didn't have enough good furniture to be scorching it!

Twyla entered, eating an apple. She announced to the room at large, "Madame Vogel from the Morpheus Society is here. She wants Elinor's advice on—"

"Later!" growled my husband.

I sent out a whooshing breath, forcing myself to stop gulping air unless I wanted to hyperventilate.

"What about the bricklayer? He's here too," said Twyla. "They want a deposit up front, or they won't start work. They say the old lord still owes them for the jobs they did during the Winter Revels."

But I wasn't paying attention to my apprentice or thinking about another bill. All of my attention was going inward, to the new life wanting out of me. From below my knees, Charlotte called out encouragement. "You're doing well, Elinor. Don't brace, just let it happen. Like a wave coming over you."

Cook chatted with Melody, the Lindengaard's maid, as if my room was her kitchen. "All my years with the old lord, and I never expected to see a new babe in this house."

"The place is coming alive again," agreed Melody. Upon my return, the servant girl had adopted a proprietary air over me.

Anne-Marie gave her contribution. "Madame will have the most beautiful baby in the world."

I finally realized that it wasn't pain blurring my vision. Apparitions appeared; the ghosts of Lindengaard were gathering to see the new heir born. Women and men. Children and teenagers. One among them I recognized: Count Christoffer Westergaard, the previous owner. Thankfully, he looked only confused, not accusatory, at my appropriation of his family estate.

"Aohhhh!" I cried.

"What's wrong?" Tristan asked Charlotte.

"Nothing, Your Grace!" Her eyes looked to heaven, as she muttered, "Lord, give me the peace of the morgue."

"Thank you for coming, Charlotte. I appreciate it," I told her between gritted teeth, before crying out again, a bit louder. "Argh!"

"The baby is crowning," said Charlotte. Like I didn't know I was birthing a cannonball!

The ghosts grew closer, forming a ring around the bed. Twyla started to introduce them all. "That's Lord Belshaw — he drowned. His brother held him under the water to inherit Lindengaard. The woman with the hair down to her waist is Lady Courbet. She drank lye after finding out her husband was having an affair with her best friend."

"Twyla, not now!" said Tristan. His voice held a warning tone that would stop anyone else dead in their tracks, though it never dented Twyla's enthusiasm to inform.

"I only thought Elinor would like to know who the ghosts were," she said, hurt.

"Later, dear, later," I huffed, panting.

One of the ghosts I knew very well. The Gray Lady of Hightower, Lady Eugénie Vaux Montaine. She looked at me mournfully. All the ghosts drew back, giving her precedence as she came closer to the bed.

I shook my finger at her, yelling, "Don't you dare!"

"A momentous birth," she intoned.

Charlotte cried out, exultant. "She's here!"

"Yes, I know she's here," I snapped at my friend.

"I mean your child, Elinor," said Charlotte, laughing. "A little girl!"

Anne-Marie rushed forward, handing the doctor towels to wipe the baby clean.

"Another push, Elinor."

"Why?"

"Just push."

Exhausted, I did as she asked. My reward was that Charlotte handed me my child.

"Her face is all squish-squashed," said Twyla.

"She's perfect," said Tristan, his face close to mine as we gazed down upon our little miracle together, our hearts beating as one.

"We won't be able to use our father's names like we planned." His arm came around me as he kissed my temple. "Perhaps that's for the best, my dear. Let go of the past and have a fresh start."

Lady Montaine, the Gray Lady, said once more in her solemn tones, "A momentous birth." When she faded away, I was thankful to see the last of her wispy drapery.

"She's so small," Tristan said. His voice was reverent, as our daughter's fists waved about.

Was he crying? Another drop plopped on my forehead, and I looked up.

"Tristan," I said warningly. He followed my gaze. "Did you remember to shut the water off in the bathroom upstairs?"

"Oh, dear," he said, before springing up to cast his body over me and our new baby to shield us from the falling plaster.

Find more great reads
by Byrd Nash
at her website
ByrdNash.com

Author Notes

At this time Tristan and Elinor's adventures have come to an end. I've loved writing about them, and from reader feedback many have loved reading about them. I give you my humble thanks.

I have so many thoughts of what their future would be like, all of it filled with adventure, ghosts, and some exasperation on Tristan's part don't you think?

From the beginning of my author journey I've been blessed with some great fans who have supported my work and provided feedback. Thanks again to Davida, Giselle S., and Gloria W. for their keen eyes on hunting typos. My editor, Emma, really waded in to read a book about a pregnant lady while she was pregnant!

If you have loved the series, consider leaving me a review where ever you've bought this book, Bookbub, or Goodreads. I would love to read your thoughts.

BYRD NASH

NOTE: This fantasy world is inspired by 1910 France, but is not a part of it.

For convenience sake, American spellings have been chosen for this fantasy series. For example, instead of grey, gray is used.

For use in this fantasy world, Guardia refers to an individual police officer. Gendarmes to the police force, or a group of police officers.

CAST OF CHARACTERS

- **Elinor Chalamet** (Shall-ah-may)— A Ghost Talker residing in the city of Alenbonné (Alan-bon-ay) in the country of Sarnesse (Sar-nessie).
- **Tristan Fontaine** duke of Archambeau (Are-shembow)— is Alenbonné nobility and a fixer for King Guénard.

Tristan's circle:

- **Minette Fontaine**, the previous Duchesse de Chambaux— (deceased) wife of Tristan. We learn what happened between her and Tristan in *Spirit Guide* and *Gray Lady*.
- **The Duchesse de Chambaux** (Sham-beau)— Tristan's mother.
- **Lady Valentina Fontaine**— Tristan's sister.

Elinor's circle:

- **Dr. Charlotte LaRue** (Lah-roo)— the city's coroner and university instructor, and a friend of Elinor's.
- **Jacques Moreau** (More-row)— a childhood friend of Elinor's who is now a soldier.
- **The Gold Souls** (four women, deceased)— Renee Bassett, a flute; Louisa Bonnet, a harp; Meike Roord, a cello, and Frida Korver, a violin. These women Parnell used in *Spirit Guide* to make his Beyond palace.

Louisa, Meike, and Frida transition to the Afterlife in *Haunted Grave*.
- **Augustus Chalamet**— Elinor's father was murdered almost 13 years ago when Elinor was 17.

The Morpheus Society:

- **Twyla Andricksson**— Elinor's apprentice, assigned to her by Parnell Lafayette at the end of *Delicious Death*.
- **Leona Granger**— Elinor's mentor in The Morpheus Society. See *Spirit Guide*.
- **Parnell Lafayette**— (deceased) Elinor's former rival who committed crimes in an attempt to extend his life. See *Spirit Guide*.
- **Claire Vogel**— a member of The Morpheus Society who wants Elinor's help.
- **Lady Alouette Sarte**— (deceased) founder of the The Morpheus Society.

Law Enforcement:

- **Sven De Windt**— a senior prosecutor for the Crown who dislikes Tristan and Elinor. He wanted to arrest them in *Gray Lady*.
- **Inspector Marcellus Barbier** (Bahr-bee-er)— a police inspector who Elinor works with to solve crimes.
- **Sergeant Quincy Dupont** (Dew-pon)— Barbier's subordinate, who meets his end in *Haunted Grave*.

Nobles:

- **King Trygve Guénard**— the ruling monarch of Sarnesse. The country follows the male-preference primogeniture (cognatic primogeniture) instead of matrilineal primogeniture which is inheritance through the female line. This is why Count Westergaard's female ancestor who was first born, but female, was supplanted by a second-born brother.

- **Lady Josephine Baudelaire** (Bowed-lair)— a society lady who was once Minette's friend and whose family lives near the Chambaux family estate. She was blackmailing Valentina. See *Gray Lady* and *Haunted Grave*.
- **Lady Maryegold Talleyrand**— a member of the House of Lords, well-known for her diplomatic powers. She is closely related to the king.
- **Lady Tulip Langenberg**— goddaughter and ward of the king after the events in *Delicious Death*.
- **Lady Annabel van den Berg**— a young lady who was guest at Hartwood when she met an unfortunate accident arranged by Valentina and Josephine as a prank. Elinor convinces a ghost did it out of love for her in *Gray Lady*.
- **Lord Jansen Buckard**— A member of the nobility who tried to coerce Lady Tulip into a marriage in order to gain access to her inheritance. Tristan shoots him in *Delicious Death*.
- **Lord Lucas Bridoux**— a nobleman who is assassinated.
- **Lord Doriac**— a noble who was blackmailed over not paying taxes.
- **Count Christoffer Westergaard**— previous owner of Lindengaard who we met in *Delicious Death* and who has passed away in an institution.
- **Lord Tassin**— a member of the House of Lords.

Others:

- **Dr. Armand Devereaux**— an alienist who heals minds. An acquaintance of Charlotte's. He hypnotized Elinor in *Haunted Grave*.
- **Theodoor Vischeer**— a naturalist at the university who is friendly with the student rebels. A member of the Groendykes, a lesser noble family. We meet him first in *Delicious Death* and he asks for Elinor's help in *Haunted Grave*.
- **Olivier Maillard**— a charismatic speaker encouraging revolution.
- **Van Heerdens**— Tristan's lawyers.
- **Dr. Hagen**— the king's physician who we first meet in *Delicious Death*.
- **General Reynard Somerville**— Jacques military superior.
- **Karl Solberg**— A mediocre artist that attended the ghost parties. He had an affair with Ebbe's maid, Hannah, in *Spirit Guide*.

Servants and Helpers:

- **Anne-Marie Draper**— Elinor's servant, a daughter of a sailor.
- **Marcus**— an orphaned street urchin who occasionally helps Elinor. Tristan starts mentoring him after the events in *Spirit Guide*.
- **Stephan**— Tristan's clerk, who likes to play pranks.
- **Ruben**— a footman at the duke's townhouse, Hartwood.
- **Luca**— the duke's valet.
- **Davis**— the duke's carriage driver.
- **Madeline Cossart**— a Chambaux family servant.

- **Madame Darly**— the duke's cook at his townhouse, Hartwood, who takes a liking to Marcus.
- **Farrow and Styles**— bodyguards assigned to Elinor by Tristan.
- **Cédric Durant**— Leona Granger's manservant.
- **Brigitta Meijer**— the Chalamet maid at the time of August Chalamet's murder. She quit the day before the murder.
- **Melody Cantrell**— a servant at Lindengaard who we met in *Delicious Death*.

Hotel staff:

- **Gerhard Perdersen**— the Crown hotel's head chef who had problem with a Noise Ghost in *Delicious Death*.
- **Henri Colbert**— the Crown's manager.
- **Pierre**— Crown head waiter.

9 781954 811584